T0347454

Also by Will Kostakis

For young adults
Loathing Lola
The First Third
The Sidekicks
Monuments
Rebel Gods
The Greatest Hit

For younger readers
Stuff Happens: Sean

WE COULD BE SOMETHING

WILL KOSTAKIS

ALLEN&UNWIN

SYDNEY•MELBOURNE•AUCKLAND•LONDON

First published by Allen & Unwin in 2023

Allen & Unwin
Cammeraygal Country
83 Alexander Street
Crows Nest NSW 2065
Australia
Phone: (61 2) 8425 0100
Email: info@allenandunwin.com
Web: www.allenandunwin.com

Allen & Unwin acknowledges the Traditional Owners of the Country on which we live and work. We pay our respects to all Aboriginal and Torres Strait Islander Elders, past and present.

A catalogue record for this book is available from the National Library of Australia

ISBN 978 1 76118 017 0

For teaching resources, explore www.allenandunwin.com/resources/for-teachers

Cover and text design by Astred Hicks, Design Cherry
Cover illustration by Astred Hicks
Set in 11.5/18 pt Adobe Garamond Pro by Midland Typesetters, Australia
Printed and bound in Australia by the Opus Group

10 9 8 7 6 5 4 3 2 1

The paper in this book is FSC® certified. FSC® promotes environmentally responsible, socially beneficial and economically viable management of the world's forests.

willkostakis.com

The first book I ever signed was to my mum.
I wrote, 'Every word is for you.'

Still true.

ONE
The gays are fighting

HARVEY

1

The one night I haul my arse to sleep before ten, I'm woken at ten-thirty by my father rummaging through my wardrobe. He's getting up me for how many red shirts I own.

It hurts to open my eyes wider than a squint. 'Huh?'

'Red shirts,' he says, like any of this is making sense to me.

I blink. The orange glow of the hallway lamp is hitting him like a spotlight. He's dressed. Fresh fade, designer stubble, knitted jumper, too-tight pants, boots, duffle bag open at his feet... He's going somewhere.

He drops two red shirts onto the bag.

'Ba?'

He ignores me. He's fixated on the shirts. 'I've counted seven.' He runs his thumb down the stack. 'Eight.'

'*Ba.*'

'This one's nice.' He waves a V-neck at me before letting it fall. 'That's three.'

'What are you doing?' I ask.

He smacks his lips. 'If you had to go an indefinite period with a reduced wardrobe, how many red shirts would you need?'

'Me?'

'That's what *you* means.'

He's packing my bag. 'What have I done?'

'Just tell me how many.'

Kinda putting me on the spot here. 'No idea. Five?'

'Tough. Three's enough.'

'Then why did you ask?'

'You can wear one on the plane. That's four.'

Right. I'm wide awake now. 'I'm getting on a plane?'

Ba's moved on to shorts. He plucks out a striped pair and instinctively checks the crotch for holes. Bingo. Two of them. He discards that pair and checks another, cream-coloured, and to his delight, no holes. He lets the shorts fall onto the bag.

'Hello?' I ask. 'You're gonna need to give me some—'

'I'm leaving your father.' He says it as if it's some big revelation, as if I haven't clued into the fact that they low-key hate each other.

They groan and bicker, and for ages, I've been wishing they'd get on with it. Have the big fight. Say the horrible thing they can't take back. Split up. Move on. It'd be rough, sure, but they'd be better in the long run.

I figured they were too chickenshit. But they're doing it. Ba's leaving.

Wait. He's packing *my* bag. *I'm* getting on a plane.

'I'm coming with you?'

He groans. 'Yes, Harvey.'

I'm in bed. 'Now?'

'Right now.'

'Sydney?'

He nods.

'For real?'

I must light up, because he tells me not to look so happy about it.

I fix my face.

My mates and I have a pool going. Ten bucks each in the kitty; the first one to bail on school without being expelled or imprisoned gets the lot. Dropping out in Perth is tricky, unless you wanna suffer an apprenticeship or some shit. In Sydney, all you have to do is turn seventeen, and I've done that.

I've had zero luck convincing my parents to let me move east, but that's what's happening now, right? Ba's fleeing and he's taking me with him.

'*Now*, Harvey.' And he's out the door with the duffle bag.

I stare after him.

Now, Harvey.

I kick off my doona. I throw on the closest shirt and shorts and follow Ba as far as the spot in the hallway where Dad's loitering. There's nothing to suggest he hasn't been there the whole time, looking like a shot of depresso between two framed family portraits. In 2014's, we're sailors on the pier. In 2019's, a choir on the vineyard.

I lean against the opposite wall. Dad shrugs. He's dressed after-dinner casual — singlet, trackpants. I'm itching to ask how a night implodes like this.

He reads my mind. 'The manure,' he explains.

Oh, they've graduated from bickering over trivial shit to bickering over literal shit. That tracks.

'The bag has been sitting in the laundry for eight days, Jeremy!' Ba calls from the master, where I assume he's packing his own luggage. 'You promised it would be sorted over the weekend and it's Wednesday.'

Dad exhales and asks me if I'm okay.

'I'm fine.' I sound too fine, so I exhale in solidarity. 'How are you? Do you want me to stay?'

He shakes his head. 'Go to Sydney with your father.'

I tell him I don't have to.

The answer comes from their bedroom. 'Harvey doesn't have a choice,' Ba says. 'He's coming. I've bought the ticket.'

Dad doesn't protest. 'Try east-coast life on for size.' He conjures a reassuring smile. My parents have always been a united front when it comes to Sydney, but I had an inkling Dad was open to the idea of me dropping out. 'You never were built for school.'

Vindication. 'Exactly!'

'What time's your flight?' he asks.

'How should I know?'

Dad sputters a laugh. He isn't talking to me.

'Soon,' Ba calls.

'Have you booked a taxi?'

No response. Dad raises both eyebrows. The silence perseveres.

'I'll drive you,' he says eventually.

Ba is adamant. 'You're *not* driving us.'

Dad's phone syncs the moment he starts the car. I dunno what song he'd choose to soundtrack the breakdown of his marriage, but a Nicki Minaj banger about starships and their propensity to fly probably ain't it. I cackle before I can stop myself. Dad scrambles to kill the track.

'You didn't have to drive us,' Ba insists. His voice sounds brittle.

Dad lets the indicator do the talking. Two ticks warn any oncoming cars, then he pulls out of the park.

The air in here is thick.

I watch the constant stream of streetlights, half-expecting Ba to renege on the break-up by the time we reach the Shell on Thomas Street. The right turn onto the freeway. Swan River. He holds firm.

They're doing it. They're finally doing it.

And I get Sydney.

I post a GIF in the group chat, this brick shithouse of a man accepting a gold medal. I tell them to pay up. Owen's always tethered to his computer keyboard. He asks for details, then adjudicates my win. No school rules flaunted. No laws broken. Fifty dollars to my bank account.

It's not how I pictured it, but I'm glad I'm slinking off into the night. Makes for an easier goodbye. No build-up. No half-slurred two a.m. speeches. No pretending we're more than what we are. When I mute the group chat, I'm not twisted up about it. We're not friends like that. They're good fun. That's all. They'll react in the morning, then they'll carry on, share memes, bitch about the usual teachers, and me not responding will become so normal, they won't even notice when I quit the group.

At the airport, Ba can't get out of the car fast enough. Dad says goodbye and asks me to text him when we land. I feel like I have to reassure him. I tell him Ba will come to his senses somewhere over South Australia.

'That's sweet of you to say.'

I yawn. The gentle rumble of the cabin is doing its thing. Only a matter of time before I'm dreaming. I look to Ba across the narrow aisle. We were assigned either side of an emergency exit row. I try to read his expression. He can be a ridiculous man and this is him at his most ridiculous. 'Manure, huh?' I ask.

He doesn't face me. 'It was more than that.'

But he won't say.

He massages his bare ring finger. The cabin lights dim. He becomes a dark silhouette. And I catch myself feeling…Um. My parents are splitting up and I'm actually sad for them.

I let my eyes close and the rumble lulls me to sleep.

2

My grandmother has two children she loves equally, Ba and the cafe on Victoria Street. It was an Italian place when she was hired to rescue it in the eighties. Her impact was immediate. People would say they were going to Gina's, and ignore the regular menu for the daily special – whatever my great-grandmother had whipped up the night before. Dolmádes. Spanakópita. All the favourites nobody can pronounce. After a while, the owner got the hint and offered Gina the joint. My family sold their old place and what they made on that was the down payment on the entire terrace. They've lived above the cafe ever since.

When our taxi pulls up at the intersection with the huge Coke signs, I know we're close.

Ba arches an eyebrow at me. 'Look alive.'

I groan. It should take longer to fly across a country, long enough for a solid eight hours.

There's a truck in the cafe's loading zone, so the taxi driver lets us out a fair way down Victoria Street, by a vacant shopfront. The floor at its entrance is tessellated with unopened mail and Domino's coupons.

Ba grunts. He struggles with his stubborn suitcase handle. 'Bastard left us in the next suburb over.'

I help him out. The handle extends for me. 'We're not *that* far.'

Seventy metres, tops. Ba exhales like we're facing Everest.

'You okay?'

He just starts walking, the loose wheels of his battered suitcase rattling behind him. I catch up.

'What's the strategy?' I ask.

'Be honest. Tell your grandmother you're dropping out of school and moving here.'

'I meant about you leaving Dad.'

His silence says everything.

'You can't not tell her. She'll know what's up.'

'Not necessarily.'

'Yes, necessarily. We fled in the night.'

'We didn't *flee*.'

Gina's wiping down a wonky table on the footpath. She's got her white shirt tucked into black pants, hair pulled back severely. Nature's facelift. When she clocks us from a distance, she shrieks. She startles the customer beside her, but she couldn't give less of a shit.

'Ah, fuck,' Ba mutters. 'Is it too late to get a hotel?'

'Yep.'

She ditches the rag and barrels towards us.

'I didn't leave your father, okay? Distract her. Not that your head won't distract her plenty.'

'My head? Oh.' He means my *hair*. People above a certain age can't handle the skullet. Buzz cut up front, mullet in the back; it breaks their brains. But even then, I doubt it'll keep Gina from noticing her son has left his husband.

She throws her arms around me. The hug is... a lot. She has all the energy of an overwhelming Greek grandmother, but to a casual observer, she could pass for my mum, or my sister if the casual observer was hitting on her and laying it on a bit thick.

She doesn't reckon she's old enough to have a teenage grandson. Watch this.

'Hi, Yiayia.'

'Oi! Gina,' she corrects. She pulls back and gives me the once over. 'You're tall. Perfect height. Don't grow more.'

'I'll see what I can do.'

'And we're shaving your head.'

I laugh. 'Sure.'

She turns her attention to Ba and arches the same eyebrow he does. 'What are you doing here?'

I give him a few seconds, and when it's obvious he's incapable of answering, I rescue him. 'I'm dropping out of school.'

'And you wanted to see me react in person? Brave.'

'It's easier in Sydney.' I gesture at Ba. 'He's here for moral support.'

'When were you going to tell me?' she asks, finally moving to embrace her son. 'Hi, darling.' She pecks his cheek and then scans the surrounds, as if expecting Dad to pop out from behind a parked car. 'Where's my son-in-law?'

Another chance to spill the beans. This time, Ba swats it away confidently. 'He has to work.'

'He needs to be his own boss,' Gina says, peeling off her apron and leading us back the way she came. 'Éla.'

We haven't visited for a while, but we were here so much when I was a kid, the red door sandwiched between the cafe and the real-estate agency is seared into my mind. It's an effort to open. Gina blames the rain, expanding timber. 'Ah! There we go.'

She leads us up the stairs and the house aggressively reminds me that half my family is Greek. Sure, I live with someone I call Ba who has his Mediterranean moments, but he hasn't been around his family much, so it's like his stores are depleted. He's Greek-Australian fusion, and the balance is off. He's a drizzle of olive oil on a kangaroo steak. This place is... I've already counted two commemorative Parthenon plates on the walls, ANT1 is blaring from a distant room, a torrent of words I don't understand, and there's the choking smell of liváni. It might be painfully early, but my great-grandmother's already smoked the place.

We abandon our bags in the formal dining room. Nobody's ever had a meal in here. It's where they keep the antique table and cabinets. One's filled with china and treasured ornaments, and the other's stuffed with old photos and funeral pamphlets. The last time I cracked a joke about the mausoleum, Gina threatened to make room in it for me. It's stacked with pics of her brother when he was around my age. He didn't get to be much older.

I round the bend and I'm in the kitchen. There's a moment when my great-grandmother doesn't know anyone else is here. She's watching the TV in the adjoining room. But something makes her turn. She lights up. A sharp intake of breath. 'To paidí mou!' She claps her hands together.

I don't feel like I've done anything to earn the reaction. I'm just the guy from the fortnightly video calls who laughs when she bends over to kiss the screen.

'Hi.'

She's at the plastic-covered table in the centre of the kitchen, halfway through her boiled eggs and toast. She's in her robe. Her hair is thinner and whiter than it was the last time I saw her in person. Short wisps of it are combed back roughly and her face is specked with more sunspots than I remember. When I'm close enough to hug her, I notice the butterfly stitch across her left eyebrow. I realise that the most prominent sunspot is a bruise.

In Greek, a grandmother is a yiayia. A great-grandmother is a proyiayia. They're like regular grandmothers, only they've been around long enough to go pro.

Yesterday, my proyiayia lost a fight with a rubbish bin. She was in the courtyard, cleaning out the bin with the hose. She lost her grip and the lid hit her head.

'The lid did that?' Ba asks, casually inspecting the injury. 'Nasty.'

Gina's tone is severe. 'She admitted she fainted.'

My great-grandmother is defiant. 'I no faint.'

'Did your vision go black?' Gina asks.

My great-grandmother nods.

'And did you wake up on the ground?'

Another nod.

'Then you fainted.'

'Bah!'

Gina's concern doesn't rub off on my father. He squeezes Proyiayia's shoulders and says she's sturdy. He does a quick lap of the kitchen. Something's different. The cupboard doors are a different colour. Gina insists she sent him pictures when she had them done.

While they debate whether that's true, I slide into the chair beside Proyiayia. She whispers, 'I no faint,' and waggles a finger at me. I wink and she grins, a little bit of egg escaping her mouth. She doesn't notice and I don't tell her. 'I come inside. I bandage. I ring Panagiotis.'

Gina breaks off her riveting conversation about the kitchen remodel to clarify, 'Her GP.'

'GP,' Proyiayia repeats. 'He say he no help on the phone. I have to come in. I drive.'

The terrace is built into a hill. Even though we're upstairs, the courtyard to my right backs onto a narrow street.

'You drove yourself?' I ask.

'Independent.' She stresses every syllable. Then she asks me something in Greek.

I look to Ba. I got *kefáli*, but the rest...

'She wants to know what died on your head,' Ba translates. He answers on my behalf. 'A skullet.'

Disdain flashes across her face. 'Ti eínai aftó?' She tries repeating it. 'Sku...Skunk?'

'Skullet.' I dunno why I bother.

'That I say. Skunk.'

I give up. 'Yes. Skunk.'

She smiles. 'Heavy.'

Proyiayia has always had difficulty with my name. My parents didn't do what their parents did and name me after a relo. They wanted a name with a story, but the story changes every time they tell it. According to the bits they repeat most, the day my dads decided to have me, they made an appointment with a mortgage broker. They briefly flirted with the idea of guilting a friend into being their baby oven, but decided it was best to engage one of those fancy overseas surrogacy agencies. That meant they needed money. Sitting opposite their broker, they told the truth. They were two men, both in their early twenties, one with an unencumbered house, who wanted money to secure a womb. This did not impress the broker. A child was apparently not a sound financial investment. But they pleaded with him – Ba says he charmed him, but Ba's always had tickets on himself – and eventually, the broker relented. He amended their application. They weren't seeking a mortgage to pay for a surrogate, they were after cash for a *Home Addition (Non-Structural)*. They thought that would make a good name for a boy, Hans.

They started telling people about the pregnancy and they said Hans aloud enough times that they fell out of love with the name. So, they went back to the drawing board. I know they briefly considered honouring their broker. Gina was the one who vetoed Stewart. Coming up to my due date, they had no name, and then one afternoon, Ba was served by a guy called Harvey at the local chicken shop.

I probably butchered it, but the story really comes alive when they tell it – Dad and Ba, bouncing off each other. They haven't told it recently, and they haven't been like *that* around each other for I dunno how long.

'So...Sydney.' Gina leans against the counter and homes in on me. 'Where are you going to live?'

'Here,' I say. Her eyebrow twitches, so I add, 'Hopefully. Till I get a job.'

'And we're committed to this no-school thing?'

Ba reminds Gina that I'm his son, which is likely as close to telling her to back off as he's comfortable getting.

'Yes, he's your kid, but that doesn't mean you can't be wrong.' She's smirking, but her focus returns to me. 'I don't tolerate bludgers. Piss me off and you will quickly learn there are worse places to be than school.'

'Understood.'

'You can look after your great-grandmother today.'

'I was gonna explore the city, actually.'

'Let me rephrase it. You're looking after your great-grandmother today.' She's firm, like Ba in a bad mood.

Proyiayia asks me what I want for lunch.

'Ma, you're not going to baby him.'

My great-grandmother chops the air. 'Áse me!'

'No, he's seventeen.' Gina looks to me for confirmation. I nod. I am indeed seventeen. She adds, 'You're going to look after her, not the other way around.' She approaches and plants a kiss on my forehead. 'I need to get back downstairs.'

She pecks Ba, and when she's gone, he relaxes. I dunno why. He's only delayed the inevitable.

'She's gonna find out,' I warn him.

'Áse me!' he huffs.

I can't recall the last time he was exasperated at me in Greek. The house is changing him, adding a little more olive oil to the steak.

3

Ba lays claim to the spare bedroom, so I get the home office where an old single bed has been sent to die. I test the mattress. Its insides have turned to dust. Not great, but I'm in Sydney. My room might only be wide enough to fit a desk and a bed, no chair, and it might smell like water damage, but I never have to set foot in a school again.

The desk's coated with old photos, some in better nick than others. There are probably hundreds more in the yolk-coloured Kodak envelopes stacked on the floor. These must be the favourites. I snatch one up. Gina and Proyiayia sitting on a grassy incline. Gina's face is fuller. She's a teenager. Proyiayia's hair is in a dark bun. They're both beaming. I put the pic down, but not exactly where I found it, because it had been covering *OVERDUE* printed in fat red letters, and now I'm curious. I shift the layer of photos to reveal several threatening notices. Utilities. Rates. Invoices.

'Gina, you rebel,' I mutter.

Through the wall, I hear Ba's phone ring and then the curt way he answers it.

'If I wanted to talk to you, Jeremy, I'd still be in Perth.'

The gays are fighting. I climb onto the bed. I press my head against the wall and wait for what comes next. Takes longer than I expect.

'Why would I tell him not to text you?' he asks.

I recoil.

Shit. I forgot to text Dad. I scramble to fish my charger out of the duffle bag. I plug my phone in but it's too late. Ba's standing in the doorway looking aggrieved.

'Your father tells you to message him, you message him,' he says.

I sigh. 'Battery died on the plane.'

'Not my problem.'

'Well, you did yank me out of bed while it was charging.'

'Don't start me.' His voice is gravel. 'And since you need reminding of things, your great-grandmother's downstairs, where you should be.'

I love her to bits in the way you love eighty-something-year-old amateur bin wrestlers, but I dunno why she's become my responsibility. 'Why aren't you the one looking after her?'

'Because you're the one who wanted to leave school,' he says. 'I'm heading out.'

When my phone has enough charge to switch on, three messages from Dad come through. Different ways of asking if everything's all right, but ramping up the anxiety each time. I shoot him a quick apology for not texting sooner. He responds, *Okay*. I ask how his morning's been. *Okay*.

Awesome. Heaps to work with.

I redownload Grindr. It's my top suggestion in the app store. Recently searched. Recently downloaded. Recently deleted.

Having gay dads comes with a lot of pressure. You're aware of how much they paid to have you, so you're hypervigilant when crossing streets. And there's an unstated expectation that you ought to be queer. Don't get me wrong, my folks went to great pains to make sure I was comfortable identifying however I wanted, but...imagine growing up in a rainbow family and being like, 'I'm an ally.' Fucking cringe. Not a problem for me, I was in primary school when the same-sex attraction kicked in. Emmett: school vice-captain, tween heartthrob. But thanks to the great pains and a co-ed high school, I experimented with heterosexuality. Meg: debating juggernaut, radiant queen. In Year Nine, I landed on pan as my identifier of choice.

Grindr isn't meant for anyone younger than eighteen. I've had it, on and off, since I turned sixteen. Dicey, I know, but I'm not the only one who's on the app when they shouldn't be. We tend to find each other, and we migrate to Insta pretty quickly to ward off the fakes and freaks. I could start there, follow the certified snacks who haunt friends' snaps, like a few posts, and launch myself into their DMs, but that's too much work. Plus, it's nice to meet someone with zero mutuals and be the most exciting thing about each other's lives. Briefly.

It's Darlinghurst, so the grid is busy, and I'm a fresh face, so the messages come thick and fast. I don't read most of them. There's no point. The guys are three times my age.

After ten minutes, an eighteen-year-old with a pictureless profile says *hey*. Big I'm-on-the-app-when-I-shouldn't-be energy. I ask if he's seventeen.

Shit, is it that obvious? he asks.

I laugh. I tell him I'm seventeen too, and I toss him a photo. He sends one back. He has a middle part and a mole on his neck shaped like Tasmania. He's cute. His name is Brad. He's skipped school because his major work is due tomorrow.

And you're on Grindr? I ask.

Yup.

That's another ding against keeping the app permanently installed. The fucker's a time suck. One minute, you're messaging a guy, next thing you know, it's June. But Brad insists he's not avoiding his work. He's set aside an hour for recreation. He wants to know if I'm keen.

I've broken my app chastity, obviously, but it does take more than seven messages to get me into somebody's bedroom. Eight, at least.

Can we chat more?

He doesn't immediately block me. That's a good sign.

Sure.

I ask for his Insta. He knows why, because he replies with a short video. 'Harvey, this is Brad. I am not a catfish.'

I think I hear somebody say my name, and then I definitely hear somebody say my name. 'Heavy.'

I unplug my phone and drag myself to the balustrade. I peer over.

Proyiayia's standing at the foot of the stairs. She smiles. 'Shopping?'

I suspect the trip to Coles hasn't been sanctioned by Gina because Proyiayia insists we leave the back way. I don't rat her out. I can handle a simple escort mission and I like having an excuse to leave the house. Coles isn't far; it's in the basement of the building with the giant Coke signs, but we make our way at Proyiayia's pace.

More than once, my gaze drifts to the butterfly stitch and the whopper bruise on her forehead. The third time, I ask if it hurts. 'Se ... ponáei?'

She clicks her tongue against the roof of her mouth and continues walking, more weight on one foot than the other. I know if I ask about *that*, she'll dismiss it with a tongue click.

I man the trolley. She leads me to the fruit and veg section, but she's less interested in the fruit and veg than she is in stockpiling the free plastic bags. She pulls on the roll with surprising force and wraps the connected bags around her forearm. She only stops when I tell her somebody with a name badge is watching us. She tears herself free, half the roll now padding her arm. She waves it at the bloke. He knows her name.

He's not the only one.

Apparently she's something of a celebrity at Coles Central Kings Cross. Shelf-stockers go out of their way to greet her, and when they do, she points to me. 'My *great*-grandson,' she bellows. Every time. And because I'm on my phone, on Grindr, I hide the screen. Every time. Not that I'm ashamed of it or anything. I just don't wanna look like the guy who's on a casual hook-up app while escorting his great-grandmother to the shops. Even though that's exactly who I am.

Proyiayia introduces me to Grace by the fresh meats. I hide the screen. She tells Proyiayia there are so many specials today, a note of pride in her voice. As far as I can tell, every cut has a discount sticker on it. Proyiayia isn't impressed. 'When everything special, nothing special,' she says.

Genuinely hilarious line delivery, made even better by how crestfallen Grace looks. Ten out of ten. No notes.

Unaware that she's a comedic icon, Proyiayia shuffles towards the lamb cutlets. She adds two packets to the trolley and we continue our tour. I farewell Grace and check my phone. Another three messages from Brad. He's keeping the conversation going. Which is good, because I need something to do every time Proyiayia pauses in front of the trolley without giving me notice and stares intensely at a shelf. She labours over every choice, be it meat cut, table salt or serviette. I'd hate to care that much about groceries.

We snake down the aisles one after the other, Proyiayia pausing abruptly, me pausing before I ram into her, her staring, me messaging. We're in the freezer section, Proyiayia being super deliberate about her selection of frozen peas, when Brad asks what I'm doing right now. I almost tell him the truth. Almost.

Nothing much.

'Heavy.'

I pocket my phone in an instant, as if my great-grandmother can not only read English, but identify a gay hook-up app on sight. She's prodding the freezer door. She wants me to retrieve a particular bag of peas. I do. Then it's off to the check-out. At least, that's where she says we're headed, but we end up zipping randomly around the store to collect final items that occur to her in the most inconvenient order possible. *Then* it's off to the check-out.

The total is a little shy of two hundred. She blinks down at the note sleeve in her wallet. The guy at the check-out waits patiently for all of five seconds and then starts huffing. Proyiayia's brow furrows. I intervene and tell her I've got it. I hold my phone over the EFTPOS terminal till it vibrates.

Today's shop is courtesy of Dad.

Almost two hundred dollars' worth of groceries is heavy. There's a pulling on the inside of my right elbow and I'm really regretting not talking Proyiayia out of the four-litre tin of extra virgin olive oil.

'You want help?' she asks.

I wince. 'Nah, I'm good.'

When we arrive at the back gate, I can't lower the bags fast enough. I exhale, extend my right arm. The bags have left purple imprints. I wiggle feeling back into my fingers. And Proyiayia hasn't budged. I speak up and she points to the lock.

'I don't have a key,' I tell her.

'Oh.' She's forgotten hers.

I size up the fence. I'm not a particularly adept climber, but I can hop onto a wheelie bin, and that's most of the way there. I feel an octogenarian gently nudge my foot as I climb over.

I unlock the gate from the inside. Proyiayia grabs the lightest bag and shuffles across the courtyard. I follow her, squeezing the groceries between the brick wall and the car. She leaves me to do the unpacking. She plants herself on the recliner, turns the heater on, unmutes the TV and puts her feet up.

I lug the bags onto the plastic-covered table and begin the process of laying out their contents. I'm not familiar with the kitchen and I'm already dreading figuring out what goes where. I start with the cold items. They go in the fridge or freezer, depending. And it's helpful Proyiayia's bought some things without fully running out, so I can keep the new cheese with the...four other packets of cheese and the milk with the... two other cartons. It's a trend. There's an unopened four-litre tin of extra virgin olive oil in the pantry. In fact, the whole pantry is very well stocked.

Half of this stuff must end up in the cafe.

I put everything in its place and toss the reusable bags in the cupboard under the sink. My stomach grumbles. I could do with lunch. 'Proyiayia?' I ask.

No response. I round the table. My great-grandmother's head is tilted back, cradled by her neck pillow. She snores softly.

I can't help but smile. I whip out my phone with the intention of taking a picture, but Grindr's still open and Brad's sent a new video.

'We spoken long enough yet?' he asks.

I glance back at Proyiayia. Brad isn't far. I'll only be an hour. She'll be asleep the whole time.

I swipe the keys from the fruit bowl and duck out. I must know I probably shouldn't, because I leave the back way.

4

Brad's building has a name. Savoy. It sounds like a kind of dry biscuit, but I google it and it's a cabbage. That's infinitely worse. It's written in gold paint above the entrance like they're proud of it. Savoy. When he's tracing circles on my bare chest, Brad tells me it was the name of a royal dynasty that once ruled Italy and briefly, Spain.

'Interesting.' For the sake of being a smart-arse, I'm not swayed. 'But how do you know the architect wasn't big into cabbage?'

He's chewing his bottom lip. He's not gonna give me the satisfaction of cracking. 'There's a Savoy region in France.'

'Yeah, really far away. Cabbage, though? Always close.'

Brad sputters a laugh. Got him.

The first time I knocked on a guy's door and he led me straight to his bedroom, I was a nervous wreck. Couldn't get it up. He was good about it and didn't kick me out after ten minutes, even though he probably wanted to. I mean, he'd jettisoned his clothes in the hallway. He wanted sex. So did I, but...I dunno. It felt abrupt. Not that I expected canapés on arrival or anything. We ended up chatting. Kissing a bit, but mostly chatting. I made him laugh. I didn't want him to hate me, and if he laughed, he didn't hate me. So, while I'm better at rising to the occasion now, some broken part of me reckons a tight comedy set is an essential part of hooking up. Getting a laugh is as good as getting off.

It's a difficult feat with strangers. Not that Brad and I are complete strangers. There's a lot you can learn about a guy from the walk to their bedroom. Brad's family's loaded, for one. Polished floors, little statues on marble tables in the hall, no obvious damp smell. Somebody rules the house, probably his mum, who's probably an interior designer. She doesn't give him much leeway to express himself. His walls are bare. The metal lamp by his bedside matches one from the living room, but this one has liquid-paper lightning bolts drawn on the base. Whoever rules the house hasn't noticed those.

Brad made the first move. He took off my shirt, clumsily, so I made an effort to be just as awkward with his. We kissed. He tasted like Colgate Total. We broke apart, grabbed at each other, kissed again. I guided him onto the mattress. I knew he only had an hour. Our eyes darted, his to my arms, mine from the tuft of hair on his chest down his treasure trail. I tested the elastic of his trackpants with one hand, ready to perform my magic trick where I make them disappear, but... a sharp breath. His eyes were wide. I recognised the discomfort. It was too abrupt for him. I released his trackies, lay beside him and made a crack about his building...

'What made you skip school today?' Brad asks.

'I dropped out of school. Well, I'm *dropping* out of school. One of my dads has to call and let the office know.'

'You have dads, plural?'

'Seven, actually.' When hooking up, I have to make every joke that occurs to me. It's annoyingly essential. This one's flown over his head. He seems confused. 'Only two,' I assure him. 'They're married, but they're in the process of...' I let unclasping my hands convey the intricacies.

'Divorce? Already?'

'Oh! Judgy.'

'No, I... Marriage hasn't been legal that long, has it?'

I laugh. 'They've always been pioneers.'

'Huh.' He tilts his head back while he contemplates it, and for a sec, his Adam's apple is super pronounced. 'I've never met someone with gay parents.'

'You probably have, statistically speaking.'

'True.' He asks when they split.

'Last night. Arrived from Perth this morning.'

'That's fresh. And you're okay?' He catches himself. 'Wait, is this weird? Talking about your parents?'

I wanna tell him it's the reality of having two dads. Everyone is so fascinated by the concept it's like I disappear, pushed out of frame by Ba and Dad. I pinch the air between us. 'A smidge weird talking about my dads at a hook-up.'

'Okay. Okay.' He comes closer. He smacks his lips and says, 'No more parent talk,' as sexily as he can muster.

I wince.

'That was the last...Yeah.' He kisses me slowly. A couple of gentle prods from his tongue and I'm into it. I suck in air through my nose, match his tongue prod for prod. Then he pulls himself off me like I've gone too far. 'Perth?'

'Yeah.' Breathily.

'So, you're visiting? This is a ships-passing-in-the-night situation?'

I don't answer. Well, not with words. I launch off the pillow to bring my lips to his. We are ships passing in the night, making the most of the moment. He presses his weight into me, till I'm on my back. He's on top, his knuckles grazing my thighs. He's pulling down his pants. And my phone is ringing. I urge him to kiss through it, but he slides off me and reaches for the phone tucked into my right shoe.

'Dispatch from shore,' he says, holding it out.

Gina's name is flashing. Not the best time to answer a call from my grandmother. 'It's fine.'

'I don't mind,' Brad says, all sweetness.

I take the phone and *reluctantly* – cannot stress that enough – answer the call from my grandmother. 'Hey.'

'What's wrong with your fathers?' she asks abruptly.

Stop one person talking about gay dads and the universe finds a way. 'What do you mean?' I ask, very aware that an adorable, half-naked guy is inches away with his trackies around his knees.

I can hear the cafe in the background. The espresso machine. 'Your father isn't answering my calls.'

'Ba? He went out.'

'No, Jeremy. He always answers my calls.'

I sit up. I'm not mentally prepared for this conversation. I stall. 'How many times have you phoned him?'

'Twice. And I've given him time to call back.'

'Maybe try again?'

'You've never shown up without telling me.'

I'm compelled to lie. 'We didn't want you making a fuss.'

'You like my fusses.' A pause. More cafe noise. Plates. 'Promise me everything's okay?'

I scratch my nose. She's unrelenting. If I wasn't in a stranger's bed, I might have caved. 'Honestly, everything's okay.'

That works. Gina drops it and asks how Proyiayia is. She thinks I'm upstairs, not a few blocks away in some random guy's bedroom.

The random guy is pulling up his trackpants.

'She's asleep.' As far as I know, it's the truth.

'Okay.' There's relief in her voice, then she says she has to go.

The call ends. I exhale hard and glance at Brad. He doesn't make a move. He knows the moment's passed.

'You want some Milo?' he asks.

The kitchen's spotless. We lean against opposite counters with speckled mugs, handmade, probably imported and definitely expensive. Since Brad knows my domestic situation, he asks if there's anything I wanna know about his parents. Hard pass. I ask about the major work instead. It's for English Extension 2. That's a weird name for a subject. He agrees, but he loves it. He's written a story, inspired by authors whose names I don't recognise. He asks me if I have a favourite writer. I don't, but I say, 'Sam Baker,' because I don't wanna seem like the sort of guy who doesn't have a favourite writer. Brad hasn't heard of him. Nobody has. I ask if he wants to be a writer. He's not sure.

He takes a slow sip of his Milo, then licks his top lip. 'What do you want to be?'

'No clue.'

He groans. He's desperate for the HSC to be over. He's ready to do something with his life. Be something. I tell him he could drop out, like me. One last joke before we say goodbye.

When I arrive at the first intersection, I elbow the pedestrian button, step back from the kerb and open

Grindr. Blocking Brad is a non-event. It's habit at this point. I've never met a guy off Grindr a second time. I've never even messaged them after the first.

Ships that pass in the night don't send carrier pigeons.

I bury my phone in my pocket and my hand with it. I start down Victoria Street. It's not unbearably cold, but it's chilly enough that I regret wearing shorts. Soon I'm at the red door, working my way through the keys till the third one fits. I turn it in the lock and Gina emerges from the cafe, a wet rag wrapped around the bony fingers of one hand. She stops and stares at me.

'What are you doing?' she asks.

I figure it's self-explanatory, but, 'I'm opening the door?'

She doesn't have a follow-up. Like, I wait a while.

I force a smile. 'Okay, bye.'

I climb the stairs two at a time, pass the commemorative Parthenon plates, return the keys to the kitchen fruit bowl.

'Georgina?' Proyiayia asks from the adjoining room.

'Harvey,' I correct her, stepping into view.

She's awake. One of her serials is playing. She's completely fine, but I hear the door and the approaching footsteps. My grandmother rounds the corner, still holding the rag.

'Georgina!' Proyiayia says, correct this time.

I expect her to be comforted by the sight of her mother, no harm having befallen her in my absence, but nope. Gina's nostrils flare. I go to speak—

'Not in here,' she growls. 'Upstairs.'

She stomps up those stairs like she has a vendetta against them. She leads me into the office. I keep some distance between us, not much, because there's not much distance in here to work with.

'Where did you go?' she asks.

'Out.'

'*Out?*'

I guess there's no harm in telling her. 'I met up with a guy.'

Her forehead vein bulges. 'I told you to look after her.'

'She's fine.'

I'm bombarded with the beginnings of sentences till Gina settles on one she likes. 'Do I need to spell it out for you? Your great-grandmother isn't *well*, Harvey.'

There's spittle and I laugh.

'Oh, come off it,' she growls. 'I need you to care more.'

I'm stunned by the force of it. I don't have a response and she doesn't wait for one. She charges past and she's gone. I stare after her, then down at the desk. My eyes find that photo of Gina and Proyiayia on the grassy incline. Beaming.

TWO
The first thing you do is dig

SOTIRIS

1

Writing is a numbers game.

One end-of-year merit award for excellence in creative writing.

One new Word document.

One page a night, every night.

One computer virus.

One wiped hard drive.

One restarted novel.

One page a night, then two, then three.

One rejection, then two, then three.

Forty-seven consecutive lunches in the classroom Mrs Ferguson always forgets to lock.

One package: one cover letter, three chapters, one self-addressed envelope.

One response that is nicer than the others.

One invitation to their office in the city.

One book deal.

Twenty-four copies of *Young* by Sotiris Bakiritzis.

Miss Fletcher's made a mountain out of them. It's

impossible to look elsewhere. Twenty-four boys, on twenty-four identical covers, stare at me. Some have speech bubbles tacked to their cheeks. 'Borrow me!' one boy cries.

While a roof collapse and banishment to a demountable smack bang in the middle of a basketball court might have defeated an ordinary teacher-librarian, Miss Fletcher is by no measure ordinary. She's not the sort to let eighteen months in a makeshift library under constant basketball bombardment break her resolve to put up a mean display.

'It's perfect,' I assure her, 'absolutely perfect.' Plucked from my wildest dreams, even.

Seeing your name on a book isn't something you get used to quickly, no matter how many covers you sketched in class with *Sotiris Bakiritzis* written various ways. When it's a real-life thing, it squeezes all the air out of you.

'You're a published author, Sotiris,' she says, voice raspy. She's come a long way since she first encountered my name on a school roll and it tied a knot in her brain. I told her the S was silent, and she pronounced it *odorous*. Now I tell people the second S is the silent one, and they fare better.

My eyes find another speech bubble. 'The school's pride and joy!'

The day I signed the contract, Mum warned me that if I disappeared up my own arse, she was going to tear it up. Not my arse. The contract. On the other side of the conference table, editor Eliza Buchanan laughed through gritted teeth. 'That's not how publishing contracts work,' she said, with more than a hint of condescension. Mum didn't flinch, and before either of them could rip the contract out of my hands, I began initialling the corners of each page. I vowed to keep my head clear of my own arse.

And I did, when they invited me into the office to hold a finished copy, when the press release called the book a *stunning debut from a startling new Australian talent*. But now, with my name written across twenty-four books arranged like I'm the best thing to happen to this crummy school, my head inches dangerously close.

A basketball bounces off a nearby window. Miss Fletcher squeezes my shoulder, then relaxes. 'I caught them as they were unboxing it and bought every copy they had,' she says. 'It isn't often a student publishes a book. It isn't *ever*.'

And that's when it happens. I become a human pretzel and I disappear up myself.

Mrs Wiseman never photocopies exemplar essays. She wants us to know we're capable of writing them, so she painstakingly copies them onto the board, and we have the pleasure of painstakingly copying them into our books, word for finger-cramping word. The first line starts off straight and then slants diagonally. Instead of correcting herself with the second line, she commits to the slant. If anything, it gets more severe the deeper into the essay she ventures.

Benji whispers my name from the back row. I lean to the side so he can see past me.

'Nah, turn around.'

I do. He waves a library copy of *Young* at me. Miss Fletcher's display is already working wonders. I play it cool. 'Cool,' I say.

Benji isn't my nemesis. His writing isn't good enough. Plus, he has frosted tips. I can't imagine having a nemesis who would wilfully do that to his own head. But Mrs Wiseman loves his prose. I think he's about as subtle as an ACME anvil, but my opinion doesn't matter. I have a book out and he doesn't. He might've bested me by one mark in last week's creative writing task, but I won the war.

He aims the first page at me. The bio.

We workshopped it a lot. The whole point of a bio is to introduce the author, but how do you introduce a seventeen-year-old author without making them sound insufferable? Self-deprecation. It begins, *Seventeen-year-old Sotiris Bakiritzis is ready to catch a ball four seconds after it hits him in the face.* Translation: I'm seventeen and super accomplished, but I have no hand-eye coordination so it evens out.

There had been discussions about whether it was worth mentioning my age, because I would keep ageing. Removing the mention would alleviate the need to take the piss out of myself, and I could just introduce myself via my interests, but I pushed for it. I dreamt of being a thirteen-, fourteen-, fifteen-, sixteen-year-old author. I was published at seventeen, later than I'd hoped, but earlier than most, and I wanted everyone to know.

I wanted people like Benji to know.

'Do you see it?' he asks.

See what? A well-crafted bio that humorously conveys the fact that I'm a seventen-year-old prodig—

I pause. Re-read. *Seventen*.

I blink at it. There's no way I spelt the first word wrong. We proofed it over and over. I'm *a startling new Australian talent*. I . . . can spell *seventeen*.

But there it is. *Seventen*.

Spotted by Benji. The Mixer of Metaphors.

'Easy mistake to make,' he says, 'but seven and ten actually make *seventeen*.'

I barrel towards the demountable at lunch, bag hanging off one shoulder. Bags are strictly forbidden in the library, but strictly speaking, the demountable isn't the library. I approach the display. The mountain is three books shorter. Benji wasn't the only person who was swayed to borrow it. I reach for a copy. The boy on the cover says, 'An achievement!' I check the first page. *Seventen*. I plonk it down and check another. *Seventen*. It's in all of them. Like, that's how publishing works. If the mistake's in one, it's in all of them . . . I check another regardless. *Seventen*.

My head is light. I see pink. I blink. Take a breath. Swallow hard. My heart is raging, breaking. I check over my shoulder. Miss Fletcher's distracted, playing chess with the kid in the corner. Now's as good a time as any. A better time than many. I unzip my bag and dismantle the mountain two books at a time.

The weight on my shoulder strap increases.

I can't zip the bag fast enough. I'm out. Out of the demountable. Out of the school grounds. I take the first right. I'm halfway to the next intersection before I find a wheelie bin teetering on the lip of a driveway. I dump the copies of *Young*.

Writing is a numbers game.

One typo ruins it.

2

I'm in Ancient History, but not really. Mr Daniels is sitting on his desk, legs dangling, ten minutes deep into one of his tangents about Herodotus. Nobody brings the past to life like Mr Daniels. He's a showman. He makes you lean in without realising.

While others hang off every word, I'm elsewhere. Stuck in the exercise book I always carry with me. The pages are littered with character sketches, story ideas, mock covers... I spent so long preparing to be an author that I figured, when it happened, it would be perfect.

I arrive at the pages devoted to refining my autograph. It had to be unique but repeatable, because I would be signing books until my wrist gave out. I can retrace the history of my autograph. It evolves from one that's every letter in my name to one that only suggests a few. Unique, repeated all the way down to the bottom right-hand corner. My breath catches in my throat. There's an autograph that isn't mine.

And I'm in ancient history. Not the big ancient history, the kind with texts and scrutinised sources, but the small kind, the personal kind, the buried-out-of-sight ancient history that is Dean and me on the platform at Macdonaldtown. Me asking him about my autograph. Him saying he prefers ones he can actually read. Him scribbling his own.

I suppose our history isn't all that ancient. I bet he still catches the train every afternoon. If I wanted to see him, I could. If…

I focus on Mr Daniels. Nobody else's mind is wandering. Herodotus. Interesting bloke. Apparently not as interesting as my exercise book. The autograph that isn't mine.

I take a slow breath.

I unzip my pencil case. It's half-empty and reeks of shavings. I subtly transfer my phone from my pocket to the case. I thumb my way to the oldest message in my inbox. *OK dude* from an unsaved number.

The past roars to life.

It's last year. We have the same idea to step off the train that's been stuck at Macdonaldtown because of a signal failure. Waiting in the open air is more comfortable. I'm reading, but I sneak a glance. A defiant lock of hair curls over his forehead. His lips are full. He looks like money, with his black-and-white striped tie and ridiculous blazer. He doesn't have a name yet, he's just some guy from Stanmore Grammar who recognises the book I'm holding. He catches me the next time I glance and says he's desperate to talk to somebody about who dies at the end. He's frustrated at himself when I ask, 'Somebody dies?' He apologises, promises to make it up to me the next day. Same place. Same time. He'll bring chips. The train's departing. We're encouraged to stand clear. He boards and asks if I'm coming. I'm scared to follow him so I wait an hour for another train.

Same time the next day, I stare at him from the carriage. He has a paper package in his lap. He watches the carriage doors expectantly. A pang of regret. I dart for the exit but I'm too late. The train lurches past Macdonaldtown. I hop out at Redfern. It's ages until the next train back, but a lady says the walk isn't too bad. It is bad. I'm not convinced he'll still be there, but he is. The grease-stained paper wrapping tears easily. The chips are soggy, but they're crumbed in chicken salt, so it evens out. I'm nervous. I look everywhere else but at him. I learn his name. He learns mine.

I take three days to message the number he scrawls on a sliver of paper. Can he ask a personal question? I tell him it's okay. He asks if I'm gay. Mum's in the room. She's on the couch, foot resting on the edge of the coffee table while she clips her toenails. I lie. Or maybe I think it's the truth. Or maybe I think it will become the truth if I type it. *I'm straight.* He apologises and promises to make it up to me. Chips. Again. He has one more question, though. Why am I messaging a gay kid so much? He doesn't wait for my reply. *I think you're gay too.*

I practise my autograph while I wait for him. When he shows up, he has thoughts. He signs his name. His autograph is better. I'm smiling. I can't stop smiling. I worry someone might spot us. We hop on the next train. We share a three-seater, our hands close to touching. We change at Central. Again at Circular Quay. The edge of his finger grazes mine. My heart. My *heart*. He says he'll take me somewhere.

We get off at Town Hall. I don't let him hold my hand. He leads me to the McDonald's on Pitt Street. I follow him upstairs to the men's. The cubicle is cramped. He presses against me; he's half a head shorter. I'm breathing like I've forgotten how. That makes him grin.

How nervous I am makes him grin, makes him get on his toes so his lips are almost at mine. Almost. I'm so close to that defiant curl. His lips. The restroom door whines. Footsteps. I'm certain somebody's about to count four shoes. Dean isn't fussed. He keeps grinning. Impossibly close. Water rushes, and some guy barely washes his hands before the door whines and we're alone again.

He leads me to the disabled bathroom. It's roomier and the door goes all the way to the tiled floor. We kiss for the first time. I kiss somebody for the first time. Dean's breath feels hot. His tongue is everywhere. I can't believe I'm kissing him. I'm terrified I'm kissing him. He fumbles with my belt. I take his hands in mine before he can undo the buckle. We pull apart. My heart spasms. He asks what's wrong. There's some invisible line: as long as my belt doesn't come off, I'm not gay. Forget the kiss and how hard I am. The *belt*. That'll do it. It's stupid. I know it's stupid.

He messages me a tiny black heart before bed. It freaks me out.

Our last afternoon at Macdonaldtown, I insist I'm straight. He calls me a liar. The kiss didn't make me feel good. *Liar*. I apologise. He's upset. The next train can't come soon enough.

I delete his number. I wipe every message except one, the reply to me saying I don't want to see him again.

OK dude

I stare at it every so often.

Today's the first time I reply. I ask Dean to meet me. I order hot chips from the milk bar near Lewisham station. I tear a hole in the wrapping so they don't get too soggy. I wait at Macdonaldtown longer than I probably should. I don't realise when I start eating the chips, but I realise when they're gone.

My phone vibrates beside me. I think it might be him, but it isn't. I have one missed call. Mum lets it ring once and hangs up. It's her way of prodding me. So long as I don't answer, it's cheaper than a message.

By the time my train arrives at the Cross, I have a second missed call from Mum. I leap out of the carriage and take the escalator two steps at a time. Having grown up in Darlinghurst, I'm pretty adept at swerving — past people coming at me on the footpath, between cars that definitely have the right of way. A driver slams the brakes, then the horn. I'm unfazed. I don't want to risk a third missed call.

Mum's is the busiest cafe on Victoria Street. It has the best Greek menu, not that the other place and its sub-par moussaká is really worth a mention. Of an afternoon, there's usually a mix of regulars sipping from oversized mugs and others having strangely late lunches. This afternoon's no different. But it's closer to evening than afternoon now.

I weave between the tables. The one in the corner is reserved for staff. Fran's picking apart her focaccia, loose-fitting woollen jumper over her work top. I dump my school bag by her feet and reach for her discarded apron. I tie it around my waist.

After school, it's my job to relieve the waitstaff.

'How long have you been on break?' I ask.

Fran eats a sundried tomato like it's a Tim Tam. 'Five minutes.'

Okay, not too bad.

I exhale, and with it, I shove the whole day down. The typo, waiting around for Dean like a loser. I approach the espresso machine. Without turning from the milk she's frothing, Mum tells me I'm late.

People like to think they have demanding mothers.

They haven't met mine, the mother upon which all demanding mothers are modelled.

'Sorry.' That's wog guilt at work. She expects too much of me and I hate when I fall short. 'Good day?' I ask.

'A day.' Weariness is etched on her face. 'Table five needs their order taken, then come back for this mocha.'

I snatch up the nearest docket book.

The bloke on five is scowling at the menu like it slapped his grandmother. Scowlers prefer to be handheld through everything, no exceptions. He asks about the difference between spanakópita and bouréki, and after a lengthy explanation, he opts for the spag bol, which is neither spanakópita nor bouréki. It's also nothing like either of them. Typical scowler behaviour.

Mum delivers the mocha herself. She makes a big show of it so I know I've failed her. On her way back, she rests a hand on my shoulder and asks the bloke on five if her son is looking after him well.

It's her oldest move and it works. 'Your son?' Now he's scowling at us. Then, the beginnings of a smile. 'You're too young to have a son.'

I'm off book at this point. She's a timeless...

'I'm a timeless beauty,' she says.

He's in awe. 'What's your secret?'

'Stay single and you'll never look dated.'

It was clever the first dozen times I heard it. I leave her to flirt and walk the spag bol order to Petro. He's the newest of Mum's cooks, and doesn't know me well enough to ask questions. I dig that. Especially on days like today. He hangs my docket with the other orders and tends to the steak on the grill.

I turn to the dining area. Mum doesn't like us keeping our backs to the customers. I relax against the counter. She doesn't like us leaning either, but I enjoy ten glorious seconds before she glances my way. She elongates her spine, wordlessly urging me to do the same.

I groan and stand tall.

The cafe is Mum's everything. The day there are no coffee grounds under her fingernails is the day she dies. I can't relate. I want more than to spend my life walking kilometres within eighty square metres, only to erase my footsteps with a mop after the last customer leaves.

I want to leave a mark.

Mum returns with the menu I left on the table. She says, 'You're in a mood.'

'No, I'm not.' I sound like the poster child for teens in a mood.

But what good is agreeing? Yes, I'm in a mood, but I can't tell her about *seventen*, because it's embarrassing, and I can't tell her about Dean, because...

'Don't make me beg, Sotiris. Your life's not interesting enough.'

She might think differently if she knew I tried (and failed) to reconnect with a guy I once made out with in a McDonald's bathroom. Not that I'd ever tell her.

She clicks her tongue. 'I can count from three to *you're grounded*, if you like.'

That works.

'There's a typo in my book.'

'Oh. That's it?'

'On the first page. It's mortifying. I want to die.'

'Righto.' She makes grabby hands over the counter. 'Something sharp, Petro.'

'*Mum.*'

The cook finishes slicing a tomato and offers her the knife. She shakes her head. 'Bigger.' When he plonks the cleaver down on the counter, she goads me. 'Go on, then.'

I sigh. 'It was hyperbole. People are going to open the book and think I can't write.'

Mum isn't particularly fazed. 'They'll read more and the rest will prove them wrong. Thank you, Petro.'

The cook's already taken back his blade.

'What does the librarian lady think?' she asks.

'Miss Fletcher? I don't think she knows about the typo.'

'Okay.'

'Or that I rounded up the library's available copies and dumped them in somebody's bin.'

Mum doesn't say anything, and that's bad, but then she clears her throat like she's preparing to say something substantial, and that's worse.

I pre-empt whatever it is. 'You really don't have to—'

'Let me speak.' She gives me a chance to chime in. It's a trap. I stay quiet and she continues, 'All my life, people have told me what I can't do, but then I've gone and done it. I wish a typo was my only worry. I mean, how often have you corrected something I've written on the specials chalkboard? '

'Yeah, but I can't rub this mistake out.'

'You can demand the publisher fix it. That's their job, isn't it?'

Petro rings the bell even though we're standing close

enough to notice table twelve's steak salad is ready for them.

'Take that, will you?' Mum starts towards the espresso machine. 'And get your books out of the fucking bin. Jesus.'

3

The place on Toothill Street doesn't have much of a backyard. The lawn is patchy, and the closest the garden has to ornaments are the kettle barbecue that looks like it's seen war and the wheelie bin that's...a wheelie bin.

I lift the lid and *Young*'s cover boy peers back at me. I'm not his biggest fan. He looks too much like a Lowes catalogue model and too little like the main character, Anthony. But he deserves better.

'Sorry, buddy,' I whisper.

I act swiftly. I peel off my bag and lay it open at my feet. I tilt the bin until it's flat on the lawn. I crawl inside. It reeks like holy hell. Clawing at the books, I think of my Year Four teacher, Mrs Stiles. When she awarded me that tiny certificate for excellence in creative writing, did she imagine I might one day find myself in a stranger's backyard, retrieving twenty-one abandoned copies of my debut novel from their bin?

I know every teacher dreams big for their star students, but surely not.

I come out for air.

'Can I help you?'

My stomach drops. My gaze traces an awkward line up to the source of the question, a woman on the balcony, a thin veneer of sternness masking a truckload of fear. An intruder is rummaging through her bin at half-past seven in the morning.

I swallow hard. I suppose I ought to answer the question. 'No, I'm all good.'

'That's my bin.' She folds her arms tightly over her robe.

'Is it? Oh.' I crawl into the bin to rescue the last of the books. When I emerge, I wave them. 'These are mine.'

'What are they doing in there?'

I shrug. 'I don't know. It's your bin.'

She doesn't have a comeback. The books are in my bag. I begin the complicated process of zipping it up around them. It's a struggle. The woman on the balcony has raised her voice now and honestly, it's a little confronting, so when the bag's half-zipped, I stand the bin upright and flee.

I bolt towards the school gate in time to camouflage myself among a horde of guys arriving from Lewisham station.

I march to the basketball court, sidle past the guy eating a breakfast burrito on the demountable step, and approach the trestle table that once supported the *Young* display. A kid has pulled up a chair and is diligently copying answers from the back of his maths textbook. He moves the third time I ask, mostly because that's the time I ask with my elbow. I rest my bag on the chair and begin rebuilding the mountain.

'Do I want to know?' Miss Fletcher asks on the way past.

'No, it's fine,' I assure her.

Some book edges are scuffed, and if you get too close to the display, you might catch a faint whiff of bin juice, but by and large, the copies are still in reasonable condition. I bend back one of the speech bubbles that creased in my bag. 'An achievement!' the boy on the cover says.

I take a deep breath. Yeah, it is.

4

The Five Irons Press office is on the fifty-seventh floor. It's the highest I think I've ever been. My ears always remind me around level forty. I yawn to pop them as the elevator opens onto a vast lobby. It's a marathon to the front desk, fashioned from five rusted iron rods arranged like the company logo and manned by a receptionist who whispers his half of a conversation into a bulky headset. There's a copy of *Young* propped up beside his monitor.

Definitely the highest I've ever been.

I was fifteen the first time I visited. There was a constant thrum in my head. I couldn't believe where I was. Mum came because she was adamant I was being scammed, and when it was clear I wasn't, she saw fit to provide a running commentary. She said Eliza's drop earrings made her look like a Christmas tree. Eliza laughed and ran with it. She said she lit up like one when she read my manuscript. She'd been in the role a couple of years and acquired a fair bit, but nothing from somebody *so* young. I had no idea how old she was, I still don't, but the way she stressed the *so* told me it had been a while since she was fifteen.

Returning to the office now, the thrum isn't as intense. The place hasn't lost any of its shine, I'm just used to being here. They're flaunting my book in reception for all new arrivals to see. I belong here.

When the receptionist ends the call and greets me, his voice is deeper and fuller. I introduce myself. He smiles like he already knows. 'For Eliza, yeah?' He dials her extension and while he waits for her to answer, he tells me my cover rocks.

'Oh?' It's a miracle I don't somersault. 'Have you read it?'

He keeps smiling. 'Eliza, hi.' He breaks eye contact. On the phone, he sounds like a remedial massage therapist. The call is brief. He encourages me to take a seat. I'm happy standing. Honestly, I could hear people's thoughts about my book all day. They probably train receptionists not to harass authors, but I really don't mind. Before I can say as much, he breathily answers a call. 'Five Irons Press, this is Norman.'

He's busy. I shouldn't waste his time.

I back away and start towards the tufted white leather tub chairs.

Mum suggested I barge in and demand Five Irons round up all unsold copies of *Young*, pulp them, and reprint the book without the typo. But why storm in, guns blazing, to rectify a typo when I can calmly arrange a meeting after school, lock in my next book deal and then casually mention the typo?

A sequel to *Young* has always been part of the grand plan. In the edit, Eliza asked me to remove the cliffhanger ending. I mentioned the grand plan, but she counselled me to focus on writing the best first book I could. She said the best first books were self-contained and satisfying.

'Sotiris!' Eliza is standing at the edge of the lobby. She's dyed her hair cherry red and lopped most of it off. No drop earrings today. 'Tis not the season. Leading me down a corridor of partially open doors, she asks how I am, how being published feels. I appreciate the softballs. I always need a few minutes to warm up around her and start sounding remotely human.

I'm pretty sure she knows.

Eliza's crammed too much into an office that's too small. She clears a stack of elastic-bound galleys onto the floor to make room for us on the lounge. She insists I sit first.

'I'm so glad you emailed. I usually see authors at their launches, but I know you haven't had yours yet...because of your aunt?'

'Grandmother.' Yiayia spends a sizeable chunk of every year in Greece; how sizeable depends on how many relatives she can guilt into hosting her. She was super persuasive this year. She'll be back the week before Christmas. 'She'd kill me if we celebrated without her.'

Eliza laughs. 'We could do with those sales early.' Her gaze drifts a smidge and she notices something behind me. 'Oh! Have you heard about this?' She reaches past my shoulder and retrieves an uncorrected proof. '*Riverside* by Joey Jensen. Wow!'

She thrusts the book into my hands. I stammer my thanks.

'Feel free to let everybody at school see you with it. Especially teachers. It would make for a great class text. Out September. We're hoping there's nothing libellous in this one. We had to pull his debut because of a line about...' She catches herself before she says anything libellous.

I study the front cover, initially to be polite, and then because it features a rower carrying a single scull on his shoulder. The straps of his half-peeled unisuit hang from his waist. His back is exposed. It's so wide, his lats could shelter a family of four. I thumb the spine, and I imagine tracing my fingers over that rugged, muscular terrain. No. I'm in a meeting with Eliza. I can't be ogling a guy. I check the other side, as if I'm eager to read the blurb. There's no blurb, just one line: *The powerful second novel from Joey Jensen.*

I say, 'Speaking of powerful second novels...'

Eliza's eyes narrow. 'Yeah, I'm surprised you're already thinking about that.' Her voice is scratchy in its upper register.

'It'll take a couple of years to write and edit.' I give the Joey Jensen book a little shake. 'And you said it was good for authors to pump out their follow-ups quickly.'

'I did say that.' She sighs, like she's annoyed at her past self, and then she returns to the present, sits bolt upright. 'I'm incredibly proud of our work on *Young*, but it would be terrible if you rushed your next book because you felt pressured.'

'I don't feel pressured,' I assure her. 'I'm totally ready. And it's a sequel, so the groundwork's already there.'

'That's...' She takes a breath. 'I've been thinking about what's next for you since you emailed. You're still in high school.'

'Final year. Home stretch.'

'You're figuring out who you want to be. How do you know *this* is what's next for you?' She gestures at the room, overstuffed with books.

'Oh, I've wanted this forever, don't you worry.'

She chuckles. 'And I wanted to be an astronaut,' she blurts, and when I'm not amused, she shifts her weight uneasily. 'I'm just...Again, I love *Young*, it's such a special book...But we track things like buzz and sell-in and early sales, and it doesn't look like it's connecting.'

I don't understand how she can say that. 'It's been a week.'

'Sadly, you can often tell pretty quickly.' She scrunches up her face. She hates being the messenger. 'Writing is a numbers game and truth is, the numbers don't justify a sequel. I think *Young* is one book, one *great* book we worked very hard on, but one book.'

This doesn't make sense. My book's on display. And I have a grand plan...

'But the good thing is, you are so young and talented, there are heaps of opportunities out there for you,' Eliza continues. 'After a few years, you'll come back with a dynamite idea.'

'The idea *is* dynamite.' My throat is dry. I sound hurt. I start running my mouth, plot points tumbling over each other on the way out. I'm desperate to convince her this needs to be my second book and Five Irons needs to publish it.

'Sotiris.' She lays a reassuring hand on the proof in my lap. This isn't happening. This can't be happening. 'Would you like a hot chocolate? We have a fancy machine. I guarantee you, it's better than the ones at home.'

'I live on top of my mum's cafe.' I might as well have thrown a brick through the window.

She exhales and changes tack. 'You're so young,' she repeats. 'You have all the time in the world to find your next story. And to read! Oh my god, I'm so jealous of you. The reading I did after high school...All the classics, *Jane Eyre*...And you still have *Young*. No one can take that away from you. It's such an achievement. I mean, how many seventeen-year-olds can say they have a book out?'

Not Benji, that's for sure. I remember him aiming the first page at me. The bio. The typo.

'What's the process when there's a mistake in a book?' I ask.

Eliza's thrown by the sudden change in topic. 'A mistake?' she asks, retracting her hand.

'There's a typo in my bio on the first page. It says I'm *seventen.*'

'Does it?' She tuts. 'That's a shame. No matter how many times you scour for errors, there's always a chance a sneaky bugger will get through.'

I ask her what we do about it, and she seems genuinely perplexed by the question. I elaborate. 'Does Five Irons do a recall? Like when a product is defective or poisonous?'

She laughs. 'It's a typo. I don't think anybody's going to die.'

I beg to differ. She didn't see the smug look on Benji's face; I could've been sentenced to ten years to life... 'People will think I can't spell.'

Eliza chooses her words carefully. 'As much as I would love to have the budget to do that whenever we find a typo, that's not how the industry works.'

Tears scratch at my eyes. I blink hard, I blink down. *The powerful second novel from Joey Jensen.*

They had to pull his first book, and now he gets a second one that's got a Herculean rower on the cover.

I can't even get a typo fixed. What do I have to do? Piss off some lawyers?

'What if there's something libellous in it?'

'In *Young*?'

'Yeah.'

When I look up at her, Eliza tucks her chin. She asks, 'Is there actually?'

A beat. 'No.'

'How about when we... *if* we reprint, I'll make sure we fix the typo. Sound okay?'

No, it doesn't. I want it fixed now, I want the chance to write my powerful second novel.

My eyes are stinging.

I have to go.

She can't see me crack. I don't need her concern or her hot chocolate.

I spring to my feet. I rush an apology for wasting her time. She's flustered. She asks if I'm all right. I'm not and I hope she feels bad. I can't turn back time and storm in here, but I can storm out.

And I will.

And I would've, but a question occurs to me in the doorway. I have a minute before I'm weeping uncontrollably, that's long enough to risk asking,

'What has to happen before you reprint *Young*?' I hear myself. I sound like a child.

She hesitates. 'We'd have to run out of stock in the warehouse.' And she doesn't think that's possible. Clearly. That hasn't been the subtext of the meeting so much as the neon sign she's been gesturing towards at regular intervals.

'Okay.' I steady myself, swallow hard so when I speak next, I sound half-normal. 'How many books would I need to sell?'

'Sotiris, I—'

'How many books would I need to sell?'

She gives me the number and I leave. It isn't quite storming out, but I keep a brisk pace. I retrace my steps past the partially open doors, past reception, past the book propped up on the desk. It isn't mine. It's *Orion* by Simone Chan.

The elevator doors close and I crash down to earth.

I will never leave this bedroom again. Except for the procurement of snacks and to use the bathroom. But even then, only when everyone's asleep.

'Well, *that's* a bit dramatic.' Mum's sitting on the edge of the single bed, her hand dangerously close to my hair. She's building up the courage to reassuringly stroke it, and I will not have it. 'What did Eliza say exactly?'

What didn't she say? My writing is crap. I should die.

'*Young* is a flop and I'd have to sell three thousand copies for them to consider fixing the mistake,' I mumble into the pillow.

'Right.'

'This isn't how it was supposed to go. I spent years imagining my first release – interviews in *The Sydney Morning Herald*, people lining up outside bookshops at midnight to be the first to buy it, movie rights sold. I've had full conversations with Steven Spielberg in the shower.'

'Maybe don't tell anyone else that last part,' Mum coos.

I'm sure she wishes this is one of those times where a bad joke can fix everything. Tending to a wounded teenager isn't what anybody needs after fourteen hours on their feet in a cafe. Plus, she hates my bedroom. She only ventures in here to throw stuff out. She's adamant it has an odour.

'Just leave,' I mumble.

She sighs. She's not going anywhere.

'From the moment the doctor told me I was having a boy, I imagined the man you'd grow into. A doctor. Maybe a lawyer. And look who I got!'

'Thanks.' Dripping sarcasm.

She sneaks a callused palm onto my cheek for the briefest moment. 'What I'm saying is, things rarely turn out how we imagine them. That doesn't make them unfair. Spielberg isn't making *Young* into a film. Okay. That doesn't mean he won't someday. He might not. You imagined a dream run and nobody is owed that. Honestly, I'm glad you didn't have it.'

I don't think she gets that she's not meant to rub salt on any exposed wounds.

'You want movies and midnight launches and I want them for you,' she continues, 'but you want your career to be a skyscraper. How do you build one of those?'

I twist around and search her face for clarification. It gives me none. All I can tell in the creamy glow of the bedside lamp is that her contact dermatitis is flaring again. There are raised bumps along her jaw that cast tiny shadows.

'What do you mean?'

'What I asked. How do you build a skyscraper?'

It's obvious. 'You erect one storey and then you erect a storey on top of that and then another.'

'Wrong. Build a skyscraper like that and it'll topple over. How many people have written huge hits and then disappeared?'

'I don't know.'

'*Heaps*, I'm sure. When you're building a skyscraper, the first thing you do is dig. It feels like you're going backwards, but you've got to lay a sturdy foundation. And only when you've got that can you start building up. The moment you reach the heights that you're supposed to, what you've built is sturdy enough to withstand anything. I want you to get your dream run, Sotiris, and I want it to last.'

The whole time I've been watching her, she hasn't blinked. She doesn't now. But it isn't unnerving. She's determined.

'How many copies did Eliza say you have to sell again?'

'Three thousand.'

Mum doesn't hesitate. 'We can do that.'

THREE
Big dreams

HARVEY

1

Ba rocks up around six with a shopping bag and this big idea that he and I are cooking dinner. He fries T-bones while I mash potatoes in one of Gina's huge stainless-steel pots. She's uncomfortable having stuff done for her. She claws at the plastic covering of the dining table. She cares about the oil splashing everywhere, she cares about how much milk there is in the mashed potato, she cares too much. No wonder she reckons I don't care enough; she has her emotions dialled up so far, anybody would look bad by comparison.

The steaks are served in a patterned casserole dish. Ba plonks it on the table, Gina tuts and moves it onto a cork trivet. She likes her beef killed twice, and even though my father charred one steak to a crisp especially for her, she keeps her plate bare.

She asks about Dad.

Ba avoids her eyes. 'What about him?'

She asks how his work's going, if he still finds time for horseriding. She asks and asks, like it's only a matter of time before Ba cracks and the truth spills out. He holds firm, and when she helps herself to the remains of Proyiayia's steak, he changes the subject. He says gnawing on bones doesn't count as a balanced meal. Gina says she won't be taking diet tips from the guy who spent Year Eight fainting in class because he threw out the sandwiches she made him. And that sets them off, yelling over each other.

He's annoyed she can't let him do *one* thing without spoiling it.

She never asked for anything.

He wants her to eat the steak he cooked for her.

She refuses.

The steak is going to waste.

So what?

And I'm starting to remember why the holidays to Sydney stopped. Ba and Gina are too alike and way too deep in each other's business. They're standing on almost forty years of kindling; one errant spark and they ignite.

I try to put the fire out.

I pierce the charred-to-hell steak with my fork. It takes all my strength to cut through. I douse it in barbecue sauce just to taste something that isn't ash.

'There,' I say, mouth full. 'You two done now?'

They keep at it.

I chew hard and glance at Proyiayia. She's unbothered, enjoying her mashed potato. Gina reckons there's something wrong with her, but I dunno, she seems fine to me.

'You good?' I ask.

Proyiayia smacks her lips together. 'Good. Good.'

See?

'We go shopping tomorrow?' she adds.

It's a knife to the heart. 'No. Proyiayia, we went today.'

My great-grandmother squints at me, as if to call me a liar. The bruise looks worse than it did this morning. I can't tell if it is, or if the light is playing tricks. She nods. 'Ah.' She's pretending. I don't reckon she remembers.

Everyone's gone quiet. She's sapped the oxygen from the room. Something's wrong with her, something bigger than a bruise that makes fighting over steak seem petty.

Gina's the one who punctures the silence. She tells Ba that dinner's nice.

He avoids eye contact. 'Thanks.'

Ba clears the table and starts the dishes. Gina wordlessly assumes the spot beside him, wiping and stacking the plates when he's done with them. Like they weren't just tearing verbal shreds off each other.

I need to get out of here. I ask if I can do a quick lap of the block. Back in Perth, I wouldn't ask and Ba wouldn't mind, but Gina says I shouldn't go wandering at night, so he gives me ten minutes. It's better than none.

I swipe my great-grandmother's keys.

I feel better the moment the fresh air hits me. Being in that house, with whatever's going on with Proyiayia, and Gina and Ba at each other's throats . . . it's a lot. Coming to Sydney was mostly about getting out of school, but when I did let myself picture life after I disembarked the plane, it didn't look like this.

This isn't close.

I only have ten minutes, so I start walking. The street's pretty dead. It's mostly people heading home from the train station. There are pockets of life ahead – people spilling out of wine bars, or out of Ubers to trundle into wine bars. I'm too young to enjoy that life, but too old to be cooped up in the terrace of intergenerational warfare.

I need my own place, but that requires money I don't have.

There's an ATM in the front window of a convenience store with lights so fluorescent they burn your eyes. I withdraw the fifty bucks Owen deposited.

That's about a day's rent in Sydney, if I'm sharing a place and it's not that nice.

I need a job. I fire up Seek but I dunno where to start. I end up searching hospo jobs, but that seems silly when I have an in with a small business owner already. I ummm and ahhh about asking her for a job the whole way back.

As I climb the stairs, Gina says, 'That you, Harvey?'

'It is.'

I head straight for the office. Someone's switched the lamp on for me. I climb onto the crappy mattress and tuck the fifty-dollar note under my pillow. I twist around and Gina's in the doorway, folding a towel.

'Jesus!'

'You were fourteen minutes,' she says flatly.

Yeah, there's no way I can work for her.

'I was just plotting out my next life steps.'

I will devote myself to understanding how Seek works.

'Oh?' She sounds surprised. 'And what are we thinking?'

I will not work for her.

I...might as well ask if I can work for her.

I shimmy to the end of the bed. 'You know how you said you wanted me to care more?'

'The words sound familiar.' She hands me the towel.

I set it to the side. 'I was thinking I could help out in the cafe.'

'You want a job?' She's amused, I think. She leans against the doorframe and runs her hand through her wiry hair.

'It would free you up to stay and look after Proyiayia.'

'And I would have to pay you.'

'Legally, yeah.'

She grunts. 'I'll think about it.' She tilts her head towards Ba's bedroom. 'You're not going to tell me what's happening, are you?'

I shrug. Her gaze narrows but I don't cave.

'Good son. Shit grandson.'

I stammer a laugh.

She grimaces. 'But he's okay?' Her voice is soft. This isn't how she shows him her concern. I wonder how different their relationship would be if it was.

'I reckon. You can ask him, you know.'

'Nah.' She takes a deep breath. Her gaze is distant, like she's half here, half sorting through filing cabinets in her brain. Then the office pulls her focus. She's looking right at me. 'You start tomorrow. Five o'clock. Set an alarm.'

'Seriously?'

'Yes. And before you get smart with me, IR laws do not apply to family. You work when I say you do, and I pay you what I feel like.'

I don't protest. I want the job because I need the money, because I'm gonna get as far away from...She pushes off the doorframe and the knife wound in my heart makes me ask what's wrong with Proyiayia.

'I honestly don't know,' Gina says. 'She has an appointment with the specialist coming up. They'll sort it.' Her smile is feeble. She asks if I want the door shut. I nod.

I should sleep, but...Grindr. I scroll through the grid of mostly shirtless men. I reach the dividing line between the profiles I can interact with for free and the ones that are only there to tempt me into buying a subscription. I scroll back to the top. There's a new nearest user. Another shirtless man. This one's in a straw hat. My *father* in a straw hat. I don't drop my phone so much as I launch it across the room. *Thud*.

Could've had a quieter involuntary reaction.

Muffled by the wall between us, Ba asks, 'What was that?'

I scramble. I don't want him checking in on me. 'Nothing, nothing.' I sound panicked. That makes it more likely he'll . . . I crawl off the mattress and retrieve my phone. I handle it delicately, afraid I'll click his profile and send anything that might identify me. I recognise his profile pic from last year's Bali trip. He's cropped Dad out. Shoddily. I can make out his polo shirt's faded blue sleeve.

Should've known my days of a father-free Grindr were behind me.

I block the profile immediately. I delete the app to be sure.

I can't move out fast enough.

2

I rock up at five on the dot and Gina greets me with an apron. I was worried my outfit wasn't cafe-appropriate, but slap an apron on anything and it screams hospo worker.

She entrusts me to Isabella, a barista who's worked here long enough to know where the skeletons are buried and which supplier to phone for what. That doesn't mean my grandmother vanishes after introducing us. Nah, she flits about, moving serviette dispensers on tables, straightening chairs. Pointless busywork, basically. It isn't till Isabella throws an empty takeaway cup at her that she flits towards the exit. 'I'm going. I'm going.' She stops just shy of going. 'This dispenser...'

Isabella assures her I'll refill it, but when she's left, 'Don't bother.'

First impression? I vibe with her.

'But grab that cup for me, will you?'

I do. Isabella stops tinkering with the espresso machine long enough to inspect the cup for any obvious marks and return it to the stack. She can't be much older than me, but it's difficult to tell because her look is edgy *Play School* presenter – denim overalls, nose ring, wavy brown bob she might have cut herself. She could be nineteen, she could be twenty-nine. Her playlist has me leaning more towards nineteen. Songs I recognise from TikTok mostly.

She invites me behind the front counter and quickly explains where everything lives. Whatever she says falls out of my brain instantly, but she assures me it'll all make sense as the day goes on. The guided tour stops at the edge of the cook's territory – three square metres around a bend that's jammed with toasters and grills and Marta, arms everywhere like a cartoon organist. The kitchen is a no-go zone, unless I'm heading out back to the sad little sink and dishwasher.

The first few customers order takeaway coffees. There's enough time between them that Isabella can work the register and make the drinks. It's my job to smile and watch. When she's confident I have a handle on the touchscreen's menu system, she sticks to the espresso machine. She only intervenes when I have a question, or when I tell a customer their soy decaf cappuccino is seventeen dollars, which it obviously shouldn't be.

A few customers dine in. Isabella sends me out with menus and water. But she doesn't let me take any orders. The iPad she uses is ancient, its screen shattered to oblivion. Getting it to do what it's supposed to takes some skill, which she must possess because the tiny printer near Marta never fails to spit out dockets.

So long as I'm getting paid, I'm happy being an extra pair of hands, somebody to walk the hot chocolate to table nine, to clear seven, to loiter by the desserts fridge, to deal with the mess of plates and pans that's accumulated out back.

Makes no sense. It's like this sad little sink belongs to a version of the cafe from an alternate universe, one that's actually busy. There's so much to wash crammed into an area barely larger than the average bathroom cubicle. Isabella's head appears at a tiny window every so often to leave cups and saucers on the sill and to relay things I wish I knew sooner like, 'Oh, yeah, cold water works better on yolk.'

I rinse off what I can before stacking the industrial dishwasher so it can do the rest. It's fun till the thrill of using the spray tap wears off, then it's fine, a bit monotonous. I keep an eye out for signs of a lunch rush, and when lunch does arrive, Isabella isn't exactly rushed – three tables and some takeaway orders.

I'm still out back when Dad calls. I'm not on my break, but I *am* enjoying a vegetarian focaccia somebody ordered but decided they didn't want.

'Hey, kid.' Dad's always called me kid. It irks me, but it'd be weird if he stopped now.

'Hey. What's up?'

'Oh, you know.' He sounds deflated. He's had the house to himself for a day and a half; it must be getting to him.

'I got a job.'

He laughs. 'Already? Not at—'

'Gina's, yeah.'

He's not surprised my grandmother's put me to work. I don't tell him it was my idea. He asks about my day, and I know he's killing time before he can ask about Ba without seeming desperate.

Seven minutes, give or take a few seconds.

'How's your father?'

I keep my answer brief. 'He's okay.' I have zero interest in being their go-between.

There's a beat. I hear Isabella chatting to a customer while she rings up his order.

'I don't want you to worry about us,' Dad says. 'He'll come around.'

Ba's on Grindr, but sure.

I can't imagine a worse conversation, so I bail. 'Hey, I have to get back to work.'

'Right. Right.' I wonder if he thought he could sneak another question in. 'Love you, kid.'

The kitchen closes at three, but Marta's been drip-feeding me utensils and containers to wash since two, so all she has to do is wipe down the counter and say goodbye. Isabella and I are staying for Study Club. I don't expect much of a turnout, but come four p.m. the joint's busier than I've seen it all day. Eleven students from nearby schools, mostly Year Nines, spread across several tables. There's usually more of them, but apparently the older ones had assessments due today. Isabella circles, taking drinks orders and helping the kidlets (her word)

with tricky maths. She's not the greatest tutor. I mean, her help is limited to checking the answers and smiling, shrugging or wincing. But the kidlets come alive when she's near.

Squinting at a screen, Isabella guides her hair back behind one ear. She's stumped. It's a particularly tricky essay question and she...catches me looking. 'You want in?'

'Fuck no.' I notice the girl in pigtails. She's the very picture of innocence, taller sitting than standing. I correct myself. 'Fudge.'

Pigtails sneers. 'I'm in Year Seven, I know what *fuck* is, boomer.'

Isabella steadies herself on the back of a chair, struggling to contain a cackle. I dunno how to respond so I just...get back to cleaning the floor behind the counter. It's my first time mopping, and if the measure of success is making tiles wetter, then I'm a natural. I slap the drenched end of the mop against the tiles and slide it back and forth between the bar fridge and the cabinet.

Some guy asks Isabella if she wants to hear the worst joke in the world. She encourages him. He gets three words out before he's interrupted by bickering that's been perfected over half a century. Proyiayia, still walking with her limp, flanked by Gina. The argument peters out, as if they were simply entertaining themselves on the way to the cafe.

My great-grandmother and the whopper bruise on her face whip up a ton of excitement. The teens have questions. Well, they have corny one-liners mostly. You know the sort... If she looks like this, they'd hate to see the other guy. She smiles faintly at them and cuts a slow path through the cafe. She's got 'hello, darling' on repeat. She holds out a hand to the really eager ones, like she's greeting her disciples.

Or like she's an old lady who isn't well, who's trying to get to the staff table.

I'm played like some instrument. The fibres of my heart are plucked and strummed. I hate the sound.

Proyiayia takes her seat. Isabella orders her kidlets back to work, then approaches. She squats low and loops an arm around my great-grandmother. She gets two affectionate little pats in reply.

Gina sets down her bag and clocks me standing behind the counter. 'Come say hello,' she orders.

I go and say hello.

'To *her*,' she clarifies, tilting her head to Proyiayia.

I greet my great-grandmother and tell her I didn't realise she was a celebrity.

Doesn't get much of a response. That plucks my heart fibres a little more.

Isabella peels off her. 'Your great-grandmother is a rockstar in these parts.'

'A regular Mick Jagger,' Gina says dryly, removing a wad of photos from her bag and spreading them out across the table. I recognise some from the office upstairs.

Gina has a perm in one. Isabella gasps and reaches for it. 'You look so young!' She catches herself and clears her throat. 'You look so *younger*.'

'Good save,' I tell her.

Gina's unbothered, too focused on the pics. She separates the notable shots from the sequence. 'One minute, you're looking at photos of people, wondering how they could've ever been so young, and the next, you're looking at photos of yourself, wondering the same thing,' she mutters.

Pigtails has her phone out. She's experimenting with angles to get as much of my great-grandmother in the background of a selfie as possible.

I ask Mick Jagger what she got up to today.

'Ti den ékana?' she asks. It's an easy one to translate. What didn't she do?

It's a nothing answer.

'Yeah, but what?'

Proyiayia isn't listening. She's encouraging Isabella closer so she can whisper something to her.

'She's not having a coffee,' Gina says.

'I no ask for coffee.' Proyiayia is obviously asking for coffee.

Gina sighs and looks anywhere but at her mother. Her gaze lands on me. 'We went to the physio for a massage. She has a haematoma on her thigh from the fall.'

Proyiayia's reliable on defence. 'I no fall.'

'You *yes* fall,' my grandmother snaps.

Proyiayia mumbles something in Greek. I don't understand the words, but I understand the sentiment. She's annoyed. Isabella gives her a reassuring pat and wanders over to the espresso machine.

'Make it weak,' Gina says.

Isabella waves her off. 'Yeah. Yeah.'

My grandmother returns her attention to the photos. She's looking for one pic in particular. I ask if she needs help. She doesn't.

'But I do.' A girl with steel-rimmed glasses a couple of tables over is stumped by an equation.

I really don't wanna help, but Isabella's busy frothing milk. Damn it. I drag myself over.

I expect her to surrender a laptop. She doesn't. 'Where are the answers?' I ask.

She only has a question sheet. Great. I have to call upon whatever mathematical knowledge I've retained from Year Nine. We work our way through solving the equation and end up with an answer that has seven decimal places. It can't be right. The girl on my left calls me clueless.

Fair enough.

'Yes!' Gina shouts, scaring the shit out of everyone. 'Sorry,' she adds using her inside voice. 'Found my photo.'

I've never seen it before. Proyiayia and three randoms at a table. It was taken with the flash on, so everyone looks paler than they probably were and one dude's pupils are red.

'Everything on the menu used to be numbered so your great-grandmother could take orders. She would pull up a chair and they would have to tell her the numbers slowly, digit by digit,' Gina explains.

'Couldn't read or write, but she knew the numbers zero through nine.'

She holds the photo out in front of her and rotates slowly. She's finding a wall for it. The cafe is decorated with framed pictures of a Sydney that's been lost to time, strangers in milk bars, arcades. This will be the first pic that isn't of some random in a place that doesn't exist anymore.

She settles on a spot for it, right where the community notices corkboard is now.

'There,' she says, triumphant.

3

Dinner's relatively tame before Dad calls. His name flashes on the screen. Ba ignores it. He's breaking bread into chunks and dunking them into his soup like his phone isn't about to vibrate off the table. I glance at Gina. Her face is a symphony of twitches till the screen goes dark and the vibrating stops. She inhales deeply and instead of blowing up, she asks Ba what he got up to today. He's cagey. That must annoy her. She doesn't push him, though. And blissfully unaware of how close the family is to war, Proyiayia asks me if I like the fakés.

It's light out when I'm woken by my father. I sit up, groggy as hell. 'Where are we off to?'

'Funny.' He's half-dressed, in a buttoned shirt and boxers, squinting at the bookcase by the door. 'It's ten o'clock.'

I groan. 'That's six o'clock Saturday time.'

'And you were up earlier yesterday.'

'Delayed jet lag.' I dunno what I'm saying. I'm not a scientist.

And Ba's not listening. He's preoccupied. The books likely haven't been touched in years, because the way they're stacked, yank one out and they're all tumbling down. He shifts his weight onto his toes and inspects higher. 'Seen my book anywhere?'

Ba rarely talks about his life as an author. It was brief and way before my time. I googled him once. I wanted an out for a school creative writing task and told Mrs McKenzie I had an author dad. I figured having a literary pedigree meant an automatic passing mark, but I couldn't prove it. There are forty thousand Sam Bakers in the world, all heaps better at search engine optimisation. I dunno how Ba got into it, why he quit after one book, or why he keeps that book hidden away in a bedroom drawer where he thinks no one looks. I've never read it. His text messages are long enough.

'Wait, are *you* renowned author Sam Baker?' I ask.

He flicks me the bird and mutters, 'She must have a copy *somewhere*,' as he leaves.

I don't immediately hop out of bed. I pull one knee up and rest my head on it. I take a breath. Gina's tidied the desk. It's bare, save for three twenty-dollar notes tucked under a mug filled with pens. My pay. Turns out, she's much lighter on her feet than Ba, because I didn't hear her come in.

I put twenty in my wallet and forty under my pillow.

I escort Proyiayia downstairs for lunch. The hope is, Gina will see me being a doting great-grandson for an hour, and be more receptive to the idea of me bailing to explore the city solo.

Sneaking serviettes into her handbag, Proyiayia asks who my father's with.

At first, I think it's a question about his marriage, then I twist in my chair and spot him seated at table fourteen. With a woman.

'No idea.' I don't stop staring. My interest's piqued. Is she a lawyer? She has a severe middle part. Very serious, very lawyerly. But she's too underdressed. Her fluffy jumper makes her look like a loofah.

When Gina appears, busted iPad tucked under one arm, she's equally curious. 'Who's the woman with the airport runway up her scalp?'

I recycle the answer I gave Proyiayia, but that's not

good enough. My grandmother expects me to strut on over and find out.

'Grígora,' she adds.

I have no interest in hopping from her good books to her bad, so I don't protest. I get to Ba's table in time to catch the end of what the mysterious woman's saying. '...don't feel comfortable springing you on her, you know?' The maybe-lawyer notices me standing close. 'Oh, hello.' And then a gasp of recognition. 'This is him! Harvey!' A quick glance between us. 'I see the resemblance.'

'Neat.' There's zero chance I look like Ba, but it makes him sit taller. 'And you are?'

'Phoebe,' she says. 'I'm a young-adult author too.' The corners of her mouth are wet so her words squelch like sorbolene.

'Cool. Bye.' I probably could have put more effort into making the interaction feel natural, but I have the information I need. I march back to my table and tell Gina her name.

My grandmother's concerned. 'If after all this, he turns straight, I'm going to slap him.'

She doesn't strike me as the sort of person who'd appreciate a gentle lecture on the fluidity of sexuality, so I don't bother. Besides, I have it on good authority that Ba is still very interested in men. But I can't tell her about the Grindr sighting. Duh.

I assure Gina that Phoebe's just a friend, another author.

She acts like that's worse. 'Fuck.'

'Fuck?'

'Don't swear.'

'You were the one who…' I trail off. It's not an argument that's worth having. 'Why is Ba catching up with an author such a bad thing?'

She sighs. 'Writing was never good for him. He gave it everything and what did he get? No, the best thing your father – the other one, Jeremy – did was distract him from a passion that didn't love him back.' It takes a few aggressive taps for the iPad to respond. 'Now, what do you want?'

After lunch, Gina sets Proyiayia up in the corner with cutlery to polish, meaning I'm free to do whatever.

I start walking with no destination in mind. I hit water, then follow the shoreline deeper into the harbour.

I buy an ice cream at Circular Quay. I use my own money. Two scoops of cookies and cream have never felt more monumental. At some point, I get bored and google *Phoebe Australian author* and several pictures of Ba's friend pop up, some recent, others from a time before the severe middle part.

Her name's Phoebe Turner.

I scroll through her book covers and that's when it all clicks into place. *Yes.* I've heard of her. They're friends in the way that if we walk into a bookshop and her latest release is prominently displayed near the front, Ba hides it. Her titles all sound like gentle threats. 'You will weep by the end,' they whisper, over colour-graded stock images. *The Heart That Aches* over a barn on a hill. *Memories of the Last Day* over a dilapidated jetty. Her name's always bigger than her titles. Maybe because they're crummy. Maybe because she's a big deal.

Her search results suggest she's a pretty big deal.

I stalk her for a bit, walk some more, buy another ice cream – not as good as the first, it's stealth gelato and I don't realise till I've had a bite. It's pushing five when I decide to make my way back.

On William Street, somebody lightly slaps my arse on the way past.

'Gotcha!' Isabella overtakes me. She's decked out in a hot-pink running singlet and grey leggings. She turns on her heel. There's mischief in her eyes, but her face is flushed and her forehead is beaded with sweat.

'Nice activewear.'

She's jogging backwards, keeping pace with me. 'It's the traditional garb...of my people...insufferable women...from the east,' she says breathily. She's smiling and wincing.

'You okay?' I ask.

'Dying, actually.' It's more wince than smile now. 'Got plans tonight?'

I shake my head.

'Study Club. I'll pick you up. Late-ish.'

It's cryptic and I don't understand, so I figure it's a joke.

My father barges into the office after a knock that barely counts as warning. He's lucky all I'm doing is browsing share house listings. He consults the bookcase again. 'It must be here,' he mutters.

I set the phone down on my chest. 'What do you need it for?'

'Nothing, it's...' A pause. He screws up his face. 'I'm writing something. I've been going to the library to work on it and I want to make sure it's better.'

'Than your first book?'

'No, than a Bunnings catalogue, Harvey.'

In hindsight, it was a stupid question. I ask an intentionally stupid one next. 'Is it about me?'

He clicks his tongue. Apparently, I wouldn't make for an interesting enough protagonist. I beg to differ. Charming but a bit of a prick, who wouldn't wanna read about me?

'Maybe she threw it out?' I offer.

He pauses his search to glare at me. The crease across his forehead is so deep it's undisputable that he shot out of Gina. 'The book?' he asks.

'Nah, a Bunnings catalogue.'

He's mad at himself for walking into that one. He looks away. 'Don't be an idiot,' he snaps.

Um. Ba keeps the book in a bedroom drawer and he wrote the damn thing, why is it hard to believe Gina, not the biggest fan of his writing, might've chucked it?

'What I'm working on has to be the best book I've ever written,' he adds. 'Phoebe and I had the same editor back in the day. She's going to help us reconnect.'

'Is she? Because it sounded like she didn't wanna spring you on somebody.'

'Phoebe will come around.' It's unclear who he's trying to convince. 'Publishing was different back then. I was too gay for my editor when I was closeted, but now she's giving every gay with an Instagram, an aesthetic and a ring light a book deal.'

'Ew.'

'What?'

'Don't work with her.'

He laughs, but not in the way you laugh when something's funny. 'Whoever I sell the new book to will have been in the industry just as long. They all said something was wrong with us, or were too scared to argue otherwise. But now we're a selling point...' He shrugs.

'That's fucked.'

'It is and it isn't.' He abandons the search and sits on the edge of the bed. He's surprised how little the mattress resists. 'The world is different. Life will be easier for you than it was for me. Is it rotten that nobody apologised? You bet. They simply switched gears when the world changed and forgot anyone they discarded along the way. But I'll let you in on a little secret.' Ba leans in closer. 'Your father's not going to let anyone forget him that easily.'

4

Gina makes a big deal of dinner being a low-effort affair...till she opens the fridge, stares down two glass jars filled with fakés and decides she's vehemently opposed to the idea of leftovers. It's almost eight, but she insists there's time to make something. She drenches a giant tray of chicken wings in olive oil and lemon juice, tosses it in the oven till we smell burning, and plonks it in the centre of the dining table. She serves Proyiayia, but leaves us to fend for ourselves. By then, it's pushing nine and I'm ravenous. I scrape two charred wings free with my fork, and Ba ignores the wings to hack away at the glistening skin that's stuck to the tray. His favourite, he says.

It's a trap.

Gina pounces. 'You've left Jeremy, yes?'

I've never seen someone almost choke on chicken skin before. Proyiayia asks if he's okay, then returns her attention to the muted soap opera playing in the next room.

Ba coughs a couple of times and asks for water. I pass the jug that makes any drink taste like plastic. He fills a glass and chugs it all.

For my grandmother, that's as good as an answer. 'Have you got a solicitor?'

'Not in front of Harvey, Mum.'

Gina rolls her eyes. 'Come off it. You're divorcing his father, whether you do it behind his back or not. Mira's daughter is in family law. Do you want her number?'

'Mum.'

'I'm just being helpful.'

And she won't stop either. I can already tell this conversation's gonna swallow up the rest of my night.

I don't count on a hero, but the back door opens and there's Isabella in a Superman T-shirt that's so faded, the S is one wash away from disintegrating. She pockets her keys. 'Hello, hello.'

The lawyer talk ceases. She works her way around the table. She introduces herself to Ba as the barista with a spare key. She embraces Proyiayia. The cutlery drawer is within reach, so Gina fetches her a fork and tells her to grab a plate. She sits to my left and helps herself to mine. 'Easy.'

It's impossible to be annoyed at her. Her smile's disarming, and even if it wasn't, she's saved me.

She hands me the wing I wasn't done with. My grandmother warns me not to get grease everywhere, as if it's my choice to eat without a plate.

'What's goss?' Isabella asks.

It's my chance to steer the conversation away from legal experts. 'Ba's started a new book.'

Isabella's a huge reader, so she asks Ba what it's about. His explanation's clumsy. He doesn't wanna spoil anything, and whatever he does reveal, he can't commit to, because it's early days and a lot can change. But Isabella hangs off every word. Her eyes are wide and she nods thoughtfully.

And it doesn't escape me that instead of watching my father, I'm watching her.

'Why is writing your big dream?' Gina asks. 'Why not something that pays a wage?'

Before he can even react, Isabella comes to bat for him. 'The same reason why you run the cafe. It's in his DNA,' she says. 'And why not dream of being one of the great Australian writers?' She plucks names from thin air and one sticks out.

'Oh, Ba's friends with Phoebe,' I say, polishing off a bone and dropping it onto Gina's plate.

Isabella's mouth hangs open. 'Shut up.'

I won't. 'He had coffee with her today.'

'In our cafe?'

Gina begrudgingly confirms. She points a greasy pinkie at her scalp. 'Runway part.'

Isabella has trouble forming full sentences. Apparently, Phoebe's the GOAT. TikTok put Isabella on to *The Heart That Aches* and she's been a fan ever since. 'Trust her to visit the one day I'm not working.'

'Darling, you like?' Proyiayia has zero interest in the subject of authors. She wants Isabella's verdict on the food.

'I do,' Isabella says. 'Your bruise looks better.'

I can't look directly at it without my heart hurting. I doubt it's any better.

Proyiayia's chuffed. 'I wait and it fix.'

Isabella nods. 'You wait and it fix, yes.' She rips a wing off the tray and leaves half of the meat stuck there. Amateur hour. 'Oops.'

'Don't I pay you enough to feed yourself?' Gina asks.

'Oh, I've already had dinner. This was just fortuitous timing,' Isabella says. 'I'm taking Harvey out.'

News to me. 'You are?'

'I told you. On William Street.'

'I thought you were kidding?'

Gina attacks the meat Isabella left behind. 'No drugs and he's home by midnight,' she says.

Ba clears his throat. It's part annoyance, part there's-still-chicken-skin-lodged-in-his-throat. 'Excuse me, I'm his dad,' he says.

My grandmother watches him expectantly. 'Go on, then.'

He crumbles under the pressure. He repeats her verbatim.

Gina smugly tosses some chicken in her mouth. 'Where are you headed?' she asks.

Isabella's coy about the shape of our night. I assume she has a small pub in mind that won't card me. She's on her second slice of Proyiayia's baklava when she gets the call and we leave in a rush.

She's parked out back. The car's fancier than I expect: a black BMW with heated front seats. It's her housemate's, and she makes a point of telling me he didn't pay for it himself. 'Christopher's a full-time adult son.'

That sounds like a sweet deal. 'Are his parents adopting?' I ask.

Isabella snorts. 'If anybody's getting free shit, it's the girl who has to share a bathroom with their slob of a son.' She regales me with horror stories – well one and a half horror stories – till we reach a tree-lined street that connects William and Oxford. She slows the car to a crawl and points vaguely at the townhouses on my left. 'It should be one of these. Ah!'

She brakes suddenly. A lanky guy's sauntered onto the bitumen. He's wearing skinny jeans, a skinnier scarf and a T-shirt that stretches to his knees. He strikes me as someone I'd mock at the beginning of the night, but make out with by the end. He approaches the car and as soon as he's close enough, he relies on the roof to balance.

'This is Felix. We're giving him a lift home,' she says.

After some effort, he manages to get the door open. 'Yo.'

'You would've met him yesterday but a bunch of Year Twelves skipped Study Club.'

Felix slides into the back seat. He smells flammable.

'Drink the whole liquor cabinet tonight, buddy?' she asks, eyeing him in the rear-view mirror.

His response is unintelligible.

'Gonna need you to enunciate, champ.'

'I *said* I didn't...drink as much...as everyone else.'

I pride myself on only having ever needed one drunken rescue. It was after a house party in Peppermint Grove. This masc-for-masc dickhead from the sticks was banging on about how gay guys should still act like men, so I let the fucker pick his bourbon premix of choice and drank him under the table. Dad said it was noble. Stupid, but noble.

When Isabella asks if Bradley's still inside, Felix exhales deeply. 'He hates it when you call him that.'

Isabella remains firm. 'Where's Bradley?'

Our passenger burps, then scowls. I know the taste – all the flavours of the night mixing with bile. 'You took him home.'

Isabella glances at me. There's weariness, then a wink. 'No, I didn't.'

'I dunno, he must have left.'

She's already dialling Bradley's number. 'What do we say, Felix?'

'Don't make me say it.' Isabella's withering look makes him say it. 'Study Club looks out for Study Club,' he drones.

'Exactly.' She tries Bradley's number a second time. 'We're not leaving until you've scoured every inch of that place for him.'

'You serious?' He throws his head back and whimpers. 'But this seat is so comfy.'

He's not fit to retrieve anyone. Isabella looks to me and I know what she's gonna ask.

5

I nudge open the front door. A golden vein of fairy lights runs the length of the narrow hallway. I follow it to a living room with a YouTube playlist projected on the wall. The guy leaning against it is camouflaged behind a Lil Nas X clip. He downs a bright drink, something mixed with OJ.

'Bradley?' I ask.

He shakes his head, then points me in the right direction. I'm grateful. I breeze through the kitchen. The girl consolidating the leftover pizza into one box scowls at me, but doesn't ask who the hell I am. I step out into the courtyard. There's a guy kneeling with his arm draped over a mop bucket.

I don't need to ask. 'Bradley?'

He stirs a little. 'Mmf.'

Great.

I move the bucket. Its contents slosh. His arm drops – all flesh, no bone. 'Ow.'

'Come on, buddy.' It's as if Isabella is speaking through me. 'We've gotta go.'

He squints up at me and for the first time I get a good look at his face. I've met him before. Brad from Grindr. There's a glimmer of recognition in his eyes. 'What are you doing here?' he asks.

I dunno what to say. His phone starts ringing in his jeans pocket. He asks if I'm the one calling.

I make an educated guess. 'It's Isabella.'

'Study Club looks out for Study Club,' he mumbles.

I stand him upright. He reeks of the reason for the bucket. There are wet patches of reason on his shirt. He asks if I know Rohan, then tells me *he* doesn't even know Rohan. I assume this is Rohan's shindig.

'I don't.'

I walk with him hanging off my shoulder. At some point between the courtyard and the car, he sighs. 'You blocked me.'

While I fasten Brad's seatbelt, Isabella speaks to him with a gentler, sweeter voice than the one she used on Felix. I shut the door and mutter a string of obscenities. My failed Grindr hook-up is one of Isabella's kidlets. If I bail now, there's a chance he'll forget who lugged him to the car.

I thought Sydney was supposed to be bigger than this.

I open my door and reach for the closest excuse. 'He chundered on me,' I lie. 'Probably better I don't hop in.'

Isabella insists. 'I've become very good at cleaning this car,' she says. 'And I need you in case he throws up again. You hear that?' She's looking at Brad now. 'If you need to spew, tell Harvey.'

Not sure how much help I'll be in the front.

I brace myself for Brad to reveal how we know each other. He doesn't. He clicks his tongue and rests his head against the window. If he's gonna be sick, he's not in any state to warn anybody.

Isabella needs a set of eyes on him while she drives. There's no avoiding this, apparently. I slip into the car, buckle up, and we're on our way before I'm mentally prepared for it. I've done nothing wrong. People have dud hook-ups all the time. But I don't want Isabella to know I had a dud hook-up with one of her kidlets. I don't wanna remind her I'm their age.

'You watching him?' Isabella asks.

I glance back. Brad's eyes are shut, thank fuck. He looks fine. Severely grog-stricken, but fine. Felix, meanwhile, is completely in his element. He's helped himself to one of the knock-off brand sports drinks in the door and a packet of chips.

Our first stop is a block of flats in Darling Point. Felix tries the door but Isabella's locked it. She won't let him out unless he tells her the worst joke in the world.

'Do I have to?' he asks, trying the door again.

'If you can't tell a bad joke, you can't climb your stairs without puking.'

He groans. 'Fine. What's the difference between an elephant and an emu?'

Isabella has a pensive moment. It isn't fruitful. 'No idea.'

'Nobody cares. Let me go to sleep.'

She sighs. It isn't a joke, but she's convinced he can climb his stairs without projectile vomiting. She unlocks the door and tells him to text her when he's safely inside. We wait in the idling car till the message comes through. Our second stop isn't far: the driveway of a mansion across from Rushcutters Bay Park. I peer up at the house. This isn't Brad's place.

'I know what you're thinking,' Isabella says.

That this place isn't where I went to bonk Brad?

'If this was where he lived,' she adds, 'I'd be holding him for ransom.'

'Why are we here, then?'

She tilts her head towards the park. 'We can't take him home in his current state.'

'But you're blocking their driveway.'

Isabella gasps. 'Live a little.'

With his arms draped over our shoulders, we lead Brad across the road and set him up under a tree. The park is dotted with lights, and excluding a handful of joggers who are either super into late-night fitness or fleeing murder scenes, we have it to ourselves. Isabella ducks back to the car, leaving me to stand guard in case the guy I blocked on Grindr topples over. Not awkward at all. Thankfully, he doesn't say anything.

Isabella returns with a packet of chips and a bottle of Greatorade. She pre-empts my joke. 'Shut up, it's like forty cents a litre.' She twists off the cap and lowers the bottle to Brad's mouth. He immediately takes to it. 'That's right, Bradley. Big gulps.'

He sighs after a particularly big gulp. 'I don't like Bradley.'

'Well, drink responsibly and I'll call you whatever you like.'

I set off towards the bay. Isabella only joins me

when she's certain Brad's capable of lifting the bottle himself.

'Study Club didn't start as this, by the way. It was strictly about studying.'

'Then you decided to spice it up?'

'No.' She punches my shoulder. 'I was walking home one night and I bumped into a kidlet looking a little wobbly. I couldn't say anything to stop him going out and getting obliterated, but I could be someone he could call if he needed a ride home. He did. And he told the others.'

'You know that's what parents are for, right?'

She waits for a jogger-slash-potential-murderer to pass before replying. 'Parents are often too involved in their own shit.' She takes two steps, and for a moment, a light nearby gives her a halo. 'Besides, like your dad's big dream is writing, this is mine.'

'What? To be the patron saint of teens who've drunk too much?'

'Helping kids.' She puffs out her chest. 'I'm gonna be a school counsellor one day... after I haul my arse to uni. Don't get me wrong, I love the cafe, love your family, but I'm not meant for it. *This*... When I do this, it's like I click into the world.' She peers over her shoulder. 'Thumbs up if you're okay, buddy.'

Brad's leaning against the tree. He takes a swig of the sports drink, raises a fist, then his thumb. 'My mouth tastes like bubblegum that burns.'

'Good boy,' Isabella says, turning back to me.

He's managing full sentences without chundering. He's sobering up. I'm on a collision course. It's only a matter of time before he reveals how we know each other...He'll make me sound like an arsehole. I'm not denying I'm an arsehole, but Isabella's out here shepherding drunk teens with a fucking halo, and I'd like her not to think I'm an arsehole.

'Don't tell your grandmother, by the way. About this or about me leaving the cafe. She's got her heart set on me being her heir.'

Gina couldn't be further from my mind. 'Sure.'

'But hey, that can be you.'

'What?'

'You can take over the cafe. I'll train you up.'

I have to cackle. 'Hell no. The moment I've got enough cash, I'm...' I whistle and point to Future Harvey vanishing over the horizon. 'I don't have some big dream, but I know it's not to stay in that place. The sooner I'm not around my family, the better.'

'You don't mean that.'

'I do. Everything feels like it's about them all the time. I've gone from being the guy with gay dads to being the guy with divorcing gay dads and an emotionally draining Greek family.' I watch that spot across the harbour where Future Harvey fled. 'Maybe that's it. Maybe my big dream's cutting loose.'

'Sounds lousy,' Isabella says.

'Huh?' I turn to her.

'I get you want to be your own man, but that's a lousy dream.'

I feel like she doesn't quite understand the intensity of my situation. 'It's my parents splitting, it's Ba on my Grindr grid, it's Gina being aggro about everything, it's whatever's up with Proyiayia.'

'Sounds like a lot.'

'It is.'

'But a dream isn't just something you have, it's something you are. It shapes you,' she says. 'If your dream's to ditch your family because they're going through an intense period, who would that make you?'

The answer's obvious. 'Somebody who doesn't need their mess.'

'See, I would grab a broom and help out. Maybe I'm a freak.' She's silent long enough for me to think that's the end of it, but something else strikes her. 'And what about other people? Friends? What if they're messy? I don't know you well, but you don't strike me as a guy who'd make a dream out of discarding people.'

I don't think she means it as a gut punch, but that's how it lands. Before I know it, I'm looking past her at Brad sucking in the night air like a cure.

I risk her thinking I'm an arsehole. I ask, 'What if I am that guy...hypothetically?'

'Then you're hypothetically aware enough to change.'

Brad's quiet the whole way back to Savoy. I can't tell if it's the shame of the recently sober, or if he hates me so much, he can't bring himself to speak. He opens the car door before we reach a complete stop. Isabella urges me to make sure he gets to his unit okay. He senses me walking behind him. He insists he's fine. And he is fine, in a one-foot-in-front-of-the-other kind of way, but I'm less interested in that than...I apologise for blocking him. Again, he's fine. Ships passing in the night. He arrives at the door, key in the lock. I maintain the distance. I can just let him go, but instead, I ask for his number.

He looks back at me, aghast. 'No, dude. Fuck.'

He lets the door slam.

6

Someone's left the TV on, so the kitchen's lit by stray colours from the next room. I drop Proyiayia's keys in the fruit bowl and find her fast asleep in her recliner, the same stray colours dancing across her face.

Across the bruise.

I don't budge.

I can leave her, waltz on upstairs and count down the days till I have enough cash to move out. Or...

I approach the couch. I'm careful not to make the noise that wakes her. I sit. I keep her company. It feels pointless, then she jerks awake. She blinks heavily, looks to her right and sees she's not alone.

'You want to go to bed?' she croaks. Like I'm the one who's been asleep.

I smile. 'Okay, Proyiayia.'

I climb the stairs behind her, hand raised in case she loses her balance. She doesn't. At the top, she says goodnight with a squeeze of my wrist. I watch her shuffle towards her bedroom.

I exhale.

FOUR
There's this guy

SOTIRIS

1

The sun sets on a bonfire in Leichhardt.

When we set the date in Homeroom on the last day of school, I pictured a metre-high stack of HSC notes engulfed in flames that threatened the sky. The reality's underwhelming, but nobody else came for the fire. They're peppered around Donovan's backyard, gripping cold beers or teasing the waistbands of chicks' pants.

I'm with the guys who don't have anyone to tune. It's all right, we're close to the outdoor tap and Jimmy brought cordial from home. He insists it mixes well with vodka, and indiscriminately spikes our drinks. Mine tastes like childhood and lighter fluid. I pretend to need the bathroom, so I can venture far enough away to pour it out.

I survey the gathering from my new vantage point. Past the glow of the fire, I spot boofhead Mark with his arm draped over Rachel's shoulder.

We were paired with girls from our sister school for the Year Eleven formal. I got Rachel. We hit it off. I was nervous, so I matched her smuggled drink for smuggled drink and we ended up in a park, clothes wet with dew, on the precipice of everything other guys bragged about. At the time, I thought it meant I might be straight. Now I know it only proved I could act.

Kissing her felt nothing like kissing Dean. There was no heat, no overwhelming sensation that there was nowhere else in the world I'd rather be. Just obligation.

I'll be obliged to say hello if she sees me. Mark won't say much, because he's Mark, but he will smirk. He'll tighten his grip on her. And I'll feel bad for not having what I don't want, because I wish I could make myself want it.

I abandon my cup. I leave a bonfire in Leichhardt.

Ace Books on Norton Street is still open. There's this guy behind the counter. He glances up from his crossword long enough to tell me they shut in twenty minutes.

I don't need that long. I stride towards the young-adult section, jammed awkwardly between the chapter books and the crime thrillers. Joey Jensen has half a row all to himself, face-out. I resist the allure of the heartthrob rower on the cover and scour the shelves for a spine with my name on it.

No luck.

When I told her I had to sell three thousand books to trigger a reprint, Mum got to work. She started with the stock Five Irons sent me. She bundled copies with coffees for fifteen dollars. She kept the money from each sale separate, and every few days, I would use that cash to buy more. Usually from the Dymocks in the city. In the early days, *Young* was easy to find. Then I had to ask for it. Then I had to duck into any bookshop I passed in the hope they had it in a cupboard somewhere.

I approach the front counter. The guy straightens, but keeps the pen close to the crossword, like five-down will suddenly occur to him. His tartan shirt, buttoned all the way to the top but untucked, hangs well from his broad shoulders. He isn't jacked, just broad. His curls are dirty blond and short, but his stubble is darker. It's patchy. *Hi*, his nametag reads, *I'm Jem*.

'Hey. I was wondering if you have *Young* by Sotiris Bakiritzis.' I say it like it isn't my own name, trip up a little over the letter salad near the end.

'I can check.' He puts the pen in his mouth and elevates a crusty keyboard onto the counter. He turns to the bulky monitor and hits the spacebar. He hits the spacebar again. He types. 'You know,' he says without turning from the screen, 'you look a lot like Sotiris Bakiritzis.' He handles the letter salad with aplomb.

'Uh.' My heart drops. I can't...Um...'Yeah, I'm him.'

He barely reacts. 'Seventeen and an author. That's impressive. Congrats.'

'Thanks.' I don't know what else to say. 'Eighteen now.'

'Oh, that's less impressive.' I can't tell if he's trying to be funny. He frowns at the monitor. 'It doesn't look like we have any, but I can order you a copy.'

'No, it's okay.' I never let them order it, because that would require leaving my name and number, and I don't want them thinking I'm an author who traipses across Sydney, only visiting bookshops to buy copies of his own work. Like Jem's thinking now, because he already knows my name.

I stammer and retreat from the counter. I need a book, any book. He needs to see me buy something I didn't write. *Jane Eyre* comes to mind, so I make a beeline for the classics. I expect to encounter Brontë early, but it starts with Steinbeck. Homer's next. Frank.

Woolf. Orwell. My gaze drifts. Jem's stumped by the crossword. His face is all knots until he's bludgeoned by the word. He doubles over and fills it in. A satisfied smile. Then *his* gaze drifts. He catches me watching and I crouch so I'm eye-level with *The Great Gatsby*.

My heart's racing, and I'm wondering if I looked gay looking at him.

I stay low so long, my thighs cramp. When I summon the courage to pull myself up, Jem's standing in the next aisle, his face centimetres from mine. I can smell his cologne. Too much cologne.

'You won't find it in the classics,' he says.

He means *Young*. It ought to be a one-hit kill, but it makes me laugh. He seems glad.

He begins to rearrange the books in his aisle. I can't tell if the section was in disarray before he came over, or if he was looking for an excuse to get closer.

It's only the two of us in here.

There's a chunk of stubble missing by his chin, a deep scar in its place.

'The classics section has stumped many a shopper,' he says. 'It's all about discovering a book you otherwise wouldn't have. It's silly. I've told my manager I hate it, but she won't listen.' He stops moving paperbacks around. His auburn eyes are trained on me. 'What are you actually after?'

'*Jane Eyre*.'

'Ah. There's your first problem. It's not one of our classics, it's one of our romance classics.' He starts towards the back of the store, where there's a wall of romances with an old-timey vibe. I follow, careful to keep some distance between us. The Brontës are exactly where they should be, after Austen, because romance readers don't tolerate nonsense. He runs an index finger along their spines. 'We're out of stock.'

'Oh, so I shouldn't take it personally?'

He laughs. It feels good to make him laugh. When he glances at me, I shrug, and that inspires an extra chuckle. Then he sighs, his shoulders relax. He raps his knuckles against the shelf and without looking at me, he says, 'I could...message you when more come in?'

There's a nervous edge to his voice, like he's being more than a helpful bookshop employee. He's asking for my number and everything is suddenly real, suddenly scary. I'm up against an invisible line, and I can't do what's on the other side of it.

'Actually, I'm rarely in Leichhardt.'

He rests his knuckles on the shelf. 'Oh.'

The collar of my shirt feels tight. 'Yeah, it's a bit of a trek.'

'I guess.' There's hurt in his eyes.

I swallow hard. 'But thanks, though.'

He changes the subject. He'll have to shut soon. He looks everywhere but at me until I'm gone.

And I'm on fire.

2

I sit at my desk, open a fresh exercise book and wait for the words. I rule a red margin, something I haven't done since primary school. I title the page, *Dynamite Idea*. I underline it. I dot the first point. Really dot it. I wait for the words.

Mum wasn't thrilled about me not applying for university. Yiayia was barely educated because of the war, so when my mother scraped through high school, she exceeded my grandmother's wildest dreams. I was supposed to do one better. Uni. To placate her, I vowed that writing would be my singular focus.

I haven't written since the meeting with Eliza.

She said I wouldn't have a dynamite idea for years. I listened. But her tenure as the final arbiter of what I am capable of is over. Today, a dynamite idea will come to me.

I add a second dot, because I am ambitious.

Less ambitious when I add a curved line and the two dots become the eyes of a sideways sad face.

Mrs Wiseman never liked how wedded I was to planning. She much preferred Benji's approach to writing. He would jot down the first words that came to him and let the story *take* him. The idea of slapping word after word on the page, hoping it all amounts to something in the end, stresses me out. Give me guardrails. Give me a destination to write towards.

All I have is a sideways sad face, and the longer I stare at it, the worse I feel. I slap down the first words that come to me. *Shawn wanders down the street.* Garbage.

I feel vindicated. Writing isn't channelling some higher power. A story can't *take* you anywhere, because you're the one doing all the work. There's no—

An image drops into my head. A boy, matted brown hair, about my age. Shawn. He's wearing a loud T-shirt. He enters a store. Jem's behind the counter. His unisuit is half-peeled, straps hanging from his waist. His pecs are boulders. He glances up from his crossword long enough to say they shut in twenty minutes.

I banish the thought. This is why I need guardrails.

Time moves slowest at International Arrivals, so it's vital you have something to do. I sit with my back against the wall, exercise book open on one thigh. A compelling story, even mildly explosive, has yet to reveal itself to me, but I have words. I'm in Shawn's world, reminded only occasionally, when I'm clipped by somebody's luggage trolley or I hear what could be my grandmother's voice, that I'm in an airport terminal.

Now that Mum trusts me with her precious 1998 Mitsubishi Magna, pick-ups are my responsibility. I'm the one-boy greeting party for every cousin who decides he wants to start a new life in Australia. They're the worst. All they do is smoke and complain. Nothing's ever as good as it is in Elláda, not the food, not the women. They never last long. They just want to be away from their old lives long enough to miss them.

When Pappou was alive, my grandparents would fight about going back. With an enormous arm gesture, Yiayia would say her bones were there. He would call her stupid and say they moved for a reason. She's gone every year since he died, usually to avoid the colder months. But no matter how eager she is to leave – her *bones* – she's always happy to be back.

Her squeal pulls me out of Shawn's world. I'm on my feet. She's all decked out in black, as expected. She has her arms outstretched. I crouch a little to embrace her. I squeeze her tightly. When the hug's over, she slaps my cheek. Playfully, but it still stings.

'Giatí den eísai xyrisménos?' Yiayia's unhappy I'm not clean-shaven. 'Póso se latrévo!' she adds.

After six months away, she was bound to bring back a word I wasn't familiar with. 'Latrévo?' I ask.

She paddles the air, as if to stir her English awake. Doesn't work. She opts for a synonym. 'S'agapó,' she says.

That I get. She loves me.

Carrying the suitcases up the narrow stairs is an ordeal. By the time they're on Yiayia's bed, she's done a lap of the cafe to greet all the regulars and brewed herself a coffee in the upstairs kitchen. She's only just met the new barista, and therefore, she doesn't trust him with her first coffee after a marathon plane journey. She appears beside me with her tiny cup. She takes a satisfied sip and directs me to open all the suitcases. It never ceases to amaze me how much she manages to smuggle through customs. I'm talking seeds, food ingredients, Mount Franklin water bottles taken to Greece for the express purpose of trafficking holy water from a church in the motherland.

I know her well enough to know none of her clothes need washing. She always launders everything before her return journey. She sets her coffee cup down on the dresser and begins unpacking. She hands me a T-shirt. She says it's a present from a cousin, but given the quality of my cousins, I wouldn't be surprised if she bought it herself.

'Lady at the store say good fabric.'

Yeah, she bought it herself.

I drape the shirt over one shoulder. It's reminded me I have a present for her. I fetch a copy of *Young* from my bedroom.

'Ah! Brávo sou!' Her voice is full of pride. She presses her palm against the front cover. 'You number one,' she says, a twinkle in her eye.

'Number one,' I echo.

Our only computer is in the living room, because that's where the family expert told Oprah it should be. I'm transferring today's rubbish words from the exercise book into Microsoft Word. My grandmother drags a dining chair from the kitchen, so she can sit and watch over my shoulder. She can't read, but she enjoys the sight of words filling the virtual page.

It's a reminder that while I haven't exceeded Mum's wildest dreams, I've exceeded hers.

3

The invitation to my first writers' festival comes at the last minute. My publicist calls on Monday, and I'm pinning a name badge to my shirt on Thursday. The entrance hall of the writers' centre is packed, and the air is thick with conversations that started without me. A volunteer encourages me to mingle. I try. The other authors have it easy. Their names were advertised and the attendees, mostly school librarians and aspiring writers, are familiar with their work. I'm Sotiris Bakiritzis, author of, 'I'm sorry, what was your book?' I'm only here because Penny Crow stumbled on a hike and broke her foot.

I'm pulled into Joey Jensen's orbit. He's in a leather jacket and taller than he has any right to be. He's talking about the reception to his work, how surprising it is that these little stories he tells to mend his own heart have resonated so profoundly. Someone squeezes past me to get closer. I want to tell them I'm an author too.

I'm on at nine in the morning, in conversation with Alex Warrick Boston Leigh. The Miles Franklin Room seats sixty in the audience and two onstage. Alex has already claimed his chair.

He's a serious man in his author photo and equally serious (if ten years older) in person. He sits with one leg crossed over the other. Not knee-over-knee; he doesn't strike me as the kind of man who'd be caught dead. Calf-on-knee. Slouch masculine. His voice is gravel when he greets me. He introduces himself with all four names, but when I use my two, he baulks at Bakiritzis and says he'll go with Sodeyerus. Close enough.

He gestures to the book on the chair beside his. 'That yours?'

It isn't, but I pick it up. *Jane Eyre* by Charlotte Brontë. I recall the nervous edge to Jem's voice when he offered to message me. Funny how *Jane Eyre* has existed my whole life, but now it's tethered to a guy I briefly encountered in a bookshop. I turn the paperback over. The price sticker says, *Ace Books*. My chest burns, but I'm certain it's just a coincidence. Must be the closest bookshop. I leave the novel on the edge of the stage where its owner can retrieve it.

I sit and drink in the view of sixty empty seats. Soon the chattering people we can hear in the hall will be in here, eyes on us.

The butterflies start.

I take a ragged breath.

Alex asks, 'You new at this?'

'Very.'

'How many do you reckon we'll get?'

'Sixty.'

He has a quiet laugh. I don't know what's funny.

A volunteer in the entrance hall reminds everybody that the first sessions will begin soon. We're up against Joey Jensen's keynote. We hear excitement, movement…Chatter coming from the hall becomes chatter dulled by a dividing wall, as the room next door fills.

The closest we get to an audience member is the guy in a sparkly vest who waltzes in, notices the two of us onstage and realises he's made an error.

Three minutes after nine, we hear the whine of feedback through the wall, and then a very long introduction to Joey Jensen. He's had many accolades heaped on him and the presenter is intent on listing every single one. Alex sighs, rises, drapes his coat over one arm. He's off to grab breakfast and I don't understand. We're supposed to be in conversation.

'We can have a conversation over pancakes,' he says. 'I know a spot on Darling Street.'

'No, in here.'

He steps down off the stage. 'There's no prize for turning down a lifeboat.' He waits and when I don't budge, he adds, 'Suit yourself.'

He strides down the aisle and I'm staring at sixty empty seats, listening to the audience applaud in the next room.

The butterflies are slaughtered. No survivors.

I don't get much warning before the tears start. A prick behind my eyes, goosebumps on my forearm, then the waterworks. I know it's pathetic. Attending the kids' and YA festival at the writers' centre wasn't even a possibility last week. The extent of my public life was flogging books in my mother's cafe and I was fine with that. But when the call came to say there was an opening, I let myself imagine more. An audience. Autographs.

Someone asks if this is the right place for the in-conversation, and it jolts me out of my self-pity. I look up from my lap. Jem from the bookshop is standing by the entrance, holding a locked cash box. I turn away and calm myself with a breath. It doesn't work. He's here. The book was him. I don't speak until after a second, steadier breath. 'Yeah, you're in the right place.'

'Where's Alex?'

My face is wet. I wipe my cheeks with the back of one hand. 'He went to have brekky.'

Jem's unimpressed. 'That's not cool.'

'Well...' I'm not sure what to say. Nothing, preferably. I want him to leave so I can wallow in private. 'But thanks for coming.'

He doesn't respond. He doesn't leave. Coins are jangling in the cash box. He's coming closer. He sets the box down on the stage. He's so close I can smell him and...A click. A whine of feedback. His voice amplifies, 'Testing, testing, one, two, three. Red leather, yellow leather...Good morning, all.'

I turn. Jem is occupying Alex's vacated chair, the microphone right up to his mouth. He's addressing the empty room.

'You don't have to...'

'My name is Jem. I'm the bookseller running the Ace Books stall. Today, I'm joined by Sotiris Bakiritzis.' He glances at me long enough to notice I'm beaming.

He tosses me a wink. 'With only one book to his name, Sotiris's CV might seem a little light, but that's only because he was born three days ago.' He crosses one leg over the other, knee-over-knee, and his gaze returns to me. 'Hey there.'

The butterflies stir. And something higher in my chest. 'Hey.'

Jem struggles against a smile. He pretends to consult an invisible sheet with all his questions on it. 'Tell me, how does a teenager come to write a book?'

Two words in, he encourages me to raise my microphone. It's pointless, but I must admit, it's cool to hear my voice amplified from the speakers. I rattle off a brief, well-rehearsed history of Sotiris Bakiritzis. Jem laughs at all the right moments. At first, there's a feeling that we're both performing for an audience on the off chance that we'll conjure one, but in time, the Miles Franklin Room falls away, and it only being the two of us doesn't bother me. I quite like it actually. He asks about *Young*. Not in the way customers in the cafe do. He doesn't care what it's about or if it's based on real life. He asks about the characters. He knows their names, he references their exploits.

He's read my book.

I'm grateful for any pause between an answer and a question. They're a chance to study his features. The kindness of his eyes. The squareness of his jaw. The plumpness of his lips.

I want to kiss him.

The applause for Joey Jensen is our cue to wrap. Jem lowers his microphone and says, 'I reckon we could've gone another hour.'

I don't want this to end. I shied away from giving him my number, but he's been tangled in my thoughts since, and now we're in the same room, I'm eager to stay here. He's on his feet and I speak up before I lose my nerve, before I think about invisible lines I'm too scared to cross. 'We can keep going.'

'Nah, they probably need this room for the next session.'

I'm persistent. 'Over brekky, then. There's a spot on Darling Street, apparently.'

'I would,' he says, stepping off the stage, 'but I've got books to sell.'

My heart drops. 'Oh.'

He bites his bottom lip. 'We can do drinks after I'm done, though?'

4

I have time.

Time to regret making plans.

Time to concoct a reason why we can't do drinks.

And yet, I'm helping Jem load two boxes of unsold books into his 1997 Toyota Corolla at the end of the day, sitting with the cash box on my lap while he drives, sliding into a booth at a pub on Parramatta Road.

It's been weeks since we met. I wonder if I sprang to his mind as often as he sprang to mine. I have *Jane Eyre* in my lap. I strum its pages. Did he think of me when he ordered more copies, hoping I'd return to Leichhardt? Did his chest burn when he heard I'd been added to the festival, the same way mine did when I saw *Ace Books* on the price sticker?

He reappears, a heady jug in one hand, two glasses in the other. 'I forgot to ask if beer's okay,' he says, lowering everything onto the table and then, after a brief calculation, sitting on my side of the booth.

'Beer's fine.' I'm not a big drinker, but I'll drink. I was brought up on occasional sips of Yiayia's VB, so I don't mind the taste.

He pours my beer first. 'Do you write full-time?'

'I work in the family cafe when needed, but yeah.'

He clinks his glass against mine and then raises it to his lips. 'Hope you didn't have plans to write this arvo.'

'No plans.'

I sip. He sculls.

'What are you working on?'

I have forty directionless pages. No dynamite idea.

He shrugs. 'Second novels are notoriously difficult. Write something that's you and you'll be fine.'

Not particularly helpful advice. I wrote a book that was me and my editor basically told me to quit. Besides, 'What's *me*? I assume you've read a ton. What sets a Sotiris Bakiritzis book apart?'

He rolls his wrist. His beer swirls but never spills. He narrows his eyes to oversell the effort he's putting in. 'The mum,' he answers finally. 'I could've read a whole book about the mother-son dynamic.'

'As a good Greek boy, I have plenty of material.'

He asks if I still live with her.

I nod.

He asks if I have to tell her where I am.

I nod.

'Where does she think you are now?' He tosses it out casually, but he must know it's a big question, because he drinks to mask the smirk.

'Catching up with an industry professional.'

'Ah. That makes me sound very influential.' He sets down his glass and studies it. 'So, she doesn't know about you?'

I haven't told him and he hasn't told me.

'Does your mum know...about you?'

'That I'm a poof?'

I'm startled by the ease with which he says the word...and struck by how it sounds. It's always had a sharpness to it, like whoever says it means to slice right through you. But it's different coming out of him.

I nod.

'Yeah. She's an actress. I was practically raised by men in tights. If she didn't conspire to make me gay, she sure as hell made it clear I could tell her I was.'

Mum owns a cafe in Darlinghurst. I've been surrounded by gay men all my life. She's lovely to them, but I hear what she says about them when they're out of earshot, when she doesn't realise she's also talking about me.

I don't want to open that can of worms. Besides, I know very little about Jem. He interviewed me for close to an hour; I need to even it out a bit. I quiz him. He grew up in Perth. His mum's still over there. He's been in Sydney a year, since school ended. He was head boy. Water polo captain. Envy of all. I sense a hint of bias in the retelling. But he makes me laugh. He puts me at ease. I don't know if that's him or the alcohol. A second jug replaces the first, then a third, paired with salt-and-vinegar chips from the bar. My hand creeps closer to him. He notices when my finger grazes his leg. He doesn't say anything, but he registers the touch. The slightest smile. I slide my hand up over the curve of his thigh. He doesn't tell me to stop.

'It's good beer,' he says.

'Very.'

His hand finds mine. He gently guides it back down between us and I worry I've pushed my luck. He trains his auburn eyes on me. They flicker.

'What?' I ask.

He leans in, says he needs to . . . He gently presses his lips against mine. It doesn't last longer than a couple of seconds, but I'm overwhelmed by the smell of him, the taste of him. Cologne. Beer.

He's hollowed me out. I am a heart beating in a husk. 'You kissed me.'

'You were copping a feel.'

'Under the table. You kissed me in *public*.'

Jem gasps. 'Did a nun see?'

'No, but...'

He tops up his beer and hovers the jug over mine. I shake my head. 'Suit yourself.' He takes a swig and then encourages me to have a go.

'What?'

He sits taller and licks his lips, his broad upper body aimed at me. 'Kiss me. A quick peck.'

'Right now?'

'In front of the whole world.'

'Shut up.'

I lean closer, nowhere near close enough to plant my lips on his. Jem puckers up. Past him, there's a woman ordering at the bar. She could turn around at any second. I inch closer. We're directly in the bartender's line of sight. He carded me. He knows my name. I know it'd hardly be the whole world watching, but still, I recoil. 'I can't. Sorry.'

Jem's amused. 'It's fine,' he says. 'You're comfortable feeling me up under the table—'

'My hand was on your thigh.'

'Like I'm a piece of meat. But a kiss is too much?'

It's not that. I want to make out. A lot. But I'm still reeling from the shock of my first public kiss, brief as it was. He might joke about my hand on his thigh, but I don't think he understands that just being here... This is the bravest I've ever been outside a Macca's bathroom.

My gaze is drawn to the gents', beside the bar.

I could go in first, he could follow after a non-suspect amount of time. Or we could enter together and pass for two regular blokes chucking a leak.

I squeeze his arm and discreetly point to the men's room. He gets exactly what I mean.

'Pash in the toilets?' he asks, upper lip curled. 'Absolutely n—'

I smack my lips against his before I lose my nerve. When we come apart, his cheeks are flushed.

I feel the difference on the bus home.

Something inside of me has shifted.

5

I invite Jem to my book launch. He believes I'm violating the sacred rules of bookselling; it's way too late in *Young*'s life for a launch, but he arranges heaps of copies through his work and sells them to me at a discount.

Mum transforms the cafe into an event space. The furniture's stacked against both walls, draped in the good sheets. There's a spread of finger food and cakes. Yiayia comes down with enough baklava to feed a Greek village, and soon enough, a Greek village descends on the cafe. Jem sticks out, pasty as a full moon. He arrives with a cover story. He removes a disposable camera from his jacket pocket and whispers, 'If anyone asks who I am, I'm the photographer.'

And not the guy I regularly make out with in Pioneers Memorial Park.

I mingle. Most of the guests are strangers to me, but they're strangers clasping copies of *Young* so when they tug on my sleeve as I pass by, I stop to answer their questions. Jem is constantly moving, committed to his cover story. He encourages people to pose for photographs. A flash will tell me where he is if I lose sight of him, but I rarely do.

I yearn for the moments when our paths intersect and he brushes up against me.

He buys a copy of *Young*, which is silly. He sold it to me for cheaper. He doesn't care. He wants my autograph.

I press the pen into the page. *Dear—*

'Can you make it out to Jeremy?' he asks. 'In case I grow out of the nickname.'

I'm smiling at him like he's more than my photographer. 'Hoping to hold on to your copy for a while?'

He shrugs. 'Possibly.'

I write his name, stew over a personalised message and then decide it's way too much pressure. I leave a gap and sign my autograph. The pen goes dry halfway through. Jem says it's fine, but it isn't. I scribble ghost circles on a serviette. I ask if he has a pen on him. He doesn't. I search for a familiar face. I spot Mum gossiping with Theía Mira, her high-school bestie, but my aunt if anybody asks. I call Mum's name, she turns and I mime signing in the air. She abruptly ends their conversation and I'm overwhelmed by a sudden sinking feeling. I've practically invited Mum over to meet Jem. She retrieves a blue biro from under the till. She approaches.

My collar's tight.

'Best behaviour,' I warn.

She stops beside Jem, surrenders the biro and then looks up at the guy I regularly make out with in Pioneers Memorial Park. 'Tall boy,' she says, like only somebody who's been hitting the ouzo can. 'Who are you?'

He introduces himself as Jeremy. 'The photographer,' he adds.

That's enough for Mum. 'Weird.'

Jem laughs. I exhale. I set to work tracing over my signature in blue. It clashes with the black *Dear Jeremy*. He reaches for the book and I pull it closer. I still owe him a personal message.

'It's fine as is,' Jem insists.

It's not. I stare at the blank space until something comes to me. I jot it down.

He snorts when he reads it. 'Nice.' He runs his eyes over the message once more.

I want to kiss him. More than anything.

I'm tasked with dismantling the towers of cafe furniture. Jem helps. When the tables and chairs are back where they ought to be, he suggests we celebrate. He invites me back to his place for a drink. We have all the alcohol we could possibly need right here, and Mum's upstairs, but I know what he really means.

He lives in a two-bedroom unit in Summer Hill. His housemate is asleep, so we slip our shoes off in the corridor. The door opens onto a bare living room. There's a chunky television on the floor in the opposite corner, and an aerial cord that snakes behind the lounge. He continues into the kitchen, to keep up the pretence that I'm not here for what I'm actually here for.

I sit. Nerves needle up my spine. My heart is beating way too fast for a body so stationary.

I stare at the television. It's the sort you turn on at three in the morning, not because there's something to watch, but because it will illuminate your bodies, drown out the whispers, the shortened breaths, the grunts...

Jem reappears with two glasses. Vodka and apple juice. He hands me one and stays standing. The first sip is overpowering. I can't tell if the drink is strong, or if it's just been too long since my last one. He sips and it barely registers on his face.

Our eyes meet. I break out in goosebumps. I tell myself it's because the drink is cold.

'You want to watch anything?' he asks.

'No, I'm good. You?'

'I'm good.'

He goes to sit, and before I can make room, he steadies my legs with a firm hold. He sets his glass down on the floor and eases himself on top of me. I can hear my heartbeat and I'm certain he can too. He takes my glass and puts it down. He stares at me, into me, tinted orange by the lamplight.

I am bulldozed by an inescapable truth: I am going to lose my virginity tonight.

He walks his fingers down my forearm.

'What are you doing?' I ask, barely louder than a whisper.

'Hanging out. You?'

I inhale deeply through my nose. 'Hanging out.'

We're both biding our time, waiting for the other to make the move. I feel the full weight of him on top of me, and it's all I can do not to reach around his back and pull him into me.

I kiss him. It's intense...and then gentler. He tastes sweet. His breath is warm. He scrambles, tugging enthusiastically at the hem of his shirt. He pulls it over his head, tosses it across the room, kisses me some more, his naked chest against me. I run my hand over the skin of his back. He twitches.

'Cold,' he whispers.

I apologise.

Our lips hardly disconnect. 'Keep kissing me,' he urges.

And I do. I don't ever want to stop. There are moments where our bodies move in sync, like we've rehearsed for this very performance, and there are moments where we give in to our frenzied excitement, and our hands are everywhere, grasping at buttons, skin, hair.

He reaches for my belt buckle.

6

I meet Jem's friends in bursts. His housemate, Maddi, barges into his room the first night I sleep over. She has a plate ('I've made too many pancakes!'), spots me in bed beside him ('Not enough pancakes!') and doubles back into the hall. His high-school mate Finn visits from Perth. We catch a movie at Broadway, and somebody watching could mistake us for three friends. I become more comfortable with his touch in public: a squeeze of my shoulder, of my waist. We do dinners with the gays, games nights with the straights. He lets me into his world.

We don't talk about it, but it must not be lost on him that outside of the book launch, he doesn't meet my people and we never venture east of Victoria Park together. I will never be too gay too close to Mum.

She's supposed to be in the cafe for the evening, but she's leaning against the doorframe while I style my hair. She peels off her shoe and massages her arch. She asks if I've heard of women in their late thirties changing shoe sizes, and in the same breath, she tells me I've been out a lot recently.

Jem hosts games night. The first time I joined him and the straights, it was the most out I'd ever been. I felt every second. But I've relaxed with each reunion. It helps that I've never not taken a board game too seriously. Tonight, it's *Monopoly*. I'm well positioned to dominate the second hour. Jem's struggling. He's many things, but ruthlessly invested in a board game with no real-world implications isn't one of them. I try to sneak him a utility but he chastises me. He doesn't need my pity.

'No, but you need my card.' He likes that. It's the sort of thing he'd say.

He takes up the dice just as the landline rings. He rolls a ten and moves his token around the board. He narrowly avoids a street I own and collects a Chance card.

'The phone,' I prompt him.

'The machine will get it.' He begins reading from the yellow card.

The answering machine on the kitchen counter plays a pre-recorded message. He and Maddi alternate every four words. It's cute. There's a loud beep. As the repercussions of the Chance card unfold and Jem mortgages the last of his properties, the caller speaks.

'Hello Jeremy, it's your mother.' She sounds older than Mum. There's a raspy quality to her voice.

I expect him to react with urgency, as I would. Instead, he collects money from the bank, and then proceeds to pay some of it back.

'I'll keep talking, in case you hear this from the other side of the apartment and need time to get to the phone,' his mother continues.

'Aren't you going to pick up?' I ask.

He shakes his head. 'Regular Friday call, I'll buzz her tomorrow,' he says.

Across from us, Greg makes a joke. Jem laughs. And true to her word, his mum keeps talking. She's onto the weather now, stalling to give her son enough time to arrive at the phone. He can hear her, but he lets the machine cut her off.

It's harsh and I'm the only one who notices.

Jem surrenders the dice to me. I have to refocus on the game. I roll a seven, and I'm thinking about his mother, desperate to talk to him. Victor moves the token for me. I land on Go and there's a debate about whether I get two hundred or more. I don't really mind, but other players whose pieces are close to Go argue that I should get double for landing on the tile and not simply passing it. There's no rulebook to consult so we settle on two hundred and the next player rolls.

I rub the hairs on Jem's forearm. 'Why didn't you answer?' I ask.

He shakes his head. 'Would've lasted an hour. I'm *here* now. She's good.' He affectionately scratches my neck.

I can't imagine sitting through Mum leaving a message like that.

I wake up in Jem's bed, alone. The digits on the clock radio are busted. It's quarter-past an hour but I don't know which. It's still dark, so I can guess. I lie there for a few minutes, expecting him to return from the bathroom. When he doesn't, I kick off the sheet, throw on underwear and investigate. The door at the end of the hall is shut, a strip of light leaking underneath. I approach and gently turn the knob.

Jem is leaning against the kitchen counter in his horse-patterned boxers. He sniffs hard, twists his body away from me. His shoulders are dusted with peeling skin, the cost of a sunny afternoon by the pool.

My voice is thick with sleep when I ask if he's okay. He clears his throat. He stands taller but keeps his back to me. He tells me he'll only be a minute. He waits for me to leave, but I don't.

He's beside the landline and the answering machine. I wonder if his mother phoned again. The time zones mean it isn't as late over there...

I take a punt. 'Was it a bad call?' I ask.

He shakes his head, still not facing me.

I risk getting closer. He flinches and then relaxes as I wrap my arms around him. I let him cry, his bare chest heaving against mine. I hold him tighter. I'm not sure what's appropriate. Do I ask questions? Or is that prying? Do I just stand here? Should I have left when he nudged me to?

His tears dry and he mutters, 'Okay.' It's my cue to loosen my hold on him. We peel apart and he runs his hand through his curls. He looks depleted. He tells me he'll meet me in the bedroom. This time, I listen. I retrace my steps.

He joins me under the sheet and we lie in the knowledge that neither of us is getting much more sleep tonight. Whether it's five minutes or fifty, I have no idea how long we're silent before he speaks.

'It was a good call,' he says.

I don't understand. If it was a good call, why did I find him shattered?

'Mum's sick,' he adds.

He's told me about her. Morsels here and there, but never much. Sylvie was once a darling of the theatre scene in Western Australia. The most famous stage actress who wasn't a soapie star looking for something different to do for three months. He grew up in dressing rooms, in the wings, in the first four rows. She was taller onstage. She would disappear into other people's lives right in front of him, but if her gaze found his, she would break character in ways that only he would notice. Twinkle her fingers by her side. As bold as a wave. It was their secret.

Tonight, he tells me more. How over time, Sylvie found it difficult to remember lines. Another one of their secrets. Until she invented an entire monologue mid-performance to keep a production of *Macbeth* moving after her memory faltered. That's when it became the whole company's secret. An MRI revealed a brain tumour behind her left eye. She had months left, a year if she agreed to surgery. She only let them remove as much as they could without affecting her daily life. She and Jem crammed everything they could into that year, but then she had another, and a third...She encouraged him to move to Sydney. His mum didn't say anything directly, but his aunt told him that she didn't want him to see her decline, didn't want him to be burdened. The way Sylvie explained it, they had two extra years together. They filled those years. They were joyous and perfect and expecting any more would be selfish of her. He had to start building a life without her.

'She's been such a good mum. She makes me want to be a dad, and I want my kid to know her, but that's...that's not happening,' he croaks. 'I'm waiting for the bad call, the one that means I have to drop everything and go back. Until then, I get the good ones, once a week. But they're sad. I can't hear about her day...I mean, she's feuding with her neighbour over the floral story of their street, and I'm laughing because I want her to hear me laugh, but my heart is breaking because she won't be around much longer. We don't have time.'

I whisper his name.

'And I don't get how you can...How can you not let your mum see who you are?'

It's a detour I don't expect. Months of avoiding everywhere east of Victoria Park weigh down on my chest.

I swallow the lump in my throat. 'I'm afraid she'll be disappointed in me.'

Jem turns onto his side. I feel his gaze before I meet it. His eyes are wide and wet. 'How could you ever disappoint her?'

7

There's probably a perfect way to come out to a Greek mother with traditional values, devised by expert homosexuals and lab-tested by scientists. But after last night, I don't care about perfect. I need the secret out of me, so I stride into the cafe and blurt it out.

Mum's balancing three plates, a mountain of breakfast food on each. I'm blocking her path. 'You're what?' she asks.

'I'm gay. I like guys.'

Her expression hardens. 'Really?' she growls. 'Now?'

She takes the long route and delivers the breakfasts to table twelve. She comes back. I go to speak, but she waves her index finger at me. The rush takes priority.

My brain is all static. I'm out. I'm gay.

Mum marches past with an omelette. 'Don't just stand there, Sotiris.'

I ditch my overnight bag and source a biro from under the till. It takes a little more effort to find a docket book, but I have one eventually. I chart a course between the tables, from one customer holding a menu to the next. I force myself through the pleasantries, even though it's hard to talk, hard to breathe. Mum avoids making eye contact. She knows I'm gay. The man on table six wants a hot chocolate. The woman on table fourteen wants a weak cappuccino and poached eggs on toast. I ask her how she'd like her eggs. She eyes me strangely. I worry I haven't written the table number clearly enough. Mum keeps her distance. She knows I'm gay. But as long as we're both working tables, I won't know the consequences. We're suspended in time. The coward in me hopes for an eternal breakfast rush, but the flow of dishes from the kitchen eventually slows and there are no new orders to take, no drinks to walk...Mum's by the counter. I approach slowly. If she's grateful for my help, she doesn't show it. She doesn't even look at me. She sends me to my room.

My bedroom is the smallest it's ever felt. I sit on the end of my bed and watch the doorway. It's pathetic. I'm eighteen and I've been sent to my room. But I'm relieved that it's not worse.

I dread Mum's arrival. The screaming match. It doesn't come. I hear the front door slam around lunchtime, but she doesn't climb the second flight of stairs to my bedroom. When it's just the two of them, Mum and Yiayia speak Greek at a frenetic pace. I never catch every word, but I always get the vibe. I strain to hear. I can't make out who they're talking about, but I know.

I don't dare leave the room.

Yiayia delivers me dinner. Kokkinistó. A beef stew in a tomato sauce, served over rice. I sit up and she cautions me not to spill any on the sheets. I want to ask if she's okay.

She pauses on her way out, considers something, then returns to my side. 'Palikári mou,' she says, throat full of love. She cups my cheek with her hand and I reach up to hold it there.

I'm woken by the weight of somebody on my mattress. I can guess who, but I open one eye anyway. Mum is lying on top of the covers in full work get-up.

It's too early to say it's morning.

'How sure are you?' she asks eventually. 'I spoke to Jeannie and she said it could be a phase.'

'I'm sure, Mum.'

She exhales. It's a struggle. 'You're making life so much harder for yourself.'

I can't imagine it's any harder than pretending.

Another laboured breath. 'When I told your grand-mother I was pregnant, she slapped me. Backhander across the face. Her ring chipped my tooth. She told me I was marrying your father, and I told her I wasn't. She had this idea of who I was and who I was going to be and I rebelled against it. She never apologised. She never told me I made the right decision. Time just... passed. I'm not sure, but I think this is like that.'

'Are you... going to slap me?'

'Say that again and I will.'

'Sorry.'

She sighs. 'I thought I knew you better than anyone. And I'm angry at you for changing, when I should be angry at myself for not... You're still my son, I still love you, I want the world for you, but I'm angry at you. I don't want you to be gay. I need time.'

It's a lot to dump on me. I don't know how to process it. 'How much time?' I ask.

She doesn't answer. Instead, she asks if there's somebody. She immediately regrets it and scrunches her eyes closed. 'No, don't tell me.'

'There's this guy.'

She shakes her head. 'Not yet. Not yet.'

I want her to accept me, wholly and completely, right now. I *told* her. She can't decide to ignore it until she's ready. Yiayia didn't put her through the rigmarole of shopping for rings and playing happy family with Dad, pretending that marrying him was ever something she was going to do... There's a fire in me and it's intensifying. She *should* be angry at herself. And then I see the tear. She's crying. Her eyes are shut, as if she's willing herself to stop, but the tears keep coming, and I'm putty, malleable. Suddenly what I want isn't important.

I lie. I tell her I'm seeing a girl called Rachel.

She doesn't open her eyes and I don't make her.

FIVE
Storms

HARVEY

1

Ba's become a regular fixture in the cafe, frowning at his laptop because he left his glasses in Perth and he's too proud to admit he needs them. I grab his empty cup, but I don't speak. I've learnt not to disturb him, even if it's been ages since I last saw him type.

I return to the counter, where Isabella alternates between steaming a jug of water and scratching at the wand with a teaspoon to clear the milk gunk. She's cursing Fabrice, the weekend barista and bane of her existence. In her ideal world, he'd be pulled off the roster for refusing to clean the machine properly, but she knows – and I suspect he knows – there's nobody else to work those shifts.

She slams down the teaspoon and looks to me, exasperated. 'Wanna learn how to make a coffee?'

Since our chat in the park, I've approached my gig in the cafe as less of a temporary thing. I walked the cash from under my pillow to the pawn shop on Darlinghurst Road. Ninety dollars didn't buy me the best iPad model they stocked, but I did manage to haggle down the price of a decent one with a scratch on the back. It's made taking orders a whole lot easier. And I'm more confident walking food and beverages, faster at clearing tables, better at washing up. I even settle bills unassisted now.

But I haven't dared get close to the hallowed espresso machine.

'You for real?' I ask.

'Should I not be? There are weekend shifts in it for you if you're not horrible.'

I've watched her work the De'Longhi. Not in a creepy way. Yes, in the weeks we've shared shifts, it hasn't been lost on me that she's gorgeous. But I've been watching to learn. My deepening appreciation for the way her face dimples when she's concentrating is purely a by-product.

She lets me get cosy with the machine. The gay in me wants to turn every knob and make it sing. I resist the temptation.

'Don't let it overwhelm you,' she says. 'You can whittle making a latte down to three simple steps: pull the shot, steam the milk, pour to combine.'

There are heaps more steps in practice, but I forgive

the subterfuge, because she closes one hand over mine to help me fasten the portafilter. It's brief, but when she releases me, I miss her touch. Only for a sec.

She doesn't sample the latte when I'm done. She's already had two. Any more and she'll be a walking earthquake simulator. I deliver it to Ba. He flashes me a smile that makes me think he might be open to disturbances. I do the supportive son thing and ask how his writing's going.

'It's going.'

He's thankful for the coffee. He needs fuel. I tell him I made it. He's still thankful, but now, a little trepidatious.

'Your first?' he asks.

I nod. 'Have to say, I reckon I'm naturally gifted.' There was a moment where I was a bit eager with one of the knobs. Steam rushed, milk sputtered, but I recovered quickly and repositioned the jug so the tip of the wand barely skimmed the milk as it spiralled.

'We'll see.' Ba sips cautiously. I've never seen somebody think so hard about their coffee before. He smacks his lips. 'Milk's burnt,' he says, with Gina's precision.

'Oh.'

I dive in to retrieve it and he slaps me away. 'I'm not done with it.' He takes a second sip. I hope it's better. 'Yeah,' Ba confirms. 'Burnt.'

I opt for levity. 'Look at me, disappointing our only customer.'

My father tuts. 'I hope you're not letting your grandmother pay you too much.'

I cringe. 'Was it that bad?' I ask.

A third sip. 'The cafe's that empty.'

2

The clinic waiting area has a vibe. The chairs have soaked up years of dread and sadness. This isn't the sort of place you wait for good news.

I pick at the crusted cappuccino stain on my apron. The invitation to Proyiayia's specialist appointment came at the last minute. Gina strode into the cafe, pointed at me and pointed at Ba. He was mid-sentence. She didn't care.

Now my father taps his closed laptop and laments the lost writing time.

'You could've written for years,' Gina says, 'an extra hour won't kill you.'

He doesn't see the point in this. Proyiayia's forgetful, but who isn't? She's fine. She's sturdy. She'll outlive us all.

Gina shushes him.

Not that Proyiayia's even listening. Her eyes are fixed on the panoramic shot of Bondi Beach hanging on the wall behind me. There isn't much else in here that's worth a second glance.

I crane my neck to get another look at it. 'Nice, huh?'

She nods and rattles off a collection of syllables that makes zero sense to me.

Makes sense to Gina. She frowns. 'What are you on about, *your bones*?' she asks her mother.

Proyiayia points a stubby finger at the photograph. 'Samos.'

'That's not Samos. That's Bondi.'

My great-grandmother scowls. 'Ti les?'

Gina opens her mouth and stops herself. The fight isn't worth it. She has a bouquet of massive medical imaging envelopes in her lap. I can see where she's tried to scratch off the seal on one of them.

Gina found Dr Tsiolkas through church. She was told the clinic had a three-month waiting list, enough time for Gina to organise the scans, stare at the scan results locked away in their sealed envelopes, scratch at the seals...After the fall, Dr Tsiolkas brought the appointment forward.

Proyiayia's name is called. Gina warns us not to say anything we don't have to, then waves at the... 'Is that the doctor?' she asks. 'He looks too young to be a doctor.'

'Mum,' my father drones.

Dr Tsiolkas approaches. He has the kind of prominent Greek nose that makes me glad my parents didn't use Ba's sperm. Gina's close to horrified as he warmly greets my great-grandmother. He calls her Sotiria and pronounces it with confidence. He asks if she's okay with him addressing her as theía. He knows her generation well. Proyiayia's charmed. He's clearly better to look at than the panoramic shot of Bondi Beach.

The doctor turns to my grandmother and calls her Georgina, which sounds weird.

She tells him he's young.

He smiles. 'Doogie Howser, right?' He tosses Ba and me a quick hello.

Gina can't get past his age. Following him across the waiting area, she asks if he's qualified. He's a trainee GP doing his extended skills term. That's all Gina needs to hear to jump to conclusions.

'So, you're not a real doctor?'

Ba groans.

Dr Tsiolkas laughs. 'Real doctor,' he assures her when we arrive at his office, 'just dabbling in a specialty.'

Gina's relieved to meet his supervisor, a severe-looking geriatrician with sun-damaged skin and a receding grey hairline. He's well past the age of dabbling in anything. When he realises there are four of us, he quietly vacates one of the chairs and stands by the door.

He's the doctor my grandmother addresses. She holds out the envelopes and Dr Tsiolkas intercepts them. 'Yeah, I'll grab those,' he says.

Gina releases them... reluctantly.

He rests the envelopes on his desk without opening them. The edge of his mouth curls when he notices the damaged seal.

Proyiayia is his patient, but his first question is for Gina. He asks how she's feeling. She's pretty good. There are cracks in her stoicism; her voice trembles a little. Dr Tsiolkas nods but he doesn't say anything. He's giving her the chance to elaborate. He read Proyiayia pretty well, but I don't think he quite knows what he's up against with Gina. She's not gonna open up to fill a silence. She said she's pretty good, move on.

'Nervous,' Gina adds. 'A little concerned.'

Ba and I catch each other's gaze. What magic is this?

Dr Tsiolkas's nod is full of understanding. He reassures her we're in the right place, and returns his attention to Proyiayia. He calls her theía again. She's practically giddy. He talks through how the consult will run, going to great lengths to make it all sound non-threatening and routine. They're just getting to know each other.

There's passing mention of the fall.

'I no fall,' Proyiayia says. He doesn't even have time to give her the silent treatment before she adds, '*Little* fall.'

Dr Tsiolkas has Proyiayia introduce us. He points to Gina.

My great-grandmother starts with, 'Beautiful,' immediately finds, 'Bossy,' then ends up recounting the time a preteen Gina split her foot open outside the house in Redfern. The doctor lets the story meander to its end, then he asks about me. She stops him. He's missed a generation. Ba. She waxes lyrical about Sotiris. When she mentions he's an author, the doctor says he'll have to read the book. People always say that when they hear Ba's an author, but they never actually mean it. Ba still inflates.

'And what about this lad?' the doctor asks, gesturing to me.

Proyiayia looks my way, exhales. 'Ah.'

We're the last ones to bed at night. In the living room after eleven, the world is ours. It smells like the Tiger Balm I rub into her stubborn shoulders and sounds like the finest Greek programming I don't understand. Can't believe I look forward to it every day, but I do.

My great-grandmother blinks at me. It's like she's been asked to describe a stranger. 'Ti boró na po?' What can she say? Something, ideally.

Her eyes narrow. She's searching... The doctor doesn't let the moment stretch too long, but as soon as he opens his mouth, she says, 'Heavy!'

She'd forgotten me. I know that in the scheme of things, I'm a recent addition and rarely seen, but she had no clue who I was... And Dr Tsiolkas thinks she's just called me fat.

'Harvey,' I clarify, the hurt still churning.

The doctor nods. 'Ah.'

The moment the cognitive test starts, I know it isn't the standard one. It's been modified for Greek folks of a certain age. I don't get why he asks the first few questions, so I'm not sure how she fares. Then he talks to her about the four items she's gonna buy when she next goes shopping – spaghetti, onions, mince and milk. He asks her to repeat what she'd buy. It's clearly a memory test and her answers are clearly wrong. She mentions fish, cheese...She pauses to think. Gina interrupts. She explains to her mother in Greek that the boy doesn't want her to tell him what she's buying next time she visits the supermarket. He wants her to repeat what he *said* she's buying. Proyiayia concentrates, really considers what's expected of her, then mentions fish, cheese...

'No, you heard him. He said spaghetti and—'

Dr Tsiolkas gently chimes in, but it might as well be a slap. Gina goes to talk back and he isn't having it. 'Let her...' he coos.

Ba doesn't say a word. His forehead is sliced in half by a deep crease. It's dawned on him. Something's fucked.

When they switch to Greek, it's beyond my comprehension level, but the impression I get from watching Gina is that the rest of the test doesn't go great. She shifts her weight in her chair, ready to leap to her mother's aid when she stammers. It's all she can do not to speak up. Ba does a bad job of hiding that he's crying.

The test culminates in Dr Tsiolkas instructing Proyiayia to draw him a clock. She stares at the pad, brow knotted, pen clasped tightly. Every second's an eternity. Gina's fighting the urge to grab the pen-holding hand and guide it to make a circle. It's a *clock*. She must know what a clock is. Rolói. Ba and I are bystanders, ordered not to say anything we don't have to. He's sniffing like the star of a Codral commercial, and I'm...

I've sat with her every night for a fortnight and she forgot me.

Proyiayia sneaks a glance at the clock on the wall, then starts drawing a circle. The doctor lets her finish. She must think she's got away with it.

She catches Gina's disapproving look. 'Ti?' she asks.

Dr Tsiolkas consults the scan results. He goes from primarily speaking with Proyiayia to straddling two conversations at once – one with his patient and one with Gina. He starts with the little fall. He asks Proyiayia for her licence. He tells her he doesn't want her driving for the time being. Gina gets the truth. Proyiayia's not getting her licence back. He wants to investigate the fainting and eliminate some possibilities. Blood sugar. Heart health. She'll see a cardiologist. It's all gingerly explained to Proyiayia; Gina's treated to the potential severity of the situation.

Proyiayia's attention wanes by the time Dr Tsiolkas mentions her brain is shrinking. He says we'll notice a significant difference in six months. He keeps bringing that up. Six months. It's happening quickly. Moderate dementia. Alzheimer's. He'll start her on tablets, but they only ease the symptoms, they don't stop it progressing. Six months to get power of attorney...Six months.

And Gina's nodding through it. Anyone can see she's a feather-knock away from collapsing. Ba's got his hand on her forearm, but I bet she's numb. The doctor assures Gina that Proyiayia won't notice what's happening. He knows we will. He wants to make sure we're gonna be okay. He wants to make sure Gina especially is gonna be okay.

'How? How can I be okay?' she whispers. The words hurt. 'I don't want to say goodbye to my mum. She's all I've ever known.'

The goodbyes are long. Proyiayia kisses Dr Tsiolkas on both cheeks. The supervising doctor too. She erupts in the elevator, though. That moró took her licence. Is he even old enough to drive?

Gina sniffs hard. She wipes her face with the back of one hand and defends the doctor. He's a good kid.

Proyiayia chops the air. I have no clue what she says next, but Gina assures her she doesn't need to go to the cemetery that often.

'Bah!'

I watch the four of us reflected in the elevator doors. So many reasons to feel shitty written all over our faces.

'What did Harvey and I coming achieve?' Ba asks. 'Were you trying to torture us?'

Gina doesn't have an answer.

He's the first out when the doors open. He storms off, laptop by his side. I get it.

'Where he go?' Proyiayia asks.

Gina's honest. She doesn't know. He's being dramatic.

I speak up. 'He's kinda right.'

My grandmother doesn't turn to me. For a while, I think she didn't hear. Then, 'I couldn't be the messenger.'

3

My parents took me down the coast for the winter holidays a few years back. They booked the shittiest Airbnb in Bunbury. Not that it was shit for them. They enjoyed the peaceful cottage retreat that the listing promised. I was treated to the shed out the back that doubled as the second bedroom. A recently renovated, carpeted shed, sure, but a shed's a fucking shed. It stormed every night and the shed was punished by the elements. I'm talking tree branches beating against the walls, the tin roof rattling and threatening to come loose. I got no sleep, convinced the place would fall to pieces. Never did.

There's a Bunbury storm inside me. It started as a churning in the doctor's office, now it's worse. The entire walk back from the clinic, I am the tin roof. Only I'm fighting to keep the storm in, not out.

I've never felt like this before.

I dunno how long I linger outside the cafe. I have a shift to finish. But I'm worried I'll burst if I so much as move...

The old bloke on table fourteen flags me down.
I can't blame him. I'm in my apron, I look like I'm here
to work. He doesn't know about the storm. I head over.
He taps his empty latte glass. He's after another. Weak
decaf. When I relay the order, Isabella says he might as
well ask for hot milk. It's all I can do to keep the storm
from showing on my face, but Isabella sees something.
She asks how the appointment went.

I cry. It's not a full-body sob, but it's enough emotion
for her to realise the news is bad. We close early. While
she cleans, she texts the kidlets individually to tell them
Study Club's off. When the last message is sent, it occurs
to her that I don't have her number.

She scrawls it on a serviette. 'In case you need
to talk.'

Gina and Proyiayia are bickering in the kitchen. It feels
wrong, like fisticuffs at a funeral. My great-grandmother
has her back to the stove, wooden spoon still in hand
but eyes off the avgolémono. Gina's taken her kleidiá.

I hear the keys jangle in my grandmother's hand.
'I'm just looking at them,' she says.

Proyiayia grunts. She must know she's being taken for a fool. Maybe not. Turning back to the soup, she spots me. I worry she won't remember who I am. 'Teleíoses?' she asks.

And the storm inside me settles. There's the warmth of relief. She's asking if work's done, so she recognises me. I dump my apron on the table. 'Teleíosa.'

She smiles and dunks the spoon in the soup. She stirs, brow furrowed.

I ask her how she's feeling.

'Good. Good.'

It's not the answer I expect. 'Even after what the doctor said?'

'Ah. Licence is bullshit.' Her eyes are defiant. 'I get back.'

'Yeah, but he—'

Gina intervenes. We're not talking about that, apparently. She won't elaborate, but she does give the keys a little wave. 'Up here,' she says, hiding them on the top shelf of the pantry, beside the cereals and well out of Proyiayia's reach.

'Is that necessary?' I ask.

She closes the doors. 'Don't start me, Harvey.'

Proyiayia glances over her shoulder. 'Ti?'

'Not you.'

My great-grandmother shrugs and her daughter makes a swift exit. She stomps up the stairs. The room is really starting to smell like lemon now. Proyiayia gestures to the wire mesh waste bin by the sink. The plastic bag she swiped from the fruit and veg section needs replacing. I tie the top as best I can and walk the rubbish out into the courtyard.

Ba's on one of the deck chairs. I have no clue how long he's been out here, if he rushed back after the appointment, or if he went for a scenic sulk around Darlinghurst. I don't wanna disturb him. I drop the bag into the bin slowly, lower the lid carefully.

'Come sit,' he says.

The other chair is pretty weathered. I saw one in better nick collapse under Owen once, so I ease myself onto it. Ba's gazing up at the sky. It's blue with bursts of milk-white clouds. I truly am a hospo worker, everything looks like latte art.

I look elsewhere. He's got his laptop by his feet. 'You been writing?'

He shakes his head. 'Ruminating.'

'Ah.' I dunno how else to respond.

'My new book's about this kid who lives above a

cafe in Darlo with his mother and her mother.' This is the first time Ba's volunteered any specifics. It sounds familiar. 'Before you ask, I have no idea where the idea came from. My mind just...'

I roll with it. 'You're a creative genius.'

'The best the world has ever known.' His laugh is half-hearted. 'I really thought fictionalising my childhood was going to be easy.'

Ba's not a huge drinker, but when he does hit the wines, he time travels. At the bottom of every glass, there's an anecdote I've never heard before, the time Gina did this, the time Proyiayia did that. I would've guessed stuffing them into a novel would be no trouble.

'No, see...I've got stories to fill a book ten times over, that's not the problem,' he says. 'The problem is plot. I have none. What are the arcs? Why does the novel start where it does and what's it all building to?' His eyes narrow like the sky's acting suss. 'I don't want it to build to this. Yiayia was supposed to live forever. Your proyiayia was supposed to live forever.' Saying that reminds him that the family doesn't end with him, that Sotiria means something to me too. Our eyes meet for the first time since I came out here. 'You okay?'

I nod.

He reckons it's funny. 'Liar.' He tries his hand at Dr Tsiolkas's power move. He keeps quiet in the hopes I come clean. But he doesn't have the gravitas of a trainee GP. He gives up pretty quickly. 'There's no shame in letting people know how you're really feeling. I mean, one of your dads is Greek. We never bottle anything. We let our emotions out, make them everyone's problem for a short time, and then they're gone. You'd probably say that's cringe.'

'Actually, you saying that is cringe.'

'Talk to someone, Harvey. It doesn't have to be me, as much as that's a dagger to my heart.'

'Ba.'

He presses a finger into his chest. 'Right here.'

'I think your heart's a little to the...' I drop the bravado. 'I'll be okay, Ba.'

He lets the finger fall. 'You know, in the interests of never bottling anything, I wanted to be Dad.'

'For real?'

'Yeah, but I'm the Greek one, so it made sense for me to be Ba and for your father to be Dad. Forget it's not something I grew up calling anyone. It made sense like Perth made sense. Like setting everything else I wanted for myself to one side made sense.'

The air's changed. Is this an opening, an opportunity to talk about the split?

No. He folds his arms and assures me he likes Ba now. It's just nice to let some things out.

'Also,' he adds, 'we're not telling her she has dementia.'

A little late to make that call. 'She was there when the doctor told us.'

'You saw her. She wasn't totally in the room.' I protest but he clicks his tongue. 'Gina's orders,' he adds flatly. I can tell there's already been a fight about it.

The soup's ready at four o'clock. It's way too early for dinner, but my father and I eat. My great-grandmother sits at the table and watches us. At one point, she asks Ba why he looks sad.

He sniffs. 'Allergies.'

I kick my shoes off at the top of the stairs, but snatch them up before Gina cracks the shits. I look to her bedroom, expecting to see her scowling. The door's shut. I'm supposed to leave her with her feelings, but I creep close enough to knock. I ask if she wants me to bring her up some dinner.

No response.

The storm isn't back, but I can feel the beginnings, the churning. I'm on my bed when I should be downstairs. It's silly to avoid Proyiayia. I told myself I wouldn't, told myself I'd slap on my trackies and head down, but I lied. I'm on Insta.

I like one of Royce's photos. It's the surest way to get a DM, and sure enough, a DM.

hey

There's an artful simplicity to his work. Royce goes to Doubleview Tech. I met him the term I tried debating. We were both second speaker, bored out of our minds, but we agreed we weren't half-bad to look at. We've never hooked up, but after a handful of messages, a saucy pic is guaranteed.

I stop myself from *hey*ing back. Better to leave him hanging after a greeting than after a pic of his junk.

There's no course-correcting the convo after that point. Like, what do I say?

Hey, appreciate the nude, but I was in the room when the great-grandmother I barely know but have a growing affection for was diagnosed with Alzheimer's and now I'm wrestling with a bunch of emotions I don't quite understand. Another time?

Ba's probably right. Maybe I do need to talk to someone. Don't think Royce is that someone.

I stare at Isabella's contact details for a good while before I call. I put it on speaker and leave the phone on my chest. She answers on the third ring. 'Isabella speaking.' She sounds stern enough to give a telemarketer second thoughts.

When I say hi, her voice changes. She sounds more like herself now. She asks how I'm going, and I'm honest with her in a way I can't be with Ba. She knows about the diagnosis, but not about Proyiayia forgetting me. I start there. Heaps to say about that. I've had my name slip somebody's mind before, but this was more than that. It'll happen again. I don't want it to. I can avoid her so I never see it. I don't want that either. My whole life, Ba's spoken about her as this huge force, and now that I'm finally starting to understand the bigness, she's...

I dunno if Isabella can tell I'm crying, but I've let everything out, and my reward is her asking if I wanna hear the worst joke in the world. She insists I brace myself. I do. She asks, 'What do you call a Greek guy coming down the stairs who thinks he's better than you?'

I have no idea.

'Con Descending.'

A Greek guy descends the stairs to spend time with his great-grandmother, finds another Greek guy on the couch.

Ba's not usually up this late. He scoots over to make room.

4

Gina stomps past the office, swearing under her breath. I peel myself off the mattress and blink hard. It's still dark out and I can hear her wrestling with the latch on the bathroom window, swearing more severely. 'Yes, you fucker!' means she's got it open. She calls down to Marta on the street. She needs five minutes. By the time I'm in the bathroom, she's gripping the sink like it's the only thing keeping her upright. The water's running... She needs more than five minutes.

Her voice is wafer-thin. She forgot she gave Fabrice the day off.

'Do you need me to head down?' It's the sort of question you ask when you already know the answer.

Gina instructs me to call Isabella – Bevan if she doesn't answer, but I'm to try Isabella twice. Their numbers are under the espresso machine. She arches an eyebrow when I say I already have Isabella's digits.

We've woken Proyiayia. She asks what's going on. Gina rushes to say everything's fine and pushes me out of the bathroom. She shuts the door before Proyiayia can see her.

My great-grandmother tightens her leopard-print robe. 'What wrong with her?' she asks.

It's my first time opening without Isabella or Gina looking over my shoulder, so I'm cosplaying as somebody who knows what he's doing. I flip all the switches that need flipping, prepare the float, make a practice latte... The first customer wanders in before Isabella arrives. Pinstripe suit on a Saturday, real-estate agent or freak or both. His slow swagger gives me an extra few seconds to brace myself.

'Latte?' I ask hopefully.

'Nah, mate, cappuccino.'

Yeah, mate, that's not gonna work for me. 'Could I interest you in a latte instead?'

He scowls. He's not used to negotiating his coffee order, but I must look completely out of my depth, because he caves. And he's surprised when he sips it. 'Not shit.'

He brushes past Isabella on his way out. She pauses

to squint at his takeaway cup, then at me. I get a nod of approval and when she's closer, a new worst joke in the world. 'What do you call a Greek guy who shrinks when he grips the road?'

I make an effort to solve this one. She tries to give me several outs, but I focus on words beginning with *con* while I refill serviette dispensers, wash dishes, polish cutle—

'Con Traction!' I shout.

Isabella raises her thumb from behind the De'Longhi.

I punch the air.

Gina hasn't emerged from her bedroom since the morning. After my shift, Ba sends me upstairs with spanakópita. I press my face against the door and say her name. I hear a sound I generously interpret as a muffled invitation to enter. The room is pitch black, except for the rectangular halo around the curtain. I'm hesitant to cross the threshold.

'I've got food.'

She's a lump under the doona. She tells me to leave the plate by the door.

'Do you need anything else?'

No response.

I'm woken by an alarm on Sunday. Gina hasn't told me to work, but she also hasn't left her bedroom in twenty-four hours. Fabrice operates the espresso machine. He's a backpacker from France with a pencil moustache and a crooked smile. He has a voice like gravel, and if we were anywhere but my grandmother's cafe at six in the morning, I'd wanna get dirty.

I ask if he wants to hear the worst joke in the world and he blanks me.

'What do you call a Greek actor who goes to war?' I ask.

His expression doesn't change. He does raise a jug and start steaming milk, though.

'Con Scripted.' I oversell it with a fat grin.

The crooked smile becomes a snarl. 'That is a stupid joke.'

The lump under Gina's doona tells me to leave dinner by the door. She barely touched yesterday's spanakópita. There's nothing stopping her from maybe having one potato and ignoring the meatballs, and me coming up with more food tomorrow, and us doing this day after day. I build up the courage to ask if she wants me to crack open a window.

'I'm fine.'

I swallow hard. She isn't fine and I shouldn't leave her. I grip the plate tighter. 'I can keep you company while you eat?'

She groans and pushes herself up to seated. The doona falls away and she adjusts her robe. 'Are you worried I'll choke?'

'More worried you haven't really spoken to anyone. You know, let it out.'

'Ah.' She holds out her hand. I walk the plate over and set it down on the bed beside her. 'Will that make it better, letting it out?'

'You might feel better.'

She laughs to herself and picks at a roast potato. 'I feel like shit because my mother's dying. I can shout it from the rooftops and I won't feel better. Because my mother's dying.'

Tough crowd. I feel wholly ill-equipped for this conversation.

She chews with her mouth open. 'Silver lining,' she says, 'when your proyiayia dies, she'll see Stavros again.'

It's a name I haven't heard in ages. My great-uncle's. I never knew him. Neither did Ba. He died young. We don't talk about how.

'Your proyiayia loved Stavros. More than me. I don't take it personally. Her generation valued sons more and he... was a son.' Gina smacks her lips together. 'The potatoes are good.'

'I know.' A fucking fantastic contribution to the conversation.

'Proyiayia died when Stavros did,' my grandmother continues. 'And then I had your father and he brought her back to life. Now God's taking her away from me and there's nothing I can do.' She clears her throat. 'And the doctor was comforting *us* and not her, because she doesn't... Your father hasn't told her, has he?'

I shake my head.

'Good,' she says. 'We're not telling her.'

It doesn't feel right to withhold this from her. It's gonna change her life profoundly; it's gonna *end* it. She has a right to be aware of that. 'I think...'

'We are *not* telling her. End of story.' Her voice is suddenly full. 'They forced your great-grandfather to retire and it was like the light behind his eyes went out. Your proyiayia has lasted this long because she's kept busy. I'm not telling her she's not capable, because then she'll believe she's not capable, and I don't want her to... If I can delay that light dimming even by one day, I'll do it. But this is gonna be a bitch of a thing. We'll want it to end and when it does, we'll wish it lasted longer.'

'What good's being up here, then?' I let it out before I think to wrap it in careful words so it doesn't hit as hard.

Gina sighs. 'You sound like me.'

The Monday wake-up is brutal. I haven't had a proper day off in a week. I brush my teeth twice and hold out hope that in the time it takes me to strip all the enamel, my grandmother will appear. She doesn't. The idea of another all-day shift is...I text Isabella to ask if she minds flying solo for a couple of hours.

She responds with a GIF of Kim Kardashian mouthing, *It seems like nobody wants to work these days.* Then she tells me to come down at eight.

Within seconds, I hit the mattress. It has never had more bounce, never felt more supportive.

I blink and it's half-past seven.

The others are still asleep, Proyiayia and Ba likely not for much longer, but Gina...I set an alarm for ten o'clock and leave my phone by her door. It isn't petty, it's me yanking her out of a rut.

I head down to the cafe.

Before she excommunicated herself, my grandmother put up more photos. They haven't been enlarged and framed yet. They're in plastic sleeves, taped to the exposed brick wall on a trial basis. There are a couple of Proyiayia the waitress, a handful of Gina with an array of embarrassing retro hairdos, and one of the cafe packed with people crammed shoulder to shoulder, their focus trained on Ba in a blazer. A bloke's admiring that pic.

A bloke I know.

'Dad?'

He turns around and beams at me. He's shaved his hair. The curls are gone and the shape of his skull is no longer a mystery. 'Hey, kid.' He pulls me into one of his tight hugs. 'Your friend told me you wouldn't be down until after eight.'

'What the fuck?' It's all I can manage. I'm flustered.

He laughs and releases me. 'I took that one.' He gestures at the hanging photo. 'It was your father's book launch.'

He starts recounting that night and I'm not processing any of it. After weeks of sporadic calls and texts, he's in Sydney. No warning, no explanation. 'What are you doing here?' I stammer.

He looks away from the photo. 'The call came,' he says with a shrug.

I picture Ba, overwhelmed by Proyiayia's diagnosis, vowing to work on their relationship in some teary late-night confession.

'The plane food was rubbish,' he adds. 'You got anything better?'

I set him and his suitcase up at table seven and dart to the counter. Isabella's making a coffee for a guy whose black skivvy says he'll corner you at a party to talk about crypto.

'I thought your folks were splitting up?' she asks.

'They are.' I grab the iPad and reconsider. 'At least, they *were*? I dunno.'

Dad gets a kick out of me waiting on him like a regular customer. He wants a big breakfast and a latte, knowing full well it's the only drink I can make with any confidence. When his food's ready, I realise Isabella sneakily added my favourite omelette to the order.

I sit opposite Dad, with a view of the foot traffic outside the cafe. He yawns between mouthfuls, but he fights to stay present, firing questions at me like he prepared a list on the red-eye.

'What's the secret to a good coffee?'

I cock an eyebrow. 'Do you really care?'

'Humour me,' he says.

'Well...' I straighten up and it's like I hit play on a recording of Isabella. 'A good barista cheats and warms the cup. It's good to keep a couple on top of the machine. In a pinch, you can run a cup under hot water before you use it. Helps retain the heat, and you have a hot coffee without burning the milk. That's the secret, not burning the milk.'

'Fascinating.'

I ask him what he's been up to. He's reluctant, but I refuse to give him the chance to quiz me on the quality of coffee beans or some shit. The weather's been good. He's been to the beach a fair bit. Cottesloe. It's not the closest to Subiaco, but it's always been his favourite.

I remember, one Saturday morning when I was a kid, he took me down there to build sandcastles. It was some stunt where a thousand people tried (and failed) to break the world record for most castles built in an hour. The one we made was an anthill with a turret, but others went overboard. They made castles a Disney princess could get lost in. Dad could've stared at them for hours, I reckon. He was so sad they wouldn't last forever.

The thought reminds me how devastated he's sounded every time we've spoken on the phone.

He's tried to hide it, but he's a horrible actor. He really thought him and Ba were forever.

What's left of my omelette hangs off my fork, and a question hangs off my tongue. Are they getting back together? Before I can ask, Ba appears. He's after eggs. He rushes past table seven and doesn't recognise the back of his estranged husband's shaved head. Dad tenses up.

'What's wrong?' I ask.

'I thought I had more time,' he says.

'Ba called you, didn't he?'

Dad doesn't respond, and it's obvious whoever called to lure him to Sydney, it wasn't his husband.

Oh, for fuck's sake.

He exhales and assures me it's okay in a way that engenders zero confidence.

Ba thanks Marta, pushes off the counter, says, 'I'm distracting your great-grandmother with breakfast,' and then notices Dad. He stops in his tracks. He's an odds-on favourite to drop the eggs, three held in one hand. His mouth is open. No words. They stare at each other for a bit. Dad rises slowly, and with cautious steps, he clears the distance between them. There's a moment's hesitation when they're close, then Ba softens and melts into him.

With Ba occupied, distracting Proyiayia becomes my responsibility. I waltz into the kitchen with three eggs, but my great-grandmother couldn't be less interested in breakfast. She's dressed for going out, black dress and wedge shoes. She rummages in the fruit bowl. 'Pou eínai ta kleidiá mou?' she asks.

She's after her keys. Nobody's told her they're on the top shelf of the pantry. Instead of us having an honest conversation about what's happening to her, we're hiding her keys and distracting her.

She starts talking to herself. I don't understand what she's saying, but I get the vibe. She's upset. Her voice cracks. And I'm supposed to placate her with eggs? Screw that.

'Where do you wanna go?' I ask her.

It's about half an hour's drive to Botany Cemetery, counting a handful of wrong turns. I have faint memories of accompanying Proyiayia on her cleaning expeditions as a kid, lying on the hot pavement in the Greek ghettos where the monuments are excessive.

Proyiayia leads me to my great-grandfather's resting place. She has a bucket of cleaning products and Orthodox paraphernalia. She fishes me out a rag. While she scrubs easier-to-reach grime, I climb onto the slab and deal with the headstone.

It reads a lot like a basic Wikipedia entry. There's my great-grandfather's name, relevant dates, a tiny portrait and some Greek I can't read. The headstone's only half-filled. There's a golden line that splits it vertically, allowing enough room for Proyiayia's basic Wikipedia entry when the time comes.

'A mental health professional's gonna find this memory one day.'

'Ti?'

Wouldn't have said it aloud if there was a chance she'd understand. 'Nothing, Proyiayia.'

I focus on the dirt that crusts the rim of her husband's portrait. They chose a black-and-white one. In it, he's young enough to still have dark hair, but old enough to have a massive widow's peak. I wonder what he sounded like. Gruff. Authoritative.

'Éla,' Proyiayia commands.

A bit like that, probably.

I climb down so she can wave the liváni over the monument, and then we're off. She refuses to extinguish the burner, so there's smoke billowing out the passenger-side window for the short drive between plots. Stavros is buried in an older part of the cemetery, where the paths are winding and there's the occasional broken step to spook an octogenarian. Proyiayia almost stumbles, but she steadies herself and laughs.

Stavros's monument is much bigger than the others. It's ridiculous and heart-shaped. Proyiayia stops in front of it and takes a deep breath. 'Hello, darling,' she says.

We're back at the terrace before twelve. The roller door is up. I could've sworn I pushed the button when we left . . . I turn into the courtyard and Gina charges out of the house. The car comes to a stop and my grandmother slams her hands down on the bonnet. Her eyes are wild.

'What were you thinking?' she growls.

It's a bit much.

She orders me out of the car. That's what I planned on doing anyway.

'We went to the cemetery,' I say.

'You can't...' She exhales. 'You can't take her out without telling anybody.'

I glance back at my great-grandmother in the passenger seat. 'She's fine.'

Gina's adamant. Anything could have happened. Proyiayia could have had another fall.

I picture it. The step. Her almost-stumble. What would I have done if it went differently?

The trip was fine. We just went to the cemetery. Proyiayia was *fine*.

'You're not a doctor!' my grandmother hisses.

Before I can stop myself: 'At least I did something for her. You're sulking in your room like she's already dead!'

Gina slaps me hard across the face.

SIX
All I ever wanted

SOTIRIS

1

I'm partial to a good snoop at a house party. When a conversation goes in circles, or somebody who microwaves their red wine gets a tad too intense about lecturer office hours, I press the small of Jem's back, lean in to his ear and tell him I'm headed to the loo. I get lost on purpose. Climb stairs I don't need to. Gravitate towards the guests who are acting the most suss. But I respect the fine line between curious and creepy. No bedrooms, no opening drawers. And so long as I look like I'm on my way somewhere, nobody bats an eyelid.

I'm on the third floor of a place in Newtown, well away from the main action of the party. Following a wall of truly hideous framed family portraits around a bend, I collide with a guy in double denim. There's a cavalcade of awkward apologies. I retreat and when there's enough distance between us, I realise I know him. His hair's longer, floppier, no frosted tips, and he's experimenting with patches of facial hair, but I *know* him.

He laughs. 'Sotiris!' Anyone pronouncing my name correctly is usually cause for celebration, but this anyone is Benji, my high-school irritation. He comes closer and loops his free arm around me. He's hugging me. We're eight months out of high school. That's not enough absence to make the heart grow fonder. At least, not for me.

He lets go, but he isn't done with me yet. He asks how I've been.

'Yeah, good.'

Benji expects an elaboration. When it doesn't come, he nods knowingly. 'You have to use the bathroom, I'm holding you up.'

'Yes!' Sweet release.

He points over his shoulder, and I have never been more excited about the prospect of locking myself in a room for ten minutes.

'I'll chill out here,' he says.

Gritted teeth. 'Great.'

I close the door with my whole body and don't budge. The room reeks of lavender. It's instantly nauseating, but I'd rather be in here than with Benji. Of all people. *Benji*. He's the first guy from school I've encountered in the wild. I only ever leave Darlinghurst to hang out with Jem, and his Sydney is so different to mine. It's populated with second-year uni students and booksellers and gay guys who wear berets... The Venn diagram of his people and my people is two circles.

Only strangers see him squeeze my non-existent bicep or peck my cheek.

I inhale, choke on the lavender, cough.

My high-school irritation is going to see me with Jem. He's going to know I'm...

And my time to freak out is up, unless I want Benji to think I am gay *and* have some unfortunate bowel situation. I flush the toilet I didn't use and run my hands under the tap. I open the door, hoping he's remembered we hate each other's guts and bailed.

He hasn't bailed.

He leads me downstairs. His crew are camped in the front room, no one I know. Benji introduces me as his friend from school, an author, and when the woman with the pixie cut asks what I write, he answers for me. 'Books for teenagers, but they're actually good,' he says. 'It's just the one at the moment, but there'll be more, right?'

It's enough to make me wonder if I've been unreliably narrating my whole life. Were Benji and I friends? No. He was a dickhead consistently.

I stumble through a half-hearted answer. 'Yeah, I'm working on something now.' A lie.

'You'll probably have your seventh book out before I finish my first,' Benji says, and the guy on his right edges closer. He's tanned, slightly older, with a beard that connects. Benji introduces him as Carlos and it takes until then to realise their fingers are interwoven.

Benji is...

While I've been living the dream as a full-time writer who doesn't write, Benji's been at Sydney Uni doing an arts degree. He walked in on the wrong tutorial early this semester, but by the time he'd cottoned on, he'd claimed a seat beside Carlos and he didn't want to give it up.

Benji asks if I'm seeing somebody.

Mum's the only person I've told I'm gay. Some people assume, like Jem and the guys who shout from passing cars. But mostly, Jem does all the telling for me. 'This is my boyfriend, Sotiris.' I step into a room with him, and the answer comes before any question.

The words stall somewhere between my brain and my lips. Benji's waiting. Behind him, Jem's in the hallway, still talking to the girl with the mug of hot wine. I raise my hand, he saunters over, and when he pecks me on the cheek, I don't have to say anything. Benji is all questions. He wants to know how we met. Jem tells the story and I watch it play out across my high-school irritation's face, the spreading smile...

When Jem's called away, I'm aware that I can escape with him, but I stay with Benji. Carlos is gone and it's just the two of us. I ask if he's writing at the moment. He describes this sprawling thing, an adult novel told through multiple perspectives across multiple time periods... I'm drowning in the details, but his fervour makes me miss it. Writing. Wrangling a huge idea onto the page. Living, breathing it when I'm not.

Benji goes quiet and I tell him I'm excited to read the book. His eyes come alive. 'Really?' I nod. The night's almost done. People are leaving or calling dibs on bedrooms, and out of nowhere, he asks, 'Do you reckon we knew about each other?'

I honestly don't have an answer.

'Maybe that's why we were...' He doesn't finish the sentence, and that manages to capture it all.

Jem burns hot in his sleep. He starts under the doona, but wriggles free in increments until he's posing for a tasteful nudie mag, with one leg and his bits covered. His exposed chest expands. He's been doing push-ups before bed, enough that I've noticed his shape change.

We've been dating so long, he's changed.

I've changed too. I haven't written in ... I can't say. There's a dam inside of me. I feel it filling with all the words I haven't put down, accumulating over days and nights and days and nights. I've neglected them for dinners and house parties, but Benji banging on about his magnum opus reminded me *I* want to bang on about a magnum opus. I am a writer. I have to write.

I have to write *now*.

I will not get a wink of sleep. I will not let me.

I roll out from under the doona, slowly so I don't wake the nudie-mag model. I feel around the floor for his footy shorts and creep into the living room. Light on. It's almost three. I snatch a page from the back of the printer, a biro from the plastic mug that's shaped like Bugs Bunny's head, minus the ears. I sit. I wait for the words the spill out of me.

I wait ten minutes, and I wait ten minutes more.

There are words inside of me, a novel's worth, I just don't know what they are. The pen hovers over the page. Nothing.

'Sotiris?' It's Jem, from the hallway.

'In here.'

I hear him piss, the toilet flush, the tap run, then his voice again. 'Come back to sleep.'

I can't tell him I'm writing, because I'm not.

He appears in his boxers, smile slanted.

'Trying to write and it's not happening,' I tell him.

He rests his head against the doorframe. 'You're up at sparrow's fart, that's why.'

'Nah, it's not that.' There were the pages I wrote and abandoned around the time I met him. They were a struggle. 'Writing is all I ever wanted and now I can't do it.'

His eyes narrow and the slanted smile becomes a smirk. 'Maybe you're only built to want one thing at a time, and right now you—'

'Don't say it.'

'—want all this.' I won't say what he does, but think: propellor.

I laugh. It's impossible not to. 'Quit it.' Still laughing. 'I've got to—'

'No. Up you get. You're just sitting there.'

'I am not.' Okay, I am. But I can't get up without writing something. The words are *there*. All I need is a way to coax them out.

He doesn't say anything, but I know he won't return to the bedroom unless I join him.

I look to the blank page. Writing is all I ever wanted, and yet...

I'm walking back to the bedroom. I'm lying on my side, his arm looped around me. I'm falling asleep, the weight of the words inside me lightening and lightening until I forget they're even there.

2

I use Yiayia's bedroom like a walk-in wardrobe when she's in Greece. The moment my clothes come off the line, I dump them on the mattress. It isn't as disorganised as it sounds. There are piles – pants, shorts, shirts, underwear. Occasionally I have to excavate for a second sock, but on the whole, it's a system that works.

Jem and I have a quiet night planned, renting a movie and ordering two-for-one pizza. But we're meeting at the bookshop, and all it takes to derail our plans is one of his co-workers mentioning the pub, so it's good to be prepared. I check my wallet. It's always dispiriting, but it's especially dispiriting this arvo. I have five dollars.

I sigh and waltz to the office. Mum's on the phone with her cake supplier, Barry. Her sixteen-inch mud cake is only fourteen and a half inches, and she has his balls in a vice. She ends up getting the cake comped and, judging by her reaction, a sincere apology. She wishes him a very nice day and drops the handset.

She makes a note in her daily planner, possibly about the size and sensitivity of Barry's balls.

She glances at me. 'You off?'

'Not yet. Soon.'

She nods and shuffles some papers. 'And you're back tomorrow?'

'Yeah.'

She never asks where I go or who I see. I leave the house and *nothing happens* until I return.

'Can I have some cash?' I ask.

Mum's other employees get envelopes every Thursday. My pay comes in dribs and drabs: fifty dollars here, ninety there. I'm never short, the schedule is just irregular. And that makes things tricky when quiet nights morph into dinners, drinks, taxis home at two o'clock.

She sighs. 'Right.' She opens the top drawer and rummages for loose notes. She finds two twenties.

I was hoping for more. 'We might head out for dinner.'

'Why are you spending more than forty dollars on dinner? You can always eat here. There's a stocked fridge.'

Yeah, and then I'll sit in a restaurant and watch everyone eat. That's not weird. 'If you pay me seventy-five bucks for Monday and Tuesday last week, that should cover me.'

Another sigh, this one's deeper. Mum lifts her handbag onto her lap like it's a huge inconvenience. She has a single hundred-dollar note in her purse. 'I'll have to go split it.'

That's too much effort. 'Take the forty back and just give me the hundred.'

'But you only need seventy-five.'

Okay, she wants to be difficult.

She leads me down to the cafe. Amanda's outside. She's a relatively new hire. She's clutching a twenty-five-kilo bag of sugar and coating a table in the stuff while she refills a dispenser.

Mum, usually a fount of unsolicited critical feedback, doesn't offer any. She tells Amanda we'll be back in a bit, then starts down Victoria Street. She could've raided the safe, but why go to some trouble, when she can go to *all* the trouble?

I jog to catch up.

When we're far enough away, Mum says, 'She's been skimming the till.'

'Who? Amanda?'

'No, Nicole Kidman.'

I check over my shoulder. The newbie's out of sight, having abandoned the twenty-five-kilo bag of sugar.

Mum must have eyes in the back of her head. 'She's visiting the bank of Gina.'

'Why not stop her?'

She tuts. 'What am I going to do? Hold her up by the ankle and shake her down? No, let her think she's smarter than me. That never works out for people.'

We turn down Liverpool Street, then take another left at the public school. Womerah Avenue. It's residential. We're supposed to be splitting a hundred-dollar note, but we're walking *away* from all the shops.

'Where are we going exactly?' I ask.

A cafe, far enough down Womerah Avenue for me to think we should've come at it from the other side. It was a corner shop not that long ago. The new owners have left the peeling lettering and the Coca-Cola branding on the awning, but the mural on the corner face reads, *Bellissimo*. It isn't particularly busy for an afternoon; there's nobody on the tiny stools out front, and only a couple and their Pomeranian inside. Not that the space is big enough to seat a rugby team or anything. We linger by the entrance, and when the guy behind the espresso machine doesn't acknowledge us, Mum sits at one of the two vacant tables.

This is weird. Mum doesn't visit other cafes. I tried taking her to one for her birthday. Big mistake. I thought it would be nice to eat somewhere new, but it stressed her out. She couldn't switch off the cafe-owner part of her brain. She practically fell out of her chair when we were served watery poached eggs. Breakfast soup, she called it. 'We have a perfectly good cafe at home, Sotiris.' Over and over.

I take my seat. Mum's already studying the menu. I ask why we're here, and her eyes widen. In a hushed voice, she says we're spying.

It's been ages since she brought me to scope out the competition, but I'd hardly call this place competition. Bellissimo could fit in our cafe ten times over. I mean, the kitchen is raised on a step and is about the size of an outhouse. At most, they can toast focaccia bread and reheat muffins in there.

Mum slides the spare menu over. 'Don't pick anything expensive.'

I scan what's on offer. By her standards, a lot of it is too expensive. I opt for the iced chocolate.

Meanwhile, Mum's inspecting the room, the ceiling. 'They took out the mouldings. A mistake.'

I need to say something. 'You're not competing with them.'

She gives the table a rock. It's disappointingly sturdy. Before the guy can pop out from behind the espresso machine to take our order, a woman in low-cut jeans ducks in. Mum mouths, 'Latte,' before the woman says it. Then we're noticed. Well, Mum's noticed. The woman greets her warmly, but there's some awkwardness. She rushes to pay and waits for her coffee on the street.

'Not competing?' she asks me. 'When people can get good coffee here, why would they walk seven minutes up the hill? The moment cafes spring up everywhere, we're fucked. Most will be shit, but no one will drive to Victoria Street on a Sunday if there's a place that's half as good around the corner.' She smacks her lips. 'Fucked, Sotiris. And what the fuck is this service?' A couple of minutes without so much as a hello and some tap water is unacceptable. 'We could move in and they wouldn't notice. Set up a couch. TV. Coffee table. No fucking clue.'

'We don't have to be here.'

'You think I want to be here?'

Mum's interrupted by a terse Italian exchange coming from the kitchen. It ends abruptly and the guy emerges from behind the espresso machine with two plates for the couple and something crunchy for their Pomeranian. The guy's name is Tony. He gently instructs us to head to the counter when we're ready to order.

Mum laughs. 'But I can tell you what we want now.' She tosses him a wink and he's unmoved.

There's a particular way things are done at Bellissimo, and Mum loses the standoff. She orders at the counter. She returns and I assure her the cafe is not a threat.

She's not having it. 'Bigger picture, Sotiris. You've got to look at the bigger picture.'

Tony calls out to Josephine, and the woman in the low-cut jeans returns to claim her latte. Mum raises her eyebrows at me. She's looking for omens where there are none. One of her regulars bought a single coffee elsewhere, that's all.

She changes the subject. 'Seventy-five dollars for dinner?' she asks.

'Not just for dinner.'

'I should charge you rent.'

I laugh. She doesn't.

'Are you serious?'

'Why not? You come and go as you please. You don't contribute much around the house – cooking, cleaning, groceries, none of that. So...rent. One hundred a week.'

'I rarely have a hundred dollars to spend.'

Mum shrugs. 'Spend less. Get another job.'

'Give me more shifts.'

'We don't have the shifts spare. If I brought you on for more, I'd have to let somebody go.'

'Great. Bye, Amanda.'

It's not that simple. 'She's a klepto, but she's good with customers. People like her.'

'I'll skim the till, then.'

'You're not as good with the customers.' She pulls the elastic out of her hair. She only does it to keep her hands busy, because she immediately reties her ponytail. 'Bigger picture, Sotiris. I let you not go to uni, I gave you time, but you're not using it wisely. I'm not doing you any favours by letting you tread water. You need a career.'

'Yeah, writing.'

'Really?' Her mouth twists. 'You're writing?'

'Yes.' It's a bold lie.

'When you go out every night?'

I'm not out *every* night, but I can't argue I haven't been busy.

'And this writing that you're doing,' she adds, 'is it paying you?'

My silence is enough.

'It's a hobby, then.'

'I'll get paid when I sell the book to a publisher.'

'For what? Three thousand dollars again? At this rate, you'll never afford a house, ki...' She stops herself, but I know what she was going to say. Kids. Not earning enough to support them isn't the reason I won't have them. But she isn't ready for that conversation. She clears her throat. 'I don't think you should work at the cafe anymore. I'll cover the rest of your shifts.'

'What?'

'If you want to set fire to your money, get it elsewhere.' She frowns. 'And don't look at me like that.'

'You're firing me, I'll look at you like this.' I don't understand how... We left the house to split a hundred because she owed me and now I don't have a job.

'You said it yourself, you have a career. But are you really motivated? Dinners and movies and parties... Where's the focus? Where's the hunger?'

'Oh, I'll go hungry without the cafe work, don't you worry.'

'I'll keep the fridge stocked, but don't shit me, Sotiris, you know I'm talking about a different kind of hunger. You used to chuck a fit if I took a pen off you and sent you to bed. Now? You're wasting time.' She leans closer. 'I want you to amount to something,' she spits.

Tony reappears and we go quiet. He places the latte in front of me and the iced chocolate in front of Mum. She swaps the drinks when he's gone. She wants me to amount to something. She wants me to amount to something. She wants me to amount to something. There was a little venom in it when she said it, but the more I think about it, the more it stings. I feel the tears scratching at my eyes.

'I am something,' I tell her. There's a tremor in my voice. 'I'm an author.'

'Don't be like that, you know what I mean.'

I refuse to speak. She can tell me exactly what she means.

'I'm very proud of you, but there's only so long you can get by on what you achieved when you were seventeen.'

'I'm eighteen.'

She raises her cup. 'Not forever.'

3

I come pretty close to cancelling on Jem twice, once at the bus stop, and once halfway down Parramatta Road. Mum's not letting me work in the cafe anymore. It's not as rough as me working four days a week only to lose most of it to rent, but it's still rough. I have eighty dollars and some change to my name. I doubt it will last long. Four dinners if I choose the cheapest thing on the menu, and that's not even factoring in how I get to those dinners and back. I have three rides left on my TravelTen, more if I don't validate my bus ticket when I board.

This is another one of Mum's hard lessons. Back in Year Seven, she caught me reading an issue of *Hyper* I'd nicked from the newsagency on Darlinghurst Road. She grabbed me under one arm and dragged me into the shop. She could've ordered me to return it to the stack of unsold video game magazines, lesson learnt, but she made me apologise to the newsagent and stand there while they negotiated the best time to take me to the police station. They were messing with me, but I didn't realise until after I'd started bawling.

Mum has a particular idea of who she wants me to be. In the long term, I don't think she wants me to be an author, and in the short term, I don't think she wants me to be able to afford spending so much time with Jem.

He beams when I enter Ace Books. He's behind the front counter with Prital. The shop's dead so they've taken to drawing facial hair on each other with an Artline marker. I attempt to hide how upset I feel. I succeed until I'm helping him shelve the bestsellers. His face drops; he asks what's wrong, but the curly moustache makes it difficult to accept he's being earnest. He covers it with his forearm and again, asks what's wrong.

I tell him about my ill-fated quest to be properly remunerated for the two shifts I worked early last week. I'm out of a job; I'll have no money in no time. It is the end of the world. I don't undersell it, but he doesn't understand.

'It's a good thing, isn't it?' Jem asks. He's stacking fresh copies of a Paul Keating biography. 'Your mum is giving you the chance to focus on your work.'

He doesn't know what she's like. Yes, there'll be a stocked fridge and a roof over my head and all the time in the world to write, but she fired me out of nowhere. What's to stop her kicking me out just as suddenly?

'She's not going to kick you out,' he assures me. 'Pass me those ugly hardcovers, will you?'

I crouch down and scoop four ugly hardcovers out of the box. He makes room and shelves them one at a time – face-out before he reconsiders. They really are ugly, but the spines less so.

'Mum doesn't want me selling another book for three thousand dollars. She doesn't think there's a viable future in me being an author, and I can see her initiating the squeeze. It won't be long before I have to pursue a different career.'

'And would that be terrible?'

My jaw hangs loose. I tilt my head and keep it tilted until he looks back at me.

'You can do something else that pays the bills,' he adds. 'That doesn't mean you're abandoning being a writer.'

'But that's what it sounds like.'

Jem taps the book with the bloodied glove and a ton of gold book-award medals on the cover. 'Felicity

Ryan, forensic cleaner for decades before she wrote *The Joy Diaries*.' He scans the bestsellers. 'Who else? Who else? Ah! Duh.' He flicks one of the ugly hardcovers. 'Grant Johnson was a chef before he released any mediocre children's books, and he's still got a couple of restaurants in the city.'

I stare at the bloodied glove on *The Joy Diaries*. I can't imagine being a forensic cleaner. I can't imagine being anything.

'What would I even do? I wanted to be an author in Year Four.'

Jem laughs. 'And I wanted to be an astronaut.' He grabs a handful of small gift books and searches for somewhere to stuff them. 'Point is, you're finding writing tough at the moment. Okay. Put it on ice. Come back to it later. Maybe you'll work as a paralegal and be inspired to write a murder mystery set in a law firm.'

'Gross.'

'It's an example.' He waits for me to say something, like admit he's right. I don't, so he continues, 'Your mum is practically offering to sponsor you to work on your next book, and if she decides that she doesn't want to anymore or you decide that you want spending money, you can get a job like everyone else our age, like the job you literally had before she fired you. And if this is all some ploy to push you into a career you can fall back on, I don't think that's necessarily a bad thing. Just because you released one novel doesn't mean you're owed a career, Sotiris. That isn't how the book world works. There are so many names I only ever see on one title. That may be you, and your mum has the foresight to make sure that if it is, you're still okay.'

Everything he's saying makes sense, and I'm glad that I didn't abandon our plans at the bus stop or halfway down Parramatta Road, because then I would've spent the night pacing my bedroom catastrophising. But while I'm more at ease about losing my job, I hate the idea of being a one-book wonder.

'I don't want it to be me.'

Jem's cheeks lift when he smiles. 'Then we'll make sure it isn't.'

We grab pizza on Norton Street and head back to Jem's. There's a tower of Blockbuster rentals beside the television, but there's been a change of plan. I sit at his desk. He retrieves a pen and some lined paper. That's enough, but soon there's a Vivaldi CD in the PS2. I keep grinning, keep glancing back at him. He's lying on the couch, one leg crossed over the other. He's reading an uncorrected proof, his neck at an angle that cannot possibly be comfortable.

Okay. Words. On the page.

I know classical music is meant to stimulate the brain, but I become very conscious of the moment's silence between the tracks. Time is slipping away and I have nothing to show for it, and soon Jem, probably proud of himself for sacrificing his night, will approach from behind, squeeze my shoulders, check the page and see I've written nothing. My stomach knots.

It's a relief when his ringtone goes off. He answers the call in his bedroom. I strain to hear, but can't over Vivaldi. And I should be writing. Words. On the page.

Jem returns and I ask who it was.

'Don't worry,' he says.

I push him. The gay twins are out for their birthday and wanted to know what we're up to.

I quite like the gay twins. Corey more than Patrick. As a set, they're a net positive. On Saturday nights at the Imperial, Corey's Annette Positive and Patrick's at the bar saying his brother's drag isn't particularly good.

They were the first friends Jem made when he came to Sydney. He's skipping their birthday so that he can support me writing exactly zero words.

'Why don't we go?' I ask.

'It's fine,' he says. 'You're working.'

I fold my arms over the page. I don't want him to see how little I've done. 'It'll be good to get inspired.'

'Only if you want to.'

We join the party at a bar in Enmore, where the music thumps and my sandshoes stick to the timber floor. The moment Corey spots Jem and me, we're pulled onto the tiny dancefloor. I last two songs, then escape to find Patrick and his more subdued friends at a table in the corner. I recognise a couple of faces, but it's mostly new people. We're far enough from the speakers that Patrick can introduce me. I'm Jem's boyfriend.

I try to cause as little an interruption as possible. I take my seat and they resume their conversation about the latest trivial drama of the local stand-up scene.

After a few minutes, the guy to my left elbows me softly.

'I'm Iain,' he says, tilting his jug. 'Beer?'

'I don't have a glass.' That's more socially acceptable than saying I'm off beer in a big way.

He isn't fussed. He's got a fresh glass. He pours me some. 'You're the writer, yeah?'

If the half-hour I spent with a pen, lined paper and Vivaldi is anything to go by, I am not.

'I'm the writer.'

'Couldn't do that,' he says. 'Where do your ideas even come from?'

I sip the beer. Swallow. Awful.

I don't have the faintest. If I did, I wouldn't be in my current position.

I'm not in the mood to talk about my craft. I'm staring down the barrel of having to become a forensic cleaner, whatever that entails beyond blood and gloves. But my mood doesn't matter. Selling books in the cafe, I learnt that every person who asks me about writing is a potential reader.

And I could always do with one more reader.

'Sometimes, I draw on my life,' I tell him. 'In my first book, *Young*, there's a mother who's a lot like my mum.'

I expect Iain to ask if there's a character like me. And he does. And I nod.

'But it's not an autobiography?'

I gulp the beer, like that'll make it taste better. The cold rushes to my temples. 'Nah. I take inspiration from real life, that's all.'

'So, it's semiautobiographical.'

That's overselling how personal my writing is. 'Something like that.'

'Oi, Iain!'

There's some contention over who did what onstage at the open-mic night in Stanmore last week, and Iain's expertise is required. He launches into a detailed account, and I might as well have vanished.

I finish my beer, and turn the word over. *Semiautobiographical.* There's something there. I fall into myself. I hear people talking around me, but there's no meaning in the sounds. *Semiautobiographical.* And then the dam wall cracks. A drip.

This is semiautobiographical

Drip. Drip.

which means I've taken creative licence.

I interrupt the gossip session. 'Does anybody have a pen?' I ask.

Patrick drinks and his friends just shake their heads.

It's the truth

I'm off my seat. The bar. They'll have a pen behind the bar.

but the explosions are bigger

My heart is pounding.

the twists are more shocking

I sidle up beside a brunette. She's next in line. She curls her upper lip so much I can assess her gum health. 'Only after a pen,' I tell her.

and I'm three to four times sexier.

I snatch up a coaster and tap it against the counter. The bartender holds out a two-dollar coin. He's told to keep the change. He pockets it, then asks the brunette what she's after. Before she can tell him what to mix with her vodka, I ask for a pen. The bartender ignores me.

This is semiautobiographical, which means I've taken creative licence.

'Pen.' I'm pointing. There's one behind him, by the spirits bottles.

It's the truth, but the explosions are bigger, the twists are more shocking, and I'm three to four times sexier.

The bartender isn't interested. The woman repeats her order.

Typical. All the times I try to write, nothing. The moment I'm drinking at a bar in Enmore, words show up.

Somebody tugs on the back of my shirt. Jem. He's holding a drink, lemonade and something. He points the tiny straw at me and shimmies his shoulders in time with the music. I'm preoccupied. Rather, I should be preoccupied, but I'm taking the straw between two fingers and sipping. It's strong. There's a double shot of petrol or something close to it. Burns when I exhale.

Jem wants me to dance.

'I can't.'

He aims his puppy-dog eyes at me, shoulders working overtime. It's not as if the bartender is all that eager to give me a pen. I surrender. Jem pulls me close. I do ask him and his brow furrows. He has no pen, and no clue why I'm asking. But it's quickly forgotten. His free hand finds my hip. We're not the greatest dancers, but we can sway in time with a beat, and I enjoy it enough not to worry about the words.

I can head to a convenience store in a couple of minutes.

Until then, I'm all Jem's, on a tiny dancefloor that's sticky with spilled alcohol. He pulls a face and I laugh, partly because he's adorable and partly because I'm relieved. I have words. I finally have words. They don't feel like they came from me. So many authors say characters speak to them, and they always sound nutty, but that's what this was. This guy, around seventeen, a bit of a smartarse, has a story to tell me.

I have words.

The song ends. I peck Jem on the lips and tell him I'll be back. I make a beeline for the exit. The air outside is ice-cold and laced with hints of kebab from two doors down. The footpath belongs to stylish people with long strides and important places to be. I match their pace and march towards Newtown. If I'm remembering right, there's a convenience store not far from here.

'Oi!'

I stop and spin. Jem's in hot pursuit like I've ditched him. I flash the blank side of the coaster and tell him I'm going to buy a pen.

He looks at me like I'm speaking Greek. 'Can't you just draft a message on your phone?'

I'm hit by a wave of yes-I-should-have-thought-of-that. I rip my mobile out of my pocket and navigate to a blank message. I type with both thumbs.

This is semiautobiographical, which means

I blink down at the screen. What does it mean? The smartarse told me, but I don't remember. Um. I wait for the words, and I might as well be back at Jem's listening to Vivaldi, because I've got nothing. Panic rises in me. Anger too.

'Shit!' I howl.

Jem recoils. 'What?'

'I had it. A character was speaking to me. Nobody gave me a pen and now I've lost it.'

'It's okay,' Jem coos. 'It'll come back if you just relax.'

'I can't relax, I...Why didn't you tell me to use my phone when I asked for a pen?'

He laughs. 'Inside? I couldn't hear you.'

I shake my head. This isn't my fault. 'You made me dance.'

'I didn't make you dance. You wanted to.'

'Because I want to do everything for you, because you're a priority, and now I've lost the beginning of a book.'

'That's bonkers, Sotiris.'

He takes a step towards me, and I take one back to maintain the distance.

'No, no, it's not.' I close my eyes and cast my mind back…I overshoot, and instead of remembering the words, I remember trying to write the morning after the Newtown house party. 'What if you were right? What if I'm only built to have one want at a time and you're that want?'

He has no idea what I'm on about. 'When did I say that?' And then, clarity. 'Come on, that was a fucking joke. I twirled my dick afterwards.'

'But what if you were accidentally onto something? Writing has been easy my whole life, but I haven't been able to do it since I met you. You're distracting, in the best way, but still distracting. I'm staying over heaps and coming to birthday parties—'

'I was happy staying in tonight.'

'But you're happier here, we both know that.'

He throws out one arm. 'We can go home right now.' His voice is vibrating.

I haven't written a word in his living room. It won't work. 'If it's a choice between you and writing, I can't be with you anymore.'

He freezes, arm out like he's hailing a taxi. 'You're not serious.'

I swallow hard. I don't want to be serious. I don't want to break up with him. But I don't want to take what I've said back, because I believe it.

His mouth twitches. He's waiting for me to say something. A Toyota hatchback blasts Turkish pop music on the way past. He blinks, inhales and lets his hand fall to his side. 'Fuck you.'

And he stomps back into the bar.

4

It's so late, it's early. I can't sleep. The songs from the bar are buzzing in my ears and Jem's parting words are eating at my heart. I made the right call. But there's a copy of *Jane Eyre* on my bedside table, taunting me.

No, this is for the best.

I can write like I did before him.

Jane Eyre's been tucked under my lamp since the writers' festival. I would've read it by now if I wasn't worried I'd crack the spine.

Before him, *Jane Eyre* was just a book Eliza mentioned.

I roll onto my other side. I punch my pillow as if its shape is why I can't sleep.

I'm lonely. I never felt lonely in this bed before him. He's never set foot in this room, but a part of me is desperate for him to climb onto the mattress, press his body against mine, and plant a kiss on my neck.

I've had him, felt him, traced lines between the freckles on his shoulder. That's changed everything.

I can only hope I write like I did before him, after him.

I breathe out the sadness, the doubt, the fear I've made a huge mistake, but then I breathe it all back in again.

The plan is to stay in bed all day, but my stomach makes demands in the early afternoon. I think I have the place to myself, then I hear the clang of cutlery and round the corner to find Mum at the kitchen table. She balances a fork on a knife on a serviette. She folds one corner over and rolls the knife and fork until they're wrapped. 'You got in late,' she says.

'I did.' It's as much as she'll get. 'You're not downstairs.'

'I'm not.' She nudges a copy of *Young* across the table. 'Somebody left it on the doorstep this morning.'

I blink down at the book. I know whose it is, but I step closer...in case. I bend the cover back. It's signed to Jeremy.

Knocks the wind right out of me.

I let the cover close. 'Okay.'

She reaches for more cutlery. She separates a serviette from the stack. She wraps. 'You going to tell me what it's about?'

'Well, the plot of *Young* is—'

'Sotiris.' Sharp enough to cut through bullshit. 'Are you going to tell me who Jeremy is and why he left his book?'

Mum wrapping cutlery up here when she has a cafe to run suddenly makes sense. This is a fact-finding expedition.

'He's nobody,' I insist.

'Nobody?'

I levelled my life to the ground last night, I'm not particularly keen on talking about it with her of all people. 'He was somebody and now he's nobody, so you don't need to worry. You got what you wanted.'

I can't believe he came all this way to return the book. He paid for it. It was his, not mine. It wasn't something that required giving back. He could have tossed it out or burnt it. I don't need this on top of everything.

'I don't want you to be unhappy,' Mum says.

'Then what *do* you want?' I snap.

My time with Jem would have been radically different if her initial reaction hadn't been what it was, if we weren't contained to his neighbourhood, if he visited the cafe often and she got to know him...

With one foot, she gently coaxes a chair out from under the table. I don't take up the offer. Her gaze bores into me. I sit, but not eagerly.

'Tell me about him,' she says.

'You have to go downstairs.'

She remains measured. 'Fucking tell me about him or I will find out myself.'

Her forehead frown line is deeper than I've ever seen it.

'Mum...'

She doesn't budge. I'm clearly not leaving this room until she knows the lot. I sigh and grab a fistful of cutlery. It'll be easier to tell her with my hands busy and my eyes elsewhere.

My story starts the night of the bonfire.

Mum goes easy on me in the days after the breakup. She doesn't probe at dinner, and if I mention that I have very little to show for the hours I've spent *trying* to write, she doesn't scold me for wasting my time.

But it does feel like I'm wasting my time.

She eventually intervenes and introduces me to Colin, a customer in his mid-to-late forties who's enjoying two slices of toast, no butter, at three in the afternoon. He works at the *Herald* and Mum's told him I'm interested in journalism.

Wiping down a nearby table, she looks particularly pleased with herself.

All I have waiting for me is a sentence I've rewritten four times that I still don't like, so I don't correct the lie.

Colin's a talker. He barely pauses to take a breath, and the longer our one-sided conversation goes, the more appealing journalism sounds. I'd be writing for a living. He bites into his toast and I seize the opportunity to ask how I'd go about getting a job. He's a big believer in cadetships, but the paper isn't recruiting at the moment. He encourages me to prepare a resume that he can collect the next time he swings by.

It's definitely something to consider on the way back to my room. After another pass at the problem sentence, I abandon my exercise book for the computer in the living room. I've never created a resume before. I start with my name and my address and I'm tinkering with the font when my phone rings.

It's Eliza.

5

Eliza has a new office, a bigger one to match her bigger role. She's a commissioning editor now. She glides to her desk, but I have to watch where I step; the floor's a minefield of chapter-book illustrations. The new chair is comfortable. I tell her so.

'Isn't it just!' She eases into her own, more impressive chair, gives it a little swivel, then asks how I am.

I don't have a succinct answer. I'm nervous. I'm unsure why I'm here. I'm excited, but history tells me I shouldn't get ahead of myself. I'm scared.

'I'm pretty good.'

The call was the first I'd heard from her since she RSVP'd no to my late launch. That felt a bit harsh, but she sent her regrets with a hamper. Its selection of jams were exquisite.

'I know I've been a bit naughty and dragged you in here without telling you why,' she says.

The nerves could literally kill me, but I assure her it's fine.

'It's not, but I couldn't not tell you in person.'

I'm really struggling not to get ahead of myself.

'I know when you last visited, I mentioned we could reprint *Young* if it performed well enough, but that was a very distant possibility.'

She opens her desk drawer, and my heart races. I'm getting a reprint. I bought copies from Jem at a discount and flogged them in the cafe, and it worked. I'm getting a reprint.

'Would you like to see *Young's* new first page, completely typo-free?' Eliza asks.

I can't say yes fast enough. She hands over the page proof and the top line reads, *Sam Baker is ready to catch a ball four seconds after it hits him in the face.*

I blink at the words. It's my bio. But... 'Who's Sam Baker?' I ask.

'This is bold, but we've been talking internally, and Sotiris Bakiritzis... doesn't exactly roll off the tongue. I've said it enough that it rolls off mine.' It doesn't. 'We've got to think about the everyman in the bookshop who's seeing it for the first time.'

They've changed my name.

'Lots of writers employ a pseudonym,' Eliza adds, 'and the Five Irons team loves it. It's strong. And get this, Eleni in sales says that Sam is the anglicised version of Sotiris, so it's still you.'

It's enough to break my brain, an Eleni who doesn't go by Helen telling people Sam and Sotiris are the same. I mean, I do like the idea of going by a name that people can pronounce. But there's history in the name I've already got. It's what I've been called my whole life. It's what's written on my merit award for excellence in creative writing.

I try the top line again. *Sam Baker is ready to catch a ball four seconds after it hits him in the face.*

It reads differently to how it used to, and not only because of the name.

They've removed any mention of my age, likely because I'm older and I'll keep getting older, but possibly because they don't trust themselves with spelling numbers...Without *seventen* they've erased the achievement, but kept the self-deprecation. I'm just some guy with no hand-eye coordination. And I'm not even me anymore.

'I'm getting you're a bit lukewarm on the pseudonym, but before you make up your mind, I want you to see this.' She has another sheet of paper, a cover mock-up for *Young* by Sam Baker.

They've ditched the boy who looked too much like a Lowes catalogue model. Instead of replacing him with another stock model, they've gone for a drawing of a piping-hot long black, with Anthony's face floating in the rising wisps of steam. He's exactly as I described him, right down to the birthmark on his cheek. It takes my breath away.

'We're thinking, instead of just reprinting it with some corrections, we go big. New cover. New name. Give it the best shot to take off.'

I love the cover. It's nothing like the ones I drew in my exercise book when getting published was a dream, it's so much better. All it'll cost me is a name that people butcher nine times out of ten.

'And who knows? If it goes well, maybe we can have a chat about what's next for Sam Baker.' She smiles like somebody who's about to get what she wants. 'What do you say?'

I approach the counter and Mum is immediately unnerved by how happy I seem. I lay down the cover mock-up. She lowers an iced chocolate onto it and says, 'Table fourteen.'

I should say something about no longer working for her, but I'm still on a high from the meeting with Eliza. I even return with an empty cappuccino cup from table seven, I'm in that good a mood.

Mum's making another coffee. There's no sign she's so much as glanced at the mock-up before she asks who Sam Baker is.

'Me.'

She purses her lips. She's unimpressed. I know it. I pre-emptively rattle off all the reasons Eliza gave for the change, and when I'm done, Mum raises a not-insignificant counterpoint. 'You're named after your grandmother.'

'I...' That didn't occur to me in the office. I deflate when I shouldn't. *Young* is getting another chance. I'm getting another chance and this is a small price to pay. I need her to be happy for me.

'I *am* happy,' she says. 'I'm assuming this means you're not giving Colin your resume.'

'*Mum.*'

She exhales. That's as close as she'll get to admitting defeat. 'I won't be calling you Sam.'

I tape the cover mock-up to my bedroom wall and step back. I could pinch myself and still believe I was dreaming. I sold enough, not only to eradicate the typo, but to warrant a new edition.

I wouldn't have this if it weren't for Jem and his Ace Books discount. The thought makes my heart burn hot, and every memory of us rises like steam. I recall our last night in Enmore, the cramped dancefloor, the words that tumbled out of me and vanished...

I still have the draft message saved.

This is semiautobiographical, which means

I read it back. With distance, it sounds less like the beginning of a story and more like a challenge.

This is semiautobiographical, which means I'll tell the truth. I'll start with the bonfire, the bookshop, Jem. It'll turn into something else, something fictional. And even if all the true bits vanish, the feelings won't.

I plant myself at my desk and crack open a fresh exercise book.

This is all I ever wanted.

SEVEN
The way through

HARVEY

1

The cemetery trip lands me in the doghouse. Proyiayia misses heaps, but she doesn't miss that. Before bed, she sneaks into the office, whispers, 'S'agapó,' and vanishes before she's caught.

Gina brushes her teeth at ten o'clock. I haven't done anything wrong, but I reckon I'm the one who'll need to extend the olive branch. I wait in my doorway. She finishes in the bathroom, flicks the light switch with her elbow and eyes the floor when she passes, massaging night cream into her arms. I say goodnight and she gives me the cold shoulder. She slams her door.

'Panagía!' my great-grandmother says.

I hear my fathers laughing. Not at this, obviously. They're downstairs in the kitchen. They were out all day. They missed the drama of Proyiayia going AWOL and the slap. They appeared during dinner. They helped themselves to Proyiayia's kota me patátes – chicken, cooked to perfection, circled by hand-cut potatoes, a little on the soft side, olive oil glistening over the lot.

It was obvious they'd been drinking and would continue drinking into the night.

I stare at Gina's bedroom door till I get bored. I don't feel like sleeping, so I follow the sound of my parents' laughter. I sit halfway down the stairs and listen. They're talking about Sydney people from before I was born. I lean my head against the baluster and enjoy them gossiping about the state of old friends' lives, who's had kids, who shouldn't have. Ba's ruthless, but Dad has his moments too. They crack each other up.

I don't think I realised how much I missed them being *them*.

It's hard not to feel shitty about wanting them to break up for so long. Gina was the one who phoned Dad, and I understand why. They get each other.

Ba tells Dad he'll fetch something from his bedroom. He wobbles into view, but collects himself the moment he notices me. After all, he's *sober*.

I let him think he's got away with it.

'Hi.'

He clears his throat. 'Hello.' He climbs the stairs like somebody who's never climbed stairs before. Instead of continuing past and grabbing whatever from his room, he sinks onto my step. 'How are you doing?'

'Gina hates me.'

'Gina hates everyone she loves.'

I scoff. 'That's convenient.'

He leans back a little. 'Be patient with her. She's going through it.'

I ask him how he's doing, and he nods. He doesn't need to say anything. It's obvious having Dad here is helping. He's a completely different person with my father in his orbit, and it reminds me of Proyiayia's second life.

'Gina mentioned Stavros yesterday.'

'Ah. The phantom uncle.'

'She reckons you brought Proyiayia back to life after he died.'

Ba laughs. 'One of my many documented miracles.'

'Gina has it wrong.'

'Oh?'

'I don't think *you* brought Proyiayia back, loving you is what did it. And as shit as losing her is gonna be, she's shown us the way through.'

'Love?' He mulls it over. 'Me and your father?'

I mean, the evidence from one day is pretty clear.

Wonder if what Dad's been for him, Isabella can be for me.

My father sighs. 'Does that mean we're going to have to get your grandmother on Tinder?'

I shouldn't find the idea funny, but I do. Should she even make sense of the app and land a date, she would break a man in minutes.

Dad calls out from the kitchen and Ba remembers why he came to the stairs in the first place. He swears and pulls himself upright.

2

Tuesday begins with the alarm I set just in case. I lurch off my cardboard mattress. Gina's door is shut, which means I'm working again. Annoying, but I get to hang with Isabella, so it's not the worst fate. After last night's chat with Ba, I've decided to ask her if she wants to catch a movie sometime.

She's at the desserts fridge by the cafe entrance. My heart flutters. She's making room for today's delivery, putting what's left of different cakes on the same dish. She turns as I approach. Her smile is warm. 'Hey.'

For the first time, I'm fucking terrified of her. 'Hi.'

'We need to sell seven tiramisu cups that expire tomorrow,' she says. 'Also . . . cleaning the bathrooms is usually Gina's stress release and the men's is a piss palace at the mo. Do you mind?'

'No!'

Can't reach for the mop fast enough. Simp behaviour.

I spend a solid hour de-pissing the palace. When I emerge, gloved, nostrils burnt by the bleach, spirit broken by the scrubbing, I decide that today's not the day I'll be asking Isabella out.

Doesn't stop my heart doing attention-seeking crap when she's near, though. I keep far and busy. At one point, when we should be experiencing a light lunch rush, I plant myself outside the cafe and try to entice passers-by with a dramatic reading of our menu.

I get a bite.

A woman with a blonde bob likes the sound of a lunchtime lasagne. Her kid protests. He's a snot factory with a mean face. She promised him Macca's and he's that particular kind of annoying that always gets his way. I won't let him cost me a sale. I end up in the Cross, ordering a McChicken and medium chips. Jeffrey at the counter attempts an aggressive upsell. For a split-second, I'm tempted to add a chocolate sundae to the order.

I deliver the snot factory his Macca's. When he's done sprinkling chips all over the floor, and his mum's done with her lasagne, I chuck a Jeffrey and offer them a tiramisu cup to go. The woman says she really shouldn't, but anybody who says that is halfway there. All it takes is some encouragement. 'Go on,' I say, and she leaves with one.

Isabella asks if it was worth it. The trip to Macca's wasn't. That's probably the hardest anyone has ever worked to sell a slice of lasagne, but I reckon, if we raise our upselling game, we can squeeze more out of the customers who do come in.

She helps me move the desserts fridge. I try to look where we're going as we carry it, and not at her concentration dimples. We set the fridge down where the community notices used to be – close to a power point, close to the register.

Anytime somebody waltzes in for an afternoon coffee, I tempt them with a tiramisu cup. I offload a couple, and three more when I start telling people they're half-price.

By the time we shut, there are two left. I offer one to Isabella, a subtle romantic gesture. She doesn't roll the dice with cream, so I walk both cups upstairs. Ba, renowned for his lactose intolerance, claims one almost immediately. He's at the fancy dining table working on his novel and too engrossed to move. 'Spoon?'

I fetch two and have this silly idea that we'll spend half an hour chatting and eating. Ba wolfs his dessert down. I'm barely past the top layer of cream when he's scratching the bottom of his plastic cup.

'Where's Dad?' I ask.

'Out for a wander,' Ba says. 'What's the new *yeet*?'

'What now?'

'All my characters talk like they're almost forty,' he explains. 'What's the new lingo? What fresh words are kids using?'

I pull one out of my arse. '*Badorka*.'

He tilts his head to the side. 'What's that mean?'

'It's fluid, but it's basically a spicier *yeet*.'

He repeats it a couple of times, mesmerised by how clunky it sounds on the way out. He lowers his cup and twinkles his fingers over the keys. 'How do I spell that?'

'B.'

He pokes the keyboard.

'A.'

Poke.

'D.'

Poke.

'Oh, I'm fucking with you. *Badorka* is not a word.'

My father scowls. 'You utter piece of shit,' he says, tapping the backspace key.

I curtsey and he tells me to piss off. In a gentler way than Gina would.

My parents are preoccupied, Gina and Proyiayia aren't around to ask anything of me...I have a free afternoon to spend however I like, so I scroll through Insta on the couch till my eyelids are heavy and I fall asleep. I probably could have made it all the way through to morning had everyone not convened in the kitchen for the loudest conversation in recorded history.

There's a seat spare beside Gina. I take it, but she doesn't acknowledge me. She's shovelling fried rice onto Proyiayia's plate. Ba claims the sweet and sour pork. He serves Dad before he serves himself, then he holds out the takeaway container for me to grab. Gina beats me to it. She pops two pieces of pork onto her mother's plate, one onto her own, then whatever's left onto mine, along with the rest of the sauce.

I thank her and she doesn't react. Instead, she asks Ba if he went to school with a Benjamin.

He nods. 'Benji Majors.'

'Thought I recognised him,' Gina says. She produces a folded clipping from the bag hanging behind her chair. It's half a page, with ads. 'I was flicking through the *Courier* at the RSL during the meat raffle.'

'How did it go?' I ask.

She ignores me. Ba's distracted by the clipping, but Dad notices. 'What was that, Harvey?'

This doesn't need to be a big thing.

'Go on,' he urges.

I repeat myself. 'How did it go?'

Dad looks at Gina expectantly, and my grandmother makes a show of realising somebody's talking to her. 'Huh? How did what go?' It's the first thing she's said to me since the slap.

'The meat raffle,' I add.

'Well, we're eating Chinese. How do *you* think it went?'

Proyiayia grunts. 'They cheat!'

I force a laugh and Dad relaxes.

'Six figures?' Ba asks from behind the clipping.

'And they're turning it into a movie,' Gina says.

'It's been optioned, that's not the same. Everybody's been optioned.'

My grandmother shrugs. 'You haven't.'

Ba pretends he doesn't hear her. Like mother, like son. He aims the clipping at Dad. 'Do you remember him?'

Dad squints. He's left his glasses upstairs. 'Nope.'

'Imagine him with a really patchy beard.'

That's past the limit of Dad's imagination. 'Can't.'

'He has fifty thousand followers on Instagram,' Gina says. 'How more than five people can follow anyone, I don't understand.'

'That's because anything more technologically advanced than a toaster confuses you.' Ba lowers the clipping and sighs. 'He actually finished the book. He's getting published.'

'And getting a movie,' my grandmother reminds him, I reckon solely as revenge for the toaster comment.

Ba straightens up. 'Good for him.' He twists his face like he is not, in fact, relishing in Benjamin's success. He glances at the guy's photo several times during dinner.

Bet you fifty bucks they bonked once.

3

I fish the cafe keys out of the fruit bowl. The noise is enough to wake somebody. Dad croaks a greeting and I jump half a metre. He's on the couch, one leg poking out from under the doona. He didn't sleep in Ba's bed. Something's happened.

'The fuck are you doing down here?' I ask.

Dad sits up. 'You know, the swearing's getting to be a bit much.'

Gina's impact, I suppose. I overcorrect and go full singsong. 'Father, why are you not upstairs? Did you and Other Father have a fight?'

He's giving me a dirty look. He doesn't have the patience for this at the arse-crack of dawn.

'Your father wanted some space last night, that's all.'

I call bullshit.

There's been drama. Trust Ba to fuck it up, barely a day after we spoke. Love is the way through. My parents can't be splitting up again. They haven't been back together long enough.

Someone's coming down the stairs. Ba's burning ears must have woken him. He's about to start a classic tiff. I look over my shoulder and...it's Gina, dressed for work. She doesn't greet me, but she does hold out her hand and say, 'Keys.' I part with them.

One look at Dad on the couch and she exhales deeply.

She tells me to go back to sleep, then she's gone. Dad's probably wondering what I did to get on her bad side, so I put him out of his misery.

'I took Proyiayia for a joyride to the cemetery and when Gina couldn't find her, she flipped.'

He yawns into his bicep. 'Sounds about right.' Another yawn. He needs more sleep.

I need more sleep.

'Your father and I are fine,' he adds.

I don't believe him.

At the first sign of life, me opening the office door at eleven o'clock to go chuck a piss, Ba calls my name. 'No,' I groan, 'not yet.' I do my business, then shuffle into his room.

He's in front of the bookcase, bouncing from foot to foot. It's obvious he's done his rigmarole – his beard is trimmed and its lines are neat, his skin has that moisturised sheen, and his belt matches his shoes. He thrusts his phone into my hands and demands I take his photo. Ba, the man who made hating Insta a central pillar of his personality, has signed up for Insta. He currently has zero posts and zero followers.

'Your handle is **sambaker4328**?' I ask.

'**sambaker** was already taken.'

'Yeah, because a million other people have that name. **sambaker4328** makes you look like a bot.'

He rests one hand on a shelf, about shoulder-level, and raises his chin. 'I don't need feedback, I need photography.'

I open the camera and squint at the screen so long, he asks if he looks okay.

'I thought you didn't need feedback?'

'*Harvey.*'

I tell him to smile more. He does, but it looks forced. Like his family's being held to ransom, but he's putting on a brave face.

'Maybe show teeth?' I suggest, but it's worse. 'Nope. Mouth closed.'

I seek out the most flattering angle, and Ba's very particular about it only being him and the bookcase in the shot.

'Make it look candid,' he instructs.

'You're posing like a French aristocrat.'

The critique confuses him, then he looks to his hand. He lets it fall. 'Better?'

'Better.' I step back to get in more of the bookcase. 'Is this because your friend got that big book deal?'

'He's not my friend.' Nobody's ever corrected the record faster. 'I don't understand how he has so many followers.'

Fifty thousand isn't that many. 'How often does he post feet?'

'Huh?'

'In his feed, were there heaps of pics of his feet?'

Ba perks up. 'Is that a thing?' he asks, a little disgusted, a little eager to kick off his shoes.

'You fucking *won't*.'

He laughs, and I take the shot. He protests, but it's a good one. Candid. He likes it when he sees it, but I do have to talk him out of adding a filter. He ummms and ahhhs over a caption, and this feels like my last opportunity to broach the subject of his shitty username.

'I can change your handle to **sotirisbakiritzis** before you post.'

He's resistant. He insists Sam Baker is how he's known professionally, which is weird, because he's practically starting over. Had I inherited his surname instead of Dad's, I'd be pissed if anyone gave it a nose job.

'Isn't this like you being too gay, though, but like, too Greek?'

Ba laughs. It's not the reaction I expect. 'Publishers love wogs, they just used to be more aggressive about making us accessible. And rightly so. People have made a mess of Sotiris Bakiritzis all my life. What good is writing under my real name if nobody can pronounce it?'

'You don't feel like you're betraying who you are?'

'Don't be silly. Authors do a lot to make themselves palatable, including adopting pseudonyms. I mean, women use the initials of their given names to pass as men so boys won't scoff at their books. They're doing what they can to get read. We all are.'

'Is there anything you won't do?'

'I'm on Instagram, Harvey, you tell me.' He dives back into his caption draft and immediately gives up. 'I need to brainstorm.'

He tosses his phone. It lands on the bed of a bachelor. The second pillow is on the floor and the doona has collected on one side...

'You know, you didn't have to wait for me this morning,' I say. 'Dad could've helped.'

Ba shakes his head. 'Don't get me wrong, it was thoughtful of him to come, and I'm glad he's here for you, but we're not... I want more for myself.'

Dad's commandeered the formal dining table. He's neglecting his work laptop in favour of a card game with Proyiayia. I think it started as the version of Snap we played when I was a kid, with a single pile and more slapping, but I suspect Dad got tired of explaining the rules along the way. My great-grandmother slaps the heap of revealed cards despite there being no pairs. Dad plays the loser. He tells her she beat him, again.

She cackles and claims the stack. 'You no good at this, Jeremy,' she says. The condescension is off the scale.

He winks at me. 'I can't keep up with you, Sotiria.'

I pull up a chair and watch Dad sacrifice card after card till his stash is spent and Proyiayia's crowned the winner. She beams. I smile, but I feel like shit.

If my parents haven't been getting along because Ba wants more, my question is, how can Ba want more than *this*?

Dad isn't some optional extra, he's *in* this family. He's down here with Proyiayia when nobody else is. Ba's making a mistake and all we can do is watch him make it.

My father collects the cards and barely shuffles them before he deals. He offers me the first one. I'm fine watching, so he starts splitting the deck between the two of them.

'Do you wanna sleep in the office tonight?' I ask. It's the least I can do. The mattress isn't great, but it's better than the couch.

'I'm good,' he says. He tries not to look bothered by the question, but I can tell he's rushing through the deck. When the final card's dealt, he asks Proyiayia if she's ready.

That delights her. 'I am ready. You never ready.'

Dad suggests lunch somewhere on Victoria Street and then a stroll, or a stroll and then lunch wherever we end up. He says it with a straight face too, like we won't pop into Gina's the moment we're out the door.

My grandmother's helping Marta in the kitchen, so Isabella takes our order – the grilled fish for Proyiayia, the daily special for Dad, and since I'm working through the menu, whatever's listed beneath yesterday's Caesar salad. I dunno if it's because I act differently around her, sit taller, speak deeper, but Dad pays attention. I feel his gaze on me when she asks the name of a Greek guy who'll transcribe a hidden meaning. It's easy. Con Notation. She gives my shoulder a squeeze on her way to the counter. Dad purses his lips, but he doesn't speak up, not till Isabella returns with our meals.

'I have one,' he says.

'One what?' I ask.

He ignores me. 'What do you call a sunbather on a Greek island who is a mezzo-soprano?'

He loses me at *mezzo*. He's big on crosswords, the more cryptic the clues, the better, so if anybody was gonna ruin our banter, it was gonna be him.

Isabella has a crack. 'I'm assuming the sunbather's a woman?'

Dad nods.

She works through the classics. Eleni...Maria...
Alexandra...She tries to build words out of them and
falls short. 'Don't know,' she concedes.

Dad's about ready to burst. 'Tanned Toula Sing.'

I don't get it. Isabella takes her time. 'Ah. *Tantalising*.'

It's too clever by half, but Dad's very proud of himself.
Isabella congratulates him, but before she leaves, she
does mention that he missed a clue in his set-up. He
should've told us the sunbather excited our senses.

What she's saying is, his joke needed more Con Text.

We go for the stroll, mindful to avoid steep hills that
might challenge Proyiayia. She's been quiet since lunch.
There's a lot of staring into the distance and not really
acknowledging what we say. At one point, she wanders
off the path. She's unsteady on her feet, but she gets
to her destination, a bench. She sits, so we take an
unscheduled break in the park across from St Vincent's.

I watch two guys by the old bandstand, about
my age, in navy-blue pants, lighter shirts and scuffed
shoes. One's vaping and the other has his back turned.

I reckon it might be Brad. We're close enough to his place. My stomach lurches, then he checks over his shoulder. Different face. Works to a point like a freshly sharpened pencil. I exhale. He's telling a story with his whole body, arms flailing. I'm hit by the sudden urge to get closer and eavesdrop.

Dad pipes up. 'A round of Questions Without Consequences?'

If Ba's desperate for information, he'll kick down my door at two in the morning and growl, 'What the fuck is up?' Okay, it's not that extreme, but he's definitely a student of the Gina School of Directness. Dad's different. He'll ruminate, stream several parenting podcasts and corner me with something cringe but well meaning like Questions Without Consequences.

'Go ahead,' I say, while the taller guy hands his mate the vape, possibly to shut him up.

'Do you regret quitting school?' Dad asks.

'No.'

He gives me time to elaborate or reconsider. I don't do either, so he asks his second question. Do I miss Perth? I know I shouldn't fear consequences, it's in the title, but I am careful when I answer. I tell him I missed *him*, not Perth.

Another question. 'Do you like Isabella?'

I sigh. Should've seen it coming. 'I do.'

'She's a fair bit older than you.'

He broke the cardinal rule. 'That's not a question.'

He apologises and rephrases. 'Isn't she older than you?'

'She's like, nineteen.'

I glance at him. He's standing in a shady spot because he's so pasty that any sun is a risk. He's watching the gents by the bandstand. 'You don't vape, do you?'

'Nope.' That's everything off his chest, but not off mine. 'Can I ask you some?'

His eyes widen like he's waited his whole life for this, then he contains himself, nods and says, 'Sure.'

I swallow. 'I know you think Ba will come around, because he always comes around, but what if he doesn't this time?'

The longer he goes without answering, the more I think this might be the first time there's a consequence for the questioner. He scratches at his slight bald spot. 'I'll wait for your father as long as I can.'

'But you...' I catch myself, rephrase. 'Can you sleep on a couch in Sydney forever?'

'Being with your father is my dream, Harvey. He has my all. If I leave, I leave without that.'

4

Gina isn't home at six, so Dad sends me down to ask if she wants him to sort dinner. I don't reckon he gets how much she hates me right now. The cafe shutters are half-down and most of the lights are off. My grandmother's at table three, organising invoices. I approach cautiously. She doesn't hear. I say her name and she practically convulses.

I laugh, then attempt to disguise it as a cough. 'Sorry.'

She reaches across the table for a particular invoice. I dunno if she needs it right this second, or if she's trying to look busy. 'What is it?' she asks.

'Do you want Dad to cook chops for dinner?'

Another invoice. She compares the pair. 'No, the mince goes off first. I'll be up soon.'

'He can start it.'

'I'll be up soon,' she stresses. She turns, enough for me to catch her face in profile. 'Did he tell you why he's back on the couch?'

She's making conversation. That's progress. I should give her a taste of her own medicine, pretend I can't hear or storm out, but I don't. 'Ba says he wants more than what they have.'

Gina sighs like she's disappointed, but not particularly surprised. 'My darling fuckwit of a son believes his name ought to be in lights. He won't stop until he's sacrificed everything for it.'

I tell her he's joined Insta.

'What?'

'Instagram.'

'Oh, good.' The sarcasm pools at her feet. 'He can be divorced *and* one of those arseholes who lets their food go cold so they can take photos of it.'

I laugh and she does too.

As far as grandmother interactions go, it's the best I've had in a while. Better quit while I'm ahead. I start retreating.

'I noticed you moved the desserts fridge.'

Fuck. Excuse me while I skip town, cut my hair, change my name...

'It was smart,' she adds. This time, when she turns, it's the whole way so she's looking right at me. 'I am grateful for all the work you've done.'

It hits me with the force of a speeding train.

I go to speak and she shushes me. She's not done. 'You should have told me you were leaving with her,' she continues. 'I was worried sick. I shouldn't have hit you. I'm sorry.' She holds my gaze for a breath. 'And we're past it.'

'Usually, people come to a consensus about when they're past something.'

She smacks her lips and returns her attention to her scattered invoices. 'I will hit you again and you will lose teeth.'

We head out for dinner. There's a place up the street that does a mean schnitzel and potato rosti. My parents treat us to a preview of this exciting new phase of their relationship. Dad's desperate to prove everything is fine between them. He asks Ba about his day, prompts him to tell the story about . . . and Ba gives him slightly more than nothing, a shrug, a single syllable.

Everything is not fine between them.

And that only becomes more obvious as we near the end of the week. Gina gives me time off, so I'm around for bursts of frustration, and the abrupt ends of conversations. Dad's needy and Ba's dismissive, which only makes Dad needier and Ba more dismissive.

A *brump* interrupts dinner on Friday. It's the Grindr alert, the sound that's outed thousands, if not millions of kids at house parties the world over. Ba acts embarrassed, but he answers the message.

It feels needlessly cruel. Dad has a quiet chuckle. Water off his back. He asks me to pass the salt.

Another *brump*.

'I put up a new photo,' Ba explains.

Brump. Brump. It's a veritable tsunami and the duck, try as he might, can't deal. Dad sets down the salt shaker. He excuses himself, his dinner half-finished and heartbreak all over his face. He leaves the back way.

Gina gives Ba a withering look. He pockets his phone and casually serves himself some steamed greens. He's proud and I let him know he shouldn't be. That wipes the smirk clean off his face, and I can tell he wishes he hadn't done that in front of me.

There's a muffled *brump* and he switches off his phone.

I watch TV with Proyiayia, but really, I'm waiting up for Dad. It's half-past ten. I'm on his bed. Gina's upgraded it, cracked out the sheets that match the doona, and lent one of her good pillows, but it's still a couch in his soon-to-be-ex-mother-in-law's house.

Dad should go back home. There's no use being here. Ba's adamant they don't have a future. If it occurs to him while he's out, I doubt he'll have the guts to tell me. He'll rock up, downplay what happened at dinner and talk up the lovely walk. I just hope that when I go to bed, I hear rolling wheels in the courtyard, a suitcase colliding with a deck chair, and come down in the morning to find him gone.

Proyiayia clears her throat violently.

'You right?' I ask.

She goes to reply and stammers. She's got that look that she had in Dr Tsiolkas's office, like she's reaching for a name that she knows should be there. She abandons the search and says, 'Paidáki mou.' She clears her throat again. She's after water.

It sucks to be forgotten, but there's no point dwelling on it, or making her feel bad about it. I smile. 'Okay.'

I fill a tall glass then halve it, because I know she'll say something about her bladder keeping her up all night. I return to the living room. She takes a slow sip, sets the glass down on top of the bulky heater and says my name her way. 'Heavy.'

It's a relief she got there, but the sadness has an echo.

There'll be a day when my name doesn't come to her, and another when it doesn't come to her and she doesn't remember it should. The days are only getting worse from here. I don't understand Ba. He has a husband and there's love there. And a lot of other shit, sure, but if love's the way through this, then why be callous? Why toss it all away?

I hear the back gate close. Dad's returned. Didn't realise he had his own key. I wait long enough for him to reach the door and my phone rings. I figure he wants to check the coast is clear before barging in, but it's Isabella's name that's flashing on my screen, not his.

'Hello?'

'Hey.' I hear her twice, once in my ear, once through the wall. 'Can you come out? I'm in the courtyard.'

5

Even at a standstill, the Mitsubishi rattles. I glance at Isabella. I wanna make a joke about the shitbox not being long for this world, but she's chewing her lip, eyes on the red light. I tell her it'll be okay, and she insists she's not worried, just annoyed. Study Club hinges on the kidlets giving her warning before they go out. Things get tricky when they call for a pick-up and she's enjoying a modest Friday night of wine, cheese and *Love Island*, and Christopher and his car are halfway to Cronulla.

'They should know better.'

The lights change. I accelerate aggressively and then keep the speedometer needle pointed at the limit. It's one thing to take Gina's car without asking (again), and another to get a fine. We zip past the pubs and darkened shopfronts of Oxford Street and Isabella apologises for ruining my night.

I laugh. 'You haven't ruined anything.'

'You could've said no. I would've dealt with the cleaning fee if they chucked up in the Uber.'

When I stepped out into the courtyard to find her leaning against the car, there was zero chance I was gonna say no. I like her. She says jump, I'm in the stratosphere.

I might regret jumping tonight.

We're driving to a block of flats in Bondi, and if Brad's there...

Isabella sighs. 'They could've told me today. They were studying in the cafe.'

My heart goes apeshit. I grip the wheel tighter and try to sound casual when I ask, 'Who?'

'Felix and Stef.'

I relax.

'Which is weird, because Felix rarely goes anywhere without Bradley.'

She says his name, and I relive him letting the door slam in my face.

'Bradley must be swamped at the moment,' she continues. 'He hasn't popped by the cafe in ages.'

I feel relieved.

And guilty. Brad's avoiding Study Club in all its forms, and there are no prizes for guessing why.

The building entrance is propped open by a bag of cat litter. Even if we didn't know the unit number, we could've followed the music up to the third floor, where the party has spilled into the hallway. Felix has Stef against the wall. He's doing all he can to make sure she goes home with a huge hickey on her neck. She's the one who spots us. Her eyes widen. She nudges Felix, but he doesn't relent till she punches his arm.

He unlatches himself. Frustrated, he asks, 'What gives?' One glance in the direction she's looking – *at us* – and he straightens up. 'You said you'd be here at one,' he tells Isabella.

'*By* one.' No remorse. 'Glad you two resolved your little will-they-won't-they.'

Felix is still stuck on the fact that their ride has already arrived. 'We've barely drunk anything.'

'The wins keep coming,' Isabella says.

Stef gives his shoulder a reassuring pat and he reaches for the bourbon by their feet.

'You're not bringing that in Gina's car.'

Felix groans and leaves the bottle where it is. It wasn't my call, but that doesn't stop him giving me the dirtiest look. He ducks into number eight to grab his shoes and bomber jacket. Stef waits with us. Her skirt gives off massive doily vibes. She looks like something Proyiayia would drape over a coffee table. But Isabella loves the skirt and asks Stef where she got it.

'Italy.'

'Ah.' Not much help to Isabella. 'Worst joke in the world?'

'We really didn't drink.'

'Humour me.'

Stef sighs. 'What do you call a Greek guy who's a happy camper?'

It stings like a betrayal. The Con jokes are *our* thing, mine and Isabella's. Who does Stef think she is? I mean, besides Stefania Mavridis, olive-skinned second-gen Greek-Aussie who's totally within her rights to mock Con as a first name.

She doesn't give us much time to solve it. 'Con Tent.'

Isabella nods. 'Of course.'

I don't like it. 'He's supposed to be a camper, not camping gear.'

Stef couldn't give less of a shit.

Felix leaves the unit in a huff, bomber jacket on, tradie boots in one hand. 'Let's go,' he says. His eyes find mine. And there it is again. The dirty look.

I can't help thinking this is about more than the bourbon. He's mates with Brad. They're usually out together. It isn't much of a stretch that Brad would tell his mate what went down between us.

He's quiet in the car, but there's the threat he'll open his mouth at any moment.

We stop at a red on Bondi Road. The chicken shop to our right catches Felix's eye. It boasts the best burgers in town and he hasn't had dinner, so I park after the intersection. The gesture doesn't win him over. He's out of the car without saying anything.

I grab a family-size chips for Isabella and me to share. We lean against the boot, the bag between us. The first chip burns the roof of my mouth. Felix and Stef are at a bench in the front of the shop. Felix is talking. I wonder if he's telling her about me and Brad.

'Where are you?' Isabella asks.

'Here,' I insist.

Isabella frowns. She doesn't believe me.

I reckon I could tell her about me and Brad. It's not a big deal, we had a failed hook-up. But I don't wanna risk saying anything that makes her think differently of me, so I tell her she's right. I'm not here. I'm thinking about Proyiayia forgetting my name tonight. I'm a wuss for hiding behind my great-grandmother, but it's not as if it isn't true. She did forget my name tonight. I am afraid the days with her are only gonna get worse. Spilling my guts, I can't help feeling *that* should've been what was troubling me. Not Felix bullshit.

Ah. Fuck. What is this? A tear? I'm fucking crying?

'I'm so sorry,' Isabella whispers.

'Don't be.' I sniff.

Goddamn it.

'Gina has this theory that Ba saved Proyiayia. She was wrecked by grief, and then Ba was born and she was better. I don't agree. I reckon Ba didn't save her. Proyiayia having someone to love…that's what saved her. She loved so much that it made life worth living. And that's how I'm gonna make it through. I'll love like she does.'

'That's a really beautiful way to think about it.'

I turn to her and manage a half-smile. She's so close, I can hear her exhale. I wanna be closer, feel the warmth of her breath on my skin, kiss her. I don't just want anybody to love, I want *her*.

It's a split-second decision. I lean in and she recoils. 'No, no. Don't do that,' she says.

We remain frozen, locked at forty-degree angles, me going in for a kiss, her eyes screaming, 'Oh, fuck no, not this!' I snap upright. Crap. Shit. Fuckity fuck. She straightens slowly and tucks her hair behind her ear.

I turn to the chicken shop. Felix and Stef are watching. My rejection had an audience. Great. Perfect.

I need to do something. I reach into the bag and grab a chip. I need to say something. 'Eat while they're still hot.' I pray it's enough to wipe all memory of the attempted kiss.

'That's not what this is,' Isabella says.

'It's okay. Seriously, eat.' I register what she's said. 'Why can't that be what this is?'

I risk a glance. Her brow is furrowed. 'You're one of the kidlets, Harvey.'

I grunt. 'No, I'm not.'

'We might work together, but we're . . . I'm twenty-four.'

All she has for me is a pitying look. I didn't want her to find out about Brad because she'd see me as one of the kidlets, but that's how she's seen me this whole time. We haven't been building a connection. I've been one of her youth projects. Someone who needs help. And I wanna cry some more. Which is fitting, being one of the kidlets and all.

'Just pretend I didn't try to kiss you. My plan to love through my grief is definitely not in tatters.'

Isabella laughs. 'Me not wanting to hook up with you doesn't...' She takes a sec to reorganise her thoughts. 'The healing power of love helping you survive grief, I get that, I've lived that, but love isn't simply shoving your tongue down somebody's throat. It's right there in your theory. Proyiayia loved Ba. That wasn't romantic. That was a grandmother's love. The love that saves you can be your love as a son, or a grandson, or a friend.' She really emphasises that last bit.

The car ride is awkward. Not because anybody does anything; it's residual awkwardness from the aborted kiss. Isabella focuses on Felix and Stef, which is wise. She asks them a ton of questions, the kind I interpreted as us growing closer. Brad brings up his brother. He's in with the wrong crowd, flirting with juvie. Feels like something he's kept to himself for a while, but Isabella gets it out with ease.

Maybe it's a skill. Or maybe people are so eager to let stuff out, they'll tell the first person who shows any interest. I mean, all she'd have to do is prod me and I'd burst. I'd fess up, say Brad going MIA is because of me. It's my fault he's lost out on Study Club.

We never went into the party proper tonight. Brad could've been there. He might still be there, drinking. Possibly in need of a lift.

I drop Stef off first, then Felix. Isabella says she's happy to walk, but I promise I won't catch feelings if I drop her at her doorstep. Her laugh's fake. I appreciate the effort.

We're gonna be fine, I reckon. A couple of rough shifts, some shit jokes and we'll be golden.

She tells me to get home safe.

She doesn't know I head back to Bondi.

I get a dream run of lights. The hope is that the party is still raging, or at least, Brad is still there with the last of them. I don't like my odds. The last thing I want is him trying to find his own way home and painting some laneway with spew because he didn't wanna face me.

The cat litter is still there. That's promising.

I take the stairs two at a time. I can hear music through the door to unit eight. It's unlocked. A girl's asleep on the couch despite a spirited argument over the best Spider-Man actor in the adjoining kitchen. Brad's sitting cross-legged on the island, makeup and lashes done on one eye, and a finger curled around the neck of a beer. He's advocating for Tom Holland despite strong opposition from a die-hard Tobey Maguire fan. He goes quiet when he notices me standing there.

We end up on the balcony, crammed between two ferns, him dangling the beer over the railing. The sea breeze is icy.

'I don't require rescuing,' he says. There's a slight slur, but he's right. I've been in far worse shape far earlier in a night.

'I know.'

'Tiff says I can crash here so Isabella doesn't have to wait for me.'

'I came alone.'

'Right.' He takes a swig, then looks down his nose at me. 'Why?'

Because I didn't like the idea of him stumbling home.

Because I regretted hurting him.

Because I . . .

'It's gonna sound stupid to say out loud.'

Brad narrows the eye with the massive drag-queen

lashes. 'Don't let yourself be intimidated by Cabbage House's finest mind.' He sells it with a burp.

I cackle. It's as if we're back in his bedroom, before I purged him from Grindr, before he rejected my number, and I have a chance to do things differently.

'I need friends my own age.'

He finishes his beer and taps the empty bottle against the railing. He's stretching the moment as long as he can. 'So, you're after more of a ships-sailing-in-tandem situation?'

'Yeah, something like that.'

6

Part of me wants to return to the terrace and find Dad's suitcase gone, his sheets and doona neatly folded. I shut the back door gently and check the couch.

Dad's fast asleep.

EIGHT
The call

SOTIRIS

1

I am perfectly capable of crossing a street. I have years of experience. I have even crossed this particular street numerous times. I suppose that's part of the problem. I'm standing on the footpath across from Ace Books, and all I can think about is how many times I've been here before and how many times Jem greeted me and how many times we snogged in that narrow excuse for a stockroom.

I exhale deeply. A woman with a pram asks if I'm okay. I manage a nod and that's all she needs to continue right past.

I'm launching a book. Jem won't be here. He isn't dim. He's realised by now that Sam Baker and Sotiris Bakiritzis are one and the same, and rostered himself off. No question.

My phone vibrates in my pocket. It's a number I don't have saved. It belongs to a new Five Irons publicist. She wants to know where I am.

'Crossing the street.'

I guess I'm crossing the street.

'Great. Wonderful.'

The bookshop's the busiest I've ever seen it. Everyone's packed in like Pringles.

Eliza pitched today as an honour, a young author opening the door for a newcomer. She sent me the uncorrected proof. On the back, *The Sound A Girl Makes When She Breaks* is described as a stunning debut from a startling new Australian talent. They spell Phoebe Turner's age right.

She's only fourteen. They'll be raiding preschools next.

I could've said no. It's not as if they're paying me. But Eliza's had the first twelve chapters of my second novel for eight weeks and missed my two follow-up emails. Us crammed in the same room together is an opportunity.

The folks at Five Irons are paying for the whole do. They've gone all out. Catering staff. Midafternoon drinks. The sales team chose a bookshop where their last stunning debut from a startling new Australian talent performed exceptionally well. Obviously, they don't know I was buying *Young* by the boxful at near-cost.

I have zero interest in bumping into any Ace Books employees, so I worm my way to the back of the shop, where a waiter tempts me with a platter of king crab rolls. I tell him I'm fine.

And I am fine. Yes, this would have all been wonderful for *Young*, but I have three-quarters of a new book, the twelve chapters Eliza has and ten more. This will be me soon. Catering staff. Midafternoon drinks. And I'll be old enough to drink them, no offence to other startling new Australian talents.

I scan the room, searching for the girl from the black-and-white photo on the back of the uncorrected proof. I find Eliza first. She's with Colleen, the other children's editor. She waves me over. I've run through our conversation a thousand times. I'm ready for this.

She asks how I've been, and I can't finish my answer fast enough because she's itching to mention the great turnout. Phoebe really deserves it. I don't know about the *really*, but I smile. They're working on her second book. Eliza hasn't even responded to me, but Phoebe's got a second book in the pipeline.

'Have you read my chapters?' I ask, out of nowhere. The thousand times I ran through our conversation, I had more tact.

Eliza laughs. 'We should chat about that soon.'

I agree completely. 'How about next week?'

She smiles to disguise something. Frustration? 'You've got a very distinctive voice, and I can see how your writing style has developed.'

'Thanks, I'm really proud of it.'

Colleen's looking everywhere but at us.

'I'm...afraid I'm not completely convinced that the story is going in the right direction.'

That's fine. She gave me plenty of guidance with *Young*. 'I'm happy to be steered.'

Eliza's stumbled into a conversation she didn't want to have. She sighs. 'The thing is, the rerelease didn't perform how we'd hoped it would, and it could be argued, not by me, that you've already had two bites of the cherry.'

'Who says it has to be a cherry?' I ask. 'Why can't it be an apple that accommodates several bites? Or a footlong?'

Eliza's laugh sounds fake. I imagine this is about as fun for her as a root canal, but I refuse to back down. This is my dream.

'The book is good,' I tell her. 'It's better than *Young*. You can see my style's developed.'

'Sometimes it's about other things. What I've seen of this new story is...You're right, it's good, but it's bold.

Bold can be risky, depending on what you're being bold about. Right now, I'm not sure I can get a book about a gay teenager through acquisitions. The schools market factors heavily into our thinking and they won't let it fly.'

The novel is semiautobiographical. I can't cut the gay teenager out. This is her saying no.

'But I'm such a fan.'

I swallow hard. 'Don't say that.' My voice cracks.

A platter of tuna rolls and a thick soy dipping sauce appears between us.

'A nibble?' the waiter asks.

Eager for the reprieve, Eliza gasps and grabs a serviette. 'I would *love* a nibble.'

Colleen finally realises that her eyes won't fall out of their sockets if she looks my way. 'Yum.' Haven't heard her say much else. Don't like her.

And I'm stewing. I can't help it. What else can I do?

'Go on.' Eliza encourages me to have a please-don't-hate-me tuna roll.

Before I can bitterly ask how many bites of it I'm allowed to have, a guy in a tuxedo shirt collides with the waiter. The tray topples over and my shirt catches most of the sauce before it hits the ground.

Ace Books doesn't have a public restroom, so I end up in the shopping centre nearby. The men's smells like food court. I'm at the sink. My shirt's off. Hot water's running. 'But I'm such a fan,' I mimic, rubbing handwash into the massive stain.

I'm supposed to be introducing Phoebe in ten minutes. I'm going to look like a damp Rorschach test.

I should bail.

But I can't do that, not to Eliza. She's *such* a fan.

I hear footsteps coming down the passageway. Perfect. The one thing worse than being the intense guy doing his laundry in a shopping centre restroom is being that intense guy without any privacy. I brace myself. The footsteps stop at the entrance. I look up, ready to make some pithy remark to dissolve the tension, but Jem's standing there. I'm staring at his reflection and he's staring at mine.

His hair's shorter and he's clean-shaven, so I can really revel in the squareness of his jaw. He looks good. And I look like an intense guy doing his laundry in a shopping centre restroom.

I risk the first word. 'Hi.'

Jem approaches the tap beside mine. He washes his hands, ten seconds without saying anything, eleven, twelve.

'I couldn't chuck a sickie,' he says, 'so I timed my break to miss some of it.'

'You didn't have to.'

'I did.' There's a firmness to how he says it. I can hear the full stop.

My throat's closing up. He barely dries his hands on his way out.

I grip the basin and it's all I can do to keep from fainting. Every breath is a struggle.

Dean vanished when I was done with him. I had expected it to be the same with Jem. But it turns out, when you're writing a semiautobiographical novel about having your first proper boyfriend, that proper boyfriend springs to mind a fair bit. You catch yourself revisiting moments. You tell yourself that's just the creative process. You don't miss him. You're only thinking about the weight of his body on yours because you *have* to get the details right.

I didn't only prepare for my chat with Eliza, I prepared for one with Jem, too. Three thousand times over, and never once did I think I'd be shirtless in a restroom.

I let him go so I could write the book without him. It's good, it's really good, and I couldn't have written it without him.

I thought up three thousand ways to say that.

Water spills onto my shoe. My shirt is blocking the drain and the sink is overflowing. I turn off the tap and wrench out the shirt. Water gushes onto the floor and Jem reappears in time to see.

'This will help.' He has his jacket over one arm. I'm hesitant and he's adamant. 'You're the author launching a book in my shop.'

I accept the jacket and immediately shield my bare chest with it.

'If you button it up the whole way,' he says, 'they won't be able to tell you've got nothing on underneath.'

He snatches my soaked top. It'll be hanging in the stockroom for me when the launch is over.

'Thanks, Jem.'

'It's literally my job.'

Before he turns to leave, he flashes me a smile. And I could weep.

The bookshop feels different. My publisher is burning money to launch their replacement child prodigy's debut and they want me here to watch. It *should* feel rotten but it doesn't. I could convince myself it's due to the confidence that comes from being secretly shirtless under a jacket, but I know it's because that jacket smells like Jem.

I'm introduced to Phoebe in the seconds before I step onto the tiny stage. She's pleasant enough. Wholly unprepared to address the crowd of mostly friends and family and publishing folks. I could let her *ummm* herself into oblivion, but the jacket, the smell of him, the fact he's watching from behind the front counter... I want to impress him. I lob her a few questions and the launch morphs into an informal Q&A.

Bev, owner of Ace Books and shell-necklace enthusiast, begins shifting her weight on her feet. It's time to wrap. I thank Phoebe for sharing her insights, which is big of me, because she shared one, tops. I'm partway through pointing out the signing table and directing attendees to make a line when Bev steps onto the stage, scored by a seashell cacophony. She breathily thanks us both, and also wants to single out somebody else. 'Our bookseller, manager, occasional bookkeeper and events coordinator, Jeremy. Friday was supposed to be his last day, but he wanted to make sure this launch went off without a hitch. Let's give him a clap too.'

I hate lurking, but I'm not too keen on there being an audience when I shed Jem's jacket. I browse the displays until the last of the stragglers are gone. I'm not particularly subtle when I lurk. Bev comes over to tell me he's out back, like I don't know. I've been in the stockroom plenty of times, but I'm not sure if the privileges of bookshop employee boyfriends transfer to bookshop employee exes. 'Just don't trip on anything because I'm not sure insurance covers you,' she adds.

I'm careful not to trip on anything. Jem's kneeling by a box, counting the books inside, and the closer I get, the more my chest feels like it might collapse in on itself.

'Hey.'

He pauses the count long enough to say I did well, but he doesn't look up.

'Cheers.'

There's only so long I can stare at the crown of his head, so I search for my shirt among the books and rolled-up posters and old dump bins that have accumulated over the years. It's on the back of a disassembled chair. I shed the jacket and rest it on a shelf. He doesn't so much as glance at me. I tug on my top. It's still damp. It clings to me when I put it on. My nipples are somehow more noticeable than they are when I'm not wearing anything. Ridiculous. Not that Jem says a word.

I swallow hard. I want Jem to say a word. Preferably more than one. A sentence. 'You're leaving the shop?'

'I am.' Two words. Okay. 'Back to Perth.' Three words. Not okay.

Perth. He's going home. I shouldn't feel like I'm losing something. I haven't seen him in ages. 'For good?'

'Think so.' He stands, and I expect the sight of me, shirt stained and nipples to attention, to light the spark in his eyes. Nope. His expression's grim. 'You been writing?'

That question from anyone else wouldn't hurt, but when he asks it, it passes through our history, that night in Enmore when I chose writing over him.

'Yeah.'

Jem smiles, but that somehow makes it worse. 'Good.'

The air is stale and heavy with dust. I wonder if it was always this unappealing back here and we were too into each other to notice.

I need to go.

Whatever I want to say about the new book and the hand he had in it, he clearly doesn't want to hear. I wish him well and I'm careful not to trip on anything as I leave.

It occurs to me too late, two-in-the-morning too late, what Jem going back to Perth must mean. He got the call. His mother's dying.

I reach across my bed for my phone. I've deleted his number and wiped every message except one. I can reply. I can call him. I can apologise for not realising *why* he'd be returning home. I can apologise for a lot of things. I can tell him I still think about him at two in the morning. I can ask if he still thinks about me.

I can but I don't.

2

I can tell a day from the first word. The stubborn ones are harbingers of pain, and the pain is never worth it. I might get a few sentences down, but reading them back, they sound about as good as a garbage disposal chewing glass.

Today's had several first words. The latest one is *fuck*. I mash backspace until it vanishes.

I can't decide what's spoiled the story more, Eliza saying it's not going in the right direction, or Jem not having the guts to tell me he's leaving. For so long, this book's been solely mine, but now I can't look at it and *not* think about the schools market and how awkward I felt in the stockroom...Jem and I didn't end things on good terms, I get that, but I didn't believe he hated me. Not until the launch. I'm not writing a true story, but it's true enough that knowing *that*...it makes me want to drag the document into the recycle bin, right-click and be done with it.

I opt for something a bit more final.

I print out the twenty-two chapters and march out the back.

Yiayia's in the courtyard. She's hanging the clothes in the afternoon sun, specifically the T-shirt from Phoebe's launch. The stubborn stain has thus far resisted my grandmother's best cleaning efforts. 'Ti eínai aftó to vásano?' she mutters as I pass.

I stop at the wheelie bin. It's empty, but it reeks. I have my twenty-two printed chapters in hand. And I hesitate.

I'm seventeen again, dumping copies of *Young* after spotting a typo. I've walked so far, but apparently, I've been on a treadmill this whole time.

The feeling that starts as a tingling at the base of my spine radiates up my back, down my arm. I adjust my grip. The top page curls in the wind.

Pins and needles in my fingers. All I have to do is let go.

Mum's voice rings out from the kitchen, 'Sotiris?'

I don't budge, so Yiayia echoes the call.

My heart is tapping something in Morse code. Does it want me to ditch the book or does it want me to persevere?

I can sense Mum's growing impatience. 'Come inside, will you?'

The top page curls again. I have no idea what I'm doing. I tuck the loose papers under my arm and cross the courtyard. Mum's imperceptible behind the dense mesh of the flyscreen. I let myself in.

She's waiting by the table. So is... My throat closes.

'Jeremy tells me he knows you.' She has an eyebrow arched. She damn well knows he knows me. 'He was standing like a sad sack at the front door.'

Jem insists he rang the doorbell.

Mum and I answer in unison, 'It's broken.'

He's briefly startled by the synchronicity, then he says, 'I was going to see if you were free to go for a walk?'

'No need.' Mum wipes her hands on her apron. 'I have to get back downstairs. There are cakes in the fridge. They're too old to serve in the cafe, but a quick zap in the microwave and you'd never know. Sotiris can give you the grand tour.'

Her exit is swift, and then I'm alone with Jem.

He asks what's under my arm.

There's no point lying. 'My new book. I was going to throw it out.'

'That bad, huh?'

I set the pages down on the table. I'm confused.

When I last saw him, he couldn't get rid of me fast enough. Now he's in my kitchen.

'There's a lot there.' He seems genuinely happy I've been productive; a surprise, all things considered.

I can't reconcile this Jem with the one from the launch, but I can't just stare, so I start towards the fridge. 'Did you want some cake?'

'Absolutely not,' he says.

That's reasonable. 'Mum botched the pitch, didn't she?'

'A little.' He grimaces and I'm lost for what to do. 'I'll take the grand tour, if you're game?'

Okay. That's something. I spin on the spot. 'This is the kitchen.'

'The stove gave it away.'

'Yeah. Duh.'

I show him around, and all the while, I'm painfully aware that this was once forbidden. Jem. In my house. He must sense how nervous I am, because when I pause at the foot of the stairs, he takes the lead. I save my room for last. I sit on my bed while he does a circuit. When he's done scanning over my CDs and trying to get my dust-coated Tamagotchi to start, he joins me on the blanket.

The tour's over and I have no clue why my ex-boyfriend is in my house.

'What's the new book called?' he asks.

'*Untitled Second Novel* until a more interesting title strikes me.'

He exhales through his nose. It's not a laugh, but it's close. He's stalling. I recognise *this*. Deep in my chest, in the vault of us, there are dozens of moments exactly like this. Us on the couch, on the bed, us filling in the gap between a call from Perth and him telling me about it. Some days, he'd need a gentle nudge...

'You got the call, didn't you?' I ask. 'About your mum?'

He nods. 'Yeah. She doesn't want me to see her. Aunt Faye is pulling rank. She doesn't want me to regret not...' He goes quiet.

There's a thigh-span between us. I want to shuffle close, reach an arm around him, but I keep still. I'm staring at the wall, as if looking at him is the scariest thing in the world.

'The whole point of working the launch was to say goodbye properly,' he says. 'Then I lost my nerve. Then I found it again. By that point, you'd gone. So, I'm in your bedroom.'

'It's weird, isn't it?'

'Very.' He sighs deeply. 'When we were together, I had it in my head that you'd come to Perth with me. I set aside money to fly you over and everything.' His laugh is fragile. 'Serves me right for making plans, huh?'

I swallow. 'For what it's worth, I'm sorry.'

'Don't be. I should know my lot in life by now and just accept the worst outcome at every turn.'

'That's bleak and dramatic.'

'My mum's dying, I'm allowed to be.' He clears his throat. 'For what it's worth, I don't regret one second of us.'

My mouth hangs open. My lungs are full, but I feel like if I exhale, I'll cry.

'I never fell in love with Sydney,' he adds, 'I fell in love *in* Sydney. I'm glad I did and I'm glad I got to see the guy's bedroom before I left. I can board the first Qantas flight on Thursday knowing I did it all.'

I laugh and that's enough to jolt a single tear loose. A slight turn of my head confirms he's watching me, watching the tear take its sweet-arse time. I smile wide enough to catch it.

Jem says he should probably get going.

I walk him out. At the door, he goes in for a hug. It's unexpected. He squeezes me and I'm overwhelmed by the smell of him.

Mum summons me to the living room with a 'Sotiris!' that could cut through steel. The telly's muted. She's folding laundry with Yiayia. She gestures limply to the mountain of clothes and suggests I help. She hates the way I fold. She's only called me down to quiz me about Jem's visit. But I play along. I kneel by the coffee table and even go through the motions of snatching a blue shirt from the heap. One of my favourites, loose around the collar. It's on its last legs.

I flatten it out, fold it twice, and add it to Yiayia's pile. It's a lumpy mess on a bed of crisp right angles.

Mum's neck tenses. She tugs the shirt, undoing my handiwork in an instant. She folds the sleeves back in midair, and closes the shirt like a book on her lap. 'What did he want?' she asks.

There it is.

Yiayia pipes up. 'Who?'

Mum points her nose in my direction. 'His boyfriend.'

It's weird coming out of her mouth. And incorrect. 'Jem is not my boyfriend.'

My mother's eyes narrow. My grandmother's eyes light up. 'Éllinas eínai?' And when we don't react, she gets her answer by osmosis. She deflates.

'He came to say goodbye,' I say. 'He's catching the first plane to Perth on Thursday and he's not coming back.'

'Kríma,' Yiayia says.

I reach for another shirt and Mum stops me. 'Please don't.'

I can't say how long I spend on the edge of my mattress. Long enough to hear Yiayia silence the talkback radio that occasionally lulls her to sleep. Long enough for Mum to call out for me to switch off my lamp. Long enough. I run my open palm over the blanket where Jem sat. The room feels different now he's gone. Emptier. He was only here minutes, and now I can't bear the thought of him never being here again.

3

Mum waltzes in at lunch. No greeting. No small talk. She slides an envelope across the dining table, then steps back like it might catch alight.

I inhale an unevenly reheated piece of spanakópita, lick my fingers and turn the envelope face-up. It isn't addressed to anyone, but...

My breath catches in my throat. 'Mum.'

She's in her work gear, but she's been elsewhere. The envelope has Flight Centre's logo in the corner.

She unclenches her jaw long enough to say, 'Open it.'

My heart's performing a drum solo. 'No.'

She doesn't flinch. She doesn't argue. She just waits for me to tear open the envelope and yank out an itinerary for Sotiris Bakiritzis.

'First Qantas flight out tomorrow,' Mum says.

I'm stunned. It's one thing to think that's what's in the envelope and another to know it. I pore over the fine print. There's no mention of when I'd come back. I turn the document over, expecting details of a return flight, but it's blank. 'One-way?' I ask, looking at her.

She sighs. 'I know you're going to tell me you're not together—'

'Because we're not together.'

'You're not living between two cities. I've watched your grandmother try and it doesn't work.'

'I have no idea what you're on about.'

'Pick a city and commit. If you go there and find something you want, stay and nurture it.'

'He's not my boyfriend. I'm not following him across the country.'

She continues, undeterred, 'Don't worry about us. We'll be fine.'

'Mum, you're not listening to me.'

'And *you* need to let me do this. You need to let me make it right.'

I am at my desk. I am working on my novel. I am not thinking about the Flight Centre envelope on my windowsill. Because Jem and I are not together. I cannot follow my ex across the country, even if he had it in his head that I would join him.

I scoop the envelope off the sill and banish it to my top desk drawer.

My gaze drifts two handles down.

I am not thinking about opening the bottom drawer.

I am not resisting the urge to open the bottom drawer.

I am...opening the bottom drawer.

It's deep and made for somebody who's mastered the art of filing folders. Its depths are lined with discarded drafts that date back years. Sitting on top, there's a first-edition *Young*. The boy on the front watches me. He wants me to get on with it.

I grab the book and carefully peel back its cover.

Dear Jeremy, the dedication on the title page reads. *Yes, I traced over the signature and it looks like shit. So what? It's not about the destination, but how you get there.*

It's my past calling out to me.

Yiayia helps me pack. Everything that goes into the suitcase must pass through her.

'Yes,' she says.

'No,' she says.

'Bullshit jumper,' she says. 'Too thin.'

She leaves her post to fetch a jacket, but returns with toilet paper. Six rolls. She stuffs them wherever they'll fit. Back in the day, she would send me on school camp with a family-size value pack of toilet paper. It was understandable. I mean, I was roughing it in the bush. But I'm going to Perth. I'm certain the city will meet all of my wiping needs. I try to explain this to her. She raises her voice. I insist. She insists louder and in Greek. I capitulate. I'm travelling to Perth with six rolls of toilet paper because I don't want to upset her before I go.

I'm used to seeing her off when she traipses back to the motherland, but this is my first time leaving her. I'll only be gone a few weeks, but I don't like the feeling. Ever since Pappou died, I've been aware that my time with her is finite. My time with everyone is finite, obviously, it's just harder to forget with her.

I fold the suitcase closed and tug on the zip. It gets caught in the usual spots. Yiayia squeezes my forearm to stop me. She's holding the stack of paper. My untitled second novel.

I shake my head. 'Áfise to.'
I'll write when I return.

Yiayia prepares lamb for my farewell dinner. Mum plates herself some, but barely eats. She spends the hour studying me. She pulls me up when I use my fork like a spoon. It's as if she's cramming in as much parenting as she can before I'm gone for good.

I assure her I'll be back before she knows it.

She doesn't believe me.

4

I don't warn Jem that I'm coming. I won't be talked out of this. I find him at the gate. He's sitting low in his seat, staring into space until he's staring at me. His brow furrows and then he's on his feet.

'What are you doing here?' he asks, all breath.

I act aloof. 'Thought you might like some company.'

He laughs like he's on the edge of tears. 'Yeah.' Despite the lack of a boarding announcement, people are congregating closer to the aerobridge. 'You're cutting it a bit fine to see me off.'

'Worst case, I can use my ticket.'

It takes him a good twenty seconds to respond. 'Your ticket?'

'I have a boarding pass in my pocket.'

The look he's giving can best be described as utter bewilderment. I relish it a little.

'There is the minor issue of me having no accommodation organised and no way to pay for any,' I add.

'Shut up. You're crashing at mine.' The offer's genuine, but I can tell he's searching for the punchline. 'You're serious?'

We were allocated seats a few rows from each other, but Jem sits beside me, and when a woman comes to claim 16B, he charms her into swapping.

This is my first time on a plane, so everything is fascinating, from the burly bloke struggling to cram a bag that clearly doesn't fit into an overhead compartment, to the armrest I can plug into and hear the radio.

Jem apologises in advance for snoring the entire trip. He didn't get much sleep last night. Neither did I, but I can't imagine snoozing on a plane. The noise this thing must make in the air…

'It'll happen,' he says. 'Trust me.'

I don't. I fasten my belt buckle. He yawns and it's contagious.

'Stop it.'

He shrugs. He's fighting a smirk. 'You look tired.'

I insist I'm not.

But my eyelids are heavy. We're on the tarmac for ages. By the time the safety demonstration starts, I'm really struggling. I give in, trusting that in the case of an emergency, there'll be someone close by who's willing to answer all my panicked questions.

I skirt on the edge of sleep, dozing off for a few seconds, waking, but never opening my eyes. I experience my first take-off in bursts. The rattle of the cabin. The wheels lifting off the tarmac. A hand gripping mine.

The slim chance we might catch Sylvie between lunch and her afternoon nap vanishes at the baggage carousel. We weasel to the front, but it's half an hour before the belt stutters to life.

Jem's bags are the last out.

We still rush to the taxi rank, though.

Sylvie's living with her sister in East Fremantle. From what I get to see on the way, Perth's an alternate-universe Sydney. It's mostly familiar, but then different in ways that jolt me. The media personalities on billboards are strangers, and the number painted across Pizza Hut windows isn't the one I know by heart.

Jem's aunt is waiting outside her bungalow. Faye has a severe face, but it cracks when her nephew approaches the picket fence. She does more of the hugging. When they pull apart and Jem introduces me, the random guy he brought with him, she raises an eyebrow and says she enjoyed my book.

I can't help but feel terrible. It's a tiny reminder that while I hid Jem away from my family, he was telling his all about me. They were reading *Young*, for God's sake.

'She awake?' Jem asks, hopeful.

Faye grimaces. 'She tried.'

'It's cool.' I don't think Jem likes the idea of his mum waiting up for him. 'We'll hang around.'

Sylvie won't wake until dinner. Faye suggests we head down to the river. There are some nice spots he can show me. Jem insists on staying. He'll be here the moment she opens her eyes.

Faye leads us inside. I don't know what makes a house a bungalow, but it seems every few decades, this one's had another room tacked on with no eye to keeping a particular style going. The house is all hardwood floors, white walls and domed light switches to start. Ten steps down the hall though, and we're thrust from the Great Depression into the seventies. The living room is autumn-coloured. The carpet has bounce and we both assume the velour couch will too. We're mistaken.

'Ow,' Jem says.

It's hard as rock.

'You'll get used to it,' Faye says. She's in the tiny kitchen. She makes sandwiches without offering. White bread, ham and whatever else she finds in the fridge. I inhale mine, careful not to get beetroot juice all over me. Jem barely touches his. He lets the plate balance on his knees. He keeps glancing at the door to the back room. I think he's scared of what's past it.

He asks his aunt how long Sylvie's been sleeping through the day like this. She's vague in that way people are when they don't want to tell you the truth, then she asks me if I've seen the collection. She means the framed photos arranged on a radiant heater by the wall. The pictures track Jem's life from beaming toddler on a wooden rocking horse to zit-strewn teen on picture day.

A big part of me wishes that the room didn't just look like the seventies, that we'd actually travelled back in time. I would write a note and wedge it between the concrete couch cushions for that zit-strewn teen to discover in the nineties.

I would tell him what's coming.

When it's time to join Sylvie for dinner, I'm suddenly afraid. I've never met somebody who's dying before. I don't know what I'll say or where I'll look. Fancy me coming all this way only to choke three metres shy of where I need to be...I tell Jem I'm happy to eat my chicken soup in the living room, but he says she'll want to meet me.

I follow him deeper into the house. I'm not sure what I expected, something akin to a hospital room maybe, not the set of a Western. At first, I think they've plonked Sylvie on a double bed in the middle of a horse's stable, but the more I avoid looking right at her, the more obvious it becomes how thought-out it all is, from the iron basket bolted to the wall for fresh towels and linen to the deep basin balancing on a barrel. This is a room designed as somewhere to spend your last days, but made to appear as if it was ripped out of the pioneer era.

I hear Jem set his mother's soup down on the bedside table. I'm staring at a stack of horseshoes on the wardrobe. Jem asks Sylvie if Jesus was born in here.

'Yes, right where your friend is standing.'

I can't not look. Sylvie smiles slightly when I do. She's propped up against a wall of pillows. It's hard not to only see the sickness. Her face is gaunt, her skin is pale and blotchy. But I recognise so much of Jem in her. They have the same kind eyes. Hers glisten in the lamplight.

'Don't ever tell Faye you like horses,' she says, 'or she'll make you sleep like one.'

'I don't mind it. It's rustic. Now let me just...' Her son rearranges the pillows.

'Jeremy. Stop fussing and sit.'

'Where? Ah.' He drags a small stool over from the corner.

His mother studies me, standing at the foot of the bed like a stunned mullet. 'Who's the bewildered nurse?' she asks.

'Sotiris.'

'Oh!' She adjusts herself. It's a process. 'You could have warned me. I would've done my hair.'

Jem laughs. 'He barely warned me.'

She tuts like that isn't good enough. 'It's a pleasure to finally meet you, Sotiris.'

'Ditto.' I regret not opting for a longer sentence. 'And your hair looks great.'

She appreciates the lie. 'I know it's intimidating,' she adds, 'but after a while, you stop noticing the big clock hovering above me that's counting down the hours I have left.'

'Mum!'

She shrugs. 'It is what it is. Have you tried the soup?'

'Not yet.'

'It's never great,' his mum concedes.

Jem offers to fetch her something from down the street. She shuts that down pretty quickly. He's having trouble suppressing his urge to fuss, so she asks him to feed her. He holds the bowl under her chin and only ever half-fills the spoon.

She tells him when she needs her first break. He intuits the timing of the others.

They don't talk much.

When she's had enough, Jem returns the bowl to the bedside table. She holds out her left hand, palm-up. He's vehemently opposed to whatever she's proposing.

'Go on,' she coos, twinkling her fingers.

'No.'

Sylvie looks to me. I'm on my own stool at this point, on the other side of the bed. 'Has he ever told you he's gifted in the art of palmistry?' she asks.

This is the first I've heard of it.

'For fun. I have no clue how it actually works,' he stresses. 'I'm not reading her palm.'

Sylvie huffs. 'Fine. Moisturise me, then.'

There's a bottle by the lamp. Jem's suspicious, but his mother doesn't have to goad him. He pumps a dollop of lotion and rubs it into her hand.

'Since you're there...'

Jem groans and his mother winks at me. She knows she's won. He carefully guides her hand closer to the light, and as he inspects her palm, she says something about him needing to send a search party to find her life line. He threatens to stop. She vows to behave. He clears his throat. I don't know how he's so stoic. If I were in his shoes, I'd be a blubbering mess.

I've never had my palm read, so it's unclear how much of it he pulls out of his arse. He talks about mounds and mentions planets and he sounds like an expert. Then he brings up her love line and a donkey-dicked man by the name of Darius.

Her laugh is like a whisper.

5

Jem grew up in Subiaco, not far from the theatre centre. His childhood home is a massive double-storey place. I roll our bags up the garden path while he fishes for the key in his wallet. His aunt pushed for us to stay at hers the night, but he was eager to show me the house. He opens the front door and flicks on the light. The living area's been cleared out. He checks the closest room. The study's empty too.

His room's untouched. From the surfing posters plastered on the walls right down to the textbooks stacked in the corner, it's exactly as he left it.

'Mum,' he whispers, 'what have you done?'

The answer's stuck to the fridge: a letter dated January 7th, 2002.

I give him space to absorb it in private, but he reads it aloud.

Slowly, Sylvie sold what she could, and tossed out what she couldn't so that when he returned, he could have a fresh start.

'*Sorry if you liked the lounge*,' he reads, '*but it was lousy and needed replacing anyway.*' He lowers the page. 'Everything's gone.' He's devastated.

'Was it a good lounge?'

'No, she's right. It was lousy.' Tears well. 'But it was *ours.*' He blinks down at the letter, then thrusts it into my hand. 'I can't. Can you?'

His mother's cursive is flawless. She's big on loops. It takes me a while to find where he's up to. '*Now, I assume you're horrified—*'

'Damn right, I'm horrified.'

I restart. '*Now, I assume you're horrified, but this is the right thing to do. When she died, your nan left me a lot. She thought it would help, and I did too. But it hurt to be reminded of her so often, and it hurt twice as much to be the one to let it all go. Better to save you the trouble.*'

'Nope,' he says. 'Not your call.'

'*I'm leaving you an empty house to fill however you please. You choose the furniture, the fixtures and the art on the walls. Raise a family here. Live a long life. And if you're still sulky . . .* Oh, she's got your number.'

'Shut up.' He steps closer to read over my shoulder.

'*And if you're still sulky, there's a box in the garage, but you're not to spend longer than an hour in there at a time. Promise me.*'

'I promise, Mum,' he says.

Nobody has lived here in months, so we open every window to air out the place. We order pizza. We splay the boxes out on the parquetry floor and pass a two-litre Coke between us. It isn't long before the disconcerting smell that haunts vacant houses is gone, or at least, overpowered by the aroma of meat and melted cheese.

Jem yawns into a slice of Hawaiian. It's getting late and neither of us has raised the bedding situation. Jem's single mattress isn't big enough for two.

'We can make it work,' he says. And then, hesitation. 'Unless that's too weird. I can sleep on the floor.'

I'm not making him sleep on the floor. I assure him it's fine. And it is. We both wear trackpants and lie on our backs. Our shoulders touch. I can feel the warmth of his body, hear every heavy breath he takes. I wait for sleep. It's dark and it's late enough in Sydney to be tired here. I wait. I wait.

When Jem asks if I'm awake, it's in the faintest whisper.

'Yeah.'

My heart thumps.

I turn onto my side.

He's staring at the ceiling. 'My brain won't stop,' he says.

I feel bad for getting swept up in the closeness of him. He's having one of the worst days of his life, what's romantic about this?

'I want to raid the box.' He exhales. 'Does that make me piss-weak?'

'No.'

It's in the garage, where his mum said it would be, beside the telly, which he's grateful she hasn't tossed out. The concrete is cold under my bare feet. The first thing he removes is a folded T-shirt. He lets it unravel and smiles at the design. He throws it over his shoulder and continues to fish. Some things don't need explaining, like the photo album, but others do, and he's more than happy to reveal the tiny histories of seemingly unremarkable objects as he sets them down around the box.

I can see what his mum meant about this stuff

hurting him. Even though the memories they conjure are happy, his eyes are sad.

Jem catches sight of something. 'Ah!' He reaches in. 'What?'

He removes a VHS tape. He checks the label on the spine, nods like a suspicion is confirmed, and then aims the label at me. *BH 1997*. 'Want to watch Mum's episode of *Blue Heelers*?' he asks.

I don't think I've ever seen somebody so excited to watch an episode of *Blue Heelers*. 'Sure.'

It's an effort. We cart the TV out into the living area, then search for the VCR. It's inexplicably in the laundry with some other electronics. While Jem hooks everything up, I drag his mattress, sheets and all, to a prime spot in front of the telly. We lie back and fold the pillows so our necks are angled just right.

The weather must've been dodgy the night they taped the episode, because there's this odd halo around people. But I get used to it. Sylvie appears about five minutes in. Jem gasps when he sees her. She guest stars as a constable who's pulled up for waving her husband through a breath-test station. Jem hangs off every word she says.

'She was so nervous when she left for Melbourne,' he tells me. 'She sat in the kitchen when it aired. She couldn't watch herself back.' He swallows hard. 'She's so beautiful.'

She really is. And young. I can't believe there are only five years between the woman on screen and the woman dying across town.

I fast-forward through the first break. It's been a while since I've watched anything on tape, but I used to be pretty good at zipping through the ads without missing any of the show. I hit play the moment the old channel logo comes up, the seven in the circle.

Jem doesn't pretend to be invested in any of the plotlines that don't involve his mum. She has a handful of scenes sprinkled through the episode, then they do her dirty, and she's run over by her drunk-driver husband. It's obviously a stunt double made up to look like her, but I still glance at Jem to check he's okay. His eyes are closed.

When I ask if he's awake, it's in the faintest whisper.

He doesn't respond.

I stop the tape and switch off the telly. The room is suddenly dark.

I drift off to sleep beside him.

I don't know what time it is when I wake. Jem's watching me. He manages a little smile. Then he inches closer. The kiss is gentle.

NINE
In tandem

HARVEY

1

Brad's a sporadic texter. A bunch in the morning, then nothing till I'm crawling into bed. I dunno if it's him exacting revenge on me for blocking him, or if Year Twelve's just that demanding. Out of nowhere one night, he asks if I'm up for a wander. I wait behind the terrace. When he appears, he's being pulled along by a cavoodle.

My left Converse gets a cursory sniff, then she moves on to an infinitely more interesting wheelie bin. 'How did I not realise you had a dog?'

'Zolda doesn't get to meet my hook-ups.'

'Ah.'

'She goes to doggy day care when Mum's at work. Lots of energy.'

'I see that.' She sinks her teeth into the wheel and growls. We both watch her with the intensity of two randoms trying on friendship, no clue if they tolerate each other let alone have any shared interests. 'Zelda, was it?'

'Zolda with an O.'

'That's not a name.'

'I'm aware. I had a cat growing up, Mario, but I had trouble with certain vowel sounds, so he was Morio, even after I could pronounce his name properly. When we got Zolda, I wanted to keep the tradition of almost infringing on Nintendo's copyright.'

It's convoluted, but cute.

'You done, sweetie?' Brad asks her. 'Yes? No? Yes. Okay.'

Zolda bolts down the street and where she goes, Brad must follow. I offer to take the lead, but he insists he's fine. I'm here to keep him entertained.

'No pressure,' he adds.

Doesn't matter, I thrive under pressure. I have stories. This bloke tried to do a runner today after a twenty-dollar breakfast. I chased him into the Cross.

Brad's suspicious when the story stops there. 'Did you catch him?'

'No.' I exhale. 'But I did stack it and scrape my shin.'

I score the first laugh of the night. 'What an athlete.'

'That's what Isabella said.'

'Oh. Your girlfriend?' He's smirking. He's heard about the attempted kiss. 'But I get it. Workplace romances can be tough.'

That gets a laugh out of me. 'Shut up.'

'And have you carry the conversation? That's negligence,' he says, before tugging my shirt.

'Huh? Oh.' He wants me to stop walking. Zolda's marking her territory under a clearway sign.

While we wait, Brad asks what working in the cafe's like. 'And be mindful,' he adds, 'I did submit my CV when I was fifteen. Got no response. I had no prior experience and my referee was my dad, but still, it's a sore point.'

'Jeez, who in my family hasn't rejected you?' The joke escapes before I can stop it. I worry it's too soon for a roast, but he howls, recovers and threatens to fuck my dad.

Yeah, I reckon we're gonna be good mates.

'The cafe's great.' I don't have another gig to compare it to, but I'm enjoying myself. After that night Brad spewed up his guts in the park, working at Gina's stopped being a means to save up enough money to leave. I started putting my stamp on the place, first with an iPad that actually works...My family has an eighty-ish-square-metre patch of the world; it's kinda cool to help make it the best it can be.

'Do you see yourself working there for a while?'

Isabella's been giving me more control over the day-to-day running of the cafe. It's happened in increments, so I don't really realise it till I'm the one on the phone to the cake supplier while she's engrossed on Insta.

'But we didn't order two sixteen-inch cheesecakes, Barry. Just because your bloke dropped them off doesn't mean we can pay for them.'

I can hear a lifetime of cigarettes in his voice when he tries some bullshit line about it being our responsibility to check deliveries when they arrive.

'No, no. That's not how this works.'

Barry launches into a gravelly monologue. I click my fingers to get Isabella's attention. I mouth, 'What's the name of another cake supplier?' and she blanks me. Fair enough. Probably difficult to lip-read.

I interrupt Barry. 'Look, Bazza, that's fine. If you can't accept we're only gonna pay for the cakes we ordered, we'll get our next batch from Nicole.'

Isabella might have earphones in, but she hears enough to lunge for the phone. I leap out of reach. I hold up a reassuring finger. I've got this.

'Who's Nicole?' Barry asks.

Good question. 'You know, Nicole.' One of Proyiayia's commemorative plates has made it onto the cafe wall. 'From Parthenon Patisserie. Great cakes, no exploitative practices. I think her stuff tastes better, but Gina believes in loyalty. How many years have you supplied us? Is it really worth throwing that all away because your driver stuffed up?'

Isabella relaxes and Barry's quick to change his tune. He comps the whole order. I was only after two free cakes, but that works.

'Bye, Barry.'

I end the call and offer Isabella a celebratory slice of cake. She shakes her head and points to our only customer, a mohawked dude nursing a macchiato like his life will end if he reaches the bottom. I add a dollop of cream to a hefty slice and walk it over.

When I return, all I get is the top of Isabella's head. I ask what gives.

She removes an earphone. 'Huh?'

'What's got you so engrossed?'

'Oh.' She disconnects her bluetooth and I hear the familiar, squelchy voice of Ba's author frenemy, Phoebe Turner. She's live on Insta.

'Lovelies, I can't quite keep up with all the messages coming through,' she says.

I roll my eyes. There's a fake softness in the way she addresses her fans, like they've just woken from a coma and she's scared she'll spook them.

Isabella taps her screen aggressively. 'Phoebe read an excerpt from her new book about two boy band members who fall in love and now everyone's spamming her asking whether it's One Direction slash fic.'

I have...no idea what those words mean, so I fetch the tub of serviettes from the stockroom and top up dispensers around the cafe.

Phoebe's voice carries. 'Oh! I see questions about...Yes, there will be a launch. Details will come as soon as I've organised a venue.'

I'm at the table closest to the photo of Ba's launch as she airily drones on about the magic of book lovers congregating. I'm bulldozed by an idea. I set down a bunch of serviettes and ask Isabella how many people are watching the stream.

'Two hundred.'

If we host the launch and get half that, and every second person buys a soft drink or a slice of cheesecake, that's some serious coin.

I'm back on my phone. I'm on Insta. I'm searching Phoebe's name. I'm in the stream. She's at her desk wearing hella distracting earrings, reading responses as they come through.

I'm typing furiously. Grígora. I tell her we've met. I'm Ba's son. She's welcome to launch her book at Gina's.

My comment is immediately pushed out of frame as more come through.

I try again. This time, my pitch lingers long enough to catch Phoebe's eye. She's enthusiastic. In the middle of a livestream with two hundred viewers, she's asking about catering. I have no fucking clue, but I assure her our packages are competitively priced.

Isabella alternates between quaking at the prospect of us hosting her favourite author's book launch and freaking out about the cafe not having any catering packages, let alone competitively priced ones.

'Oh, how special is this!' Phoebe says. 'Lovelies, this cafe is beautiful. It's in the heart of Darlinghurst, run by a fantastic author's sweet old mother.'

I'm not sure how happy Gina will be about being called sweet or old.

'For those of you who don't know Sam Baker...' Phoebe gasps. 'He should launch the book! That would be...It's perfect. This is my tenth and he launched my first. Full-circle moment. We can do an in-conversation.'

I don't need to ask. Isabella says, 'It's when two authors talk to each other about how good they think their books are.'

'And that's entertaining for people?'

She shrugs. 'I enjoy it.'

Having an in-conversation with Phoebe sounds like the sort of name-in-lights shit Ba froths over. I could make him pay me for the privilege. I could...A sharp intake of breath.

Isabella's startled. 'What?'

I've fallen arse-backwards into a way to force Ba to act less like a prick. I peel off my apron and ask her to watch the cafe.

Ba's in the office. I thought the absence of a desk chair might keep him from commandeering the space for creative endeavours, but nope, he's sitting on the unmade bed, awkwardly typing at the desk. My entrance confuses him. Why am I upstairs so early? Has somebody died? It's a weird place for his brain to go, but I ignore it. I tell him about the launch, and I don't have to convince him to do it. He reckons it's an extraordinary opportunity to introduce himself to a new generation of readers.

'Fuck,' he keeps saying, grinning ear-to-ear. '*Fuck.*'

This is big. This is huge. This is Ba proving he's looked up the thesaurus entry for *large*.

He asks what the catch is. He's joking, but I have one.

'You have to be nice to Dad.' I say it like he's trying to charge me for cheesecakes I never ordered.

'Harvey...'

'I mean it. You have to go out of your way to talk to him. And no Grindr at dinner.'

He tries my name again, but I tell him I'm on the clock.

It works.

At dinner, Ba asks Dad how his day was. Dad's flustered, caught off guard after a week of his estranged husband being a total arsehole. His answer's the longest sentence ever uttered. He trails off, embarrassed, certain he's blown it. But Ba asks another question. Dad remembers to breathe. He organises his words in shorter sentences.

Brad asks if it's a good idea.

'Yes.' Because it's working.

Zolda's supposed to be exploring as much of the park as her leash will allow, but she's mesmerised by my new sneakers. She presses a curious paw into one.

'Your dad's not going to be hurt by your other dad pretending to like him?'

'Ba likes Dad. He's just acting like he doesn't for . . . reasons.'

'Yeah, but your dad will get his hopes up. He's going to think they're getting back together.'

'He won't. They're gonna split up better, that's all.'

Brad doesn't argue. I know them best.

I can't shake what Brad says.

When Ba speaks in full sentences at dinner, or proposes they go on their own late-night strolls, and Dad seems *super* into it, I wonder if I'm hurting him. I mean, he's made it clear he's not leaving, what's the harm in Ba being civil while he's here?

Well, one morning, I am once again up at the arse-crack of dawn. I shuffle into the kitchen to console myself with a bagel smothered in Philadelphia and Dad's already up. He's made coffee. He's grinning ear-to-ear and when I'm close enough, he whispers, 'Your father's really turned a corner. We feel like we did back in the beginning.'

Fuck.

2

I shit bricks the first time I do close alone. I shouldn't. I mean, I have the experience and Isabella prepares a list. Still feels like a lot of responsibility. Gina says she might duck in and check on me, but she doesn't till my fourth solo close. I'm cleaning the espresso machine when she sits at table three and lets out an earth-shaking sigh. 'Good shift?'

'Constant.'

'Mmm.' She looks like she's run a marathon.

'Big day?' I ask.

She exhales. That's a yes. 'Had your great-grandmother's dentist appointment. Five cavities.'

'Solid effort.'

'You're telling me! She barely has that many fucking teeth. *Then* I had to get her moving so we did laps around Westfield, like I used to with you.'

I have no memory of that. Apparently, we used to do it all the time.

'Your father told me not to spoil you, but who was

I to deprive you of a jumbo chocolate shake with extra Flake when you asked?'

Okay, that's ringing bells.

'I had to tire you out so you weren't bouncing off the walls when we got home.' Gina's eyes are fixed on the floor. She's travelled back in time. She laughs a little. Blinks. And she's back. Her smile slips. 'Now I'm doing it all again with Proyiayia and I feel a hundred times older.'

'To be fair, you...' Her look is a warning. I abandon the joke.

Gina runs her hand through her hair and scrunches it. 'She's been banging on about me taking her to Greece. I swear, she's demented when it suits her. She forgets when she puts the stove on, but won't forget the islands.'

'Maybe if you told her—'

'No, no.' We've been here before. Gina's not telling Proyiayia what's wrong with her.

I don't push my luck. Instead, I scan my list of the essentials. There are some tasks, like cleaning the De'Longhi, that must be done every close. Others, like mopping, should be completed daily, but skipping them isn't a total disaster.

'You're going to mop, aren't you?' Gina asks. She must've noticed something on the floor.

I wasn't, but sure. That can be next.

I head to the sink and return with a full bucket and a mop. Gina's squinting at a flyer for Phoebe's book launch. She wasn't keen on the idea at first. An event is a big undertaking. But the cafe's not in a position where she can turn down a tidy profit on finger food and soft drinks.

'I'm losing my grip on this place,' she says, slotting the flyer back between the shakers.

'No, you're not.'

'I am.' She swallows. 'It's not a bad thing. I really thought that to keep it from falling apart, I'd have to be here every day until I died. I stepped back and now, we're selling desserts in numbers we never used to and hosting events.'

I dunk the mop and walk it towards the stockroom.

Gina clicks her fingers. She's pointing to the opposite wall. 'Start on this side.'

Her grip's loosened from vice to stranglehold. I laugh and she tells me to shut up.

I mop with broad strokes. Partway through telling me to make figure eights, she catches herself. She doesn't seem unhappy when I amend my technique, though.

I enjoy mopping. It's a bit sad, but I like the rhythm of it. Isabella would say something deep: I like leaving things better than I found them, or some shit. But I think it's just the rhythm. Brain off. Wet the mop. Drain the mop. Drag the mop. Wet the mop.

I steal glances at Gina. The day has taken it out of her. If I was that exhausted, I'd wanna have done more than visit a dentist and a shopping centre.

'Why don't you take Proyiayia to Samos?' I ask.

My grandmother rubs her cheeks. 'She's too frail, Harvey, and you...'

'I can handle this.'

Her eyes narrow, as if she's trying to detect a lie. 'You really like working here, don't you? You don't think it's small? Like you're meant for something bigger?'

She's asking if I'm like Ba. I'm not. 'Honestly, I don't think anybody is meant for anything,' I say eventually. 'You end up where you are, and if you like it, you like it.'

Me, the mop and the bucket are much closer to her by the time she speaks again. 'I could give you this,' she says. 'After I trained you properly, taught you everything.

Years down the track, mind you. Would you want that?'
Before I can reply, she adds another caveat. 'You'd have
to go to TAFE too.'

'Yiayia.'

'*Gina*,' she corrects.

It's a huge leap, going from asking if I enjoy working
here to asking if I wanna work here forever. 'How about
we take it a year at a time?'

She huffs. 'Commitment-phobes, the lot of you.'

3

Mildly tipsy miniature golf is my idea. There's a place nearby. The guy on the door doesn't suspect we've added vodka to our Greatorades, and the guy at the bar reckons Brad looks old enough not to card. It's moderately drunk miniature golf by the time we finish nine holes.

I stumble up the terrace stairs and shush myself.

It's almost one o'clock. Lamplight leaks from Ba's bedroom. I'm careful with my next step. The floorboard creaks under my weight.

Ba says my name.

I grit my teeth.

He's on his bed, hunched over his laptop. 'Fun night?' he asks.

'Yeah.'

I wait for the stream of follow-up questions that don't come. He sips his tea, which can't possibly be warm, and continues typing. I ask what he's working on.

'The same sentence I started when you left.' He folds his arms like he's about to scold his computer. 'I'm agonising over the pitch for the new book.'

He's already told me the premise. 'Isn't it about the kid who lives on top of a cafe in Darlo with his mum and her mum?'

'Yeah, but...I can't exactly say that in the cafe without looking like the autofiction wanker who thinks his life is a must-read.'

To be fair, he *is* the autofiction wanker who thinks his life is a must-read.

'Don't say it,' he warns.

The wanker has psychic abilities.

He has a week till the in-conversation. That's more than enough time to craft a riveting pitch, but he's stubborn. He's refusing to sleep before it's done.

I sit beside him. I'm jealous his mattress can support the two of us without disintegrating. 'Can I help?'

He's grateful for the offer, but I doubt he takes it seriously. My breath smells like it might strip paint off the walls.

'I can explain beat for beat what happens, but that won't excite anyone. I'm trying to capture the vibe without sounding vague,' he says. 'Phoebe's readers would lap that shit up, but I'm performing for an audience of one.'

'And I'm proud of you no matter what.'

'Not *you*. My old editor is Phoebe's publisher. She's coming on Saturday. If I can convince her the story has legs, book deal.'

Oh, shit. This is about more than impressing some rabid Phoebe Turner fans. He could really kickstart his comeback.

I ask about the vibe. I can totally help him spin vague into gold.

'What time is it?' He squints at the screen. 'Balls. I promised your father I'd do breakfast with him. And if I cancel, who knows what someone might do.' It's a lighthearted barb, but – and this might just be all the vodka – I'm sensitive to the truth in it. He must feel like I'm holding his career hostage.

'It hasn't been horrible, has it?' I ask. 'Hanging out with Dad.'

'No.' He reaches for the mug on his bedside table, but it doesn't get close to his mouth. 'I mean, is it what I want to be doing with my time? Not really. But it isn't horrible. We've spent most of our lives together for a reason. There's love there and it's nice to feel it. Especially when...It's such a mind-fuck. She's slipping away from us, Harvey.' He scratches at his beard. 'It's like I'm on a beach and there's a hole in the sand. The grief comes in waves. They knock me into that hole. I climb out, but there isn't long enough between the knocks for my clothes to dry. When I spend time with your father, when I make him laugh...I forget my socks are wet.'

I don't speak till I'm certain he's finished. 'Love is the way through this.'

'Maybe.' He smacks his lips and lowers his mug. 'If only love was enough for me.' I dunno if I imagine it, but there's a yearning in his voice, a wish that he could be fulfilled by love and love alone.

'Shouldn't it be?'

He shakes his head and points to his screen. 'This is torture, but the moment it all clicks? It's like nothing else.'

'And you can't have both? This and Dad?'

'No. When I'm with him, he is everything to me. It's scary how content I am doing his fucking laundry. At the end of my life, I'll be so angry at myself if I haven't done more.'

I yawn. It's the wrong time for it. And it's a circuit breaker. He probably realises he shouldn't be telling me any of this. Even though he's no closer to finalising his pitch, he urges me to go to sleep.

He doesn't stay up much later. I'm still awake when his lamp clicks and the hallway darkens.

4

Brad's eager to see my bedroom. It's only fair. I've seen his and where you sleep says a lot about you. I haven't really had a chance to make it my own. It's still Gina's home office, but he can discern whatever he likes from a room that's barely big enough to fit a paper-thin mattress and an old desk.

He runs his eyes over it, cornices to carpet, and nods. 'Just as I thought,' he says. 'Serial killer.'

'Shut up.'

I nudge his back and he enters. The bed's unmade, so I climb onto the mattress and hurriedly straighten the doona. I sit and invite him to do the same. He does. The shock of sinking right to the base briefly registers, then he regains his composure. He twists his left hand at the wrist and runs the back of his fingers seductively down his front. 'Try not to get H-word,' he coos.

'Shut up.' It's evergreen.

Our friendship has progressed enough in three and a half weeks that we're comfy meeting up for something tedious. Brad's memorised an English essay and he'd like to recite it for an audience. I have to follow along and if he strays too far from what's written on the four double-sided pages, I have to pull him up.

Riveting stuff.

'How do you sleep on this?' he groans. 'My arse is killing me.'

'That's what all the boys say.' It's low-hanging fruit, but it tastes sweet.

Brad's having none of it. 'Yeah, brag more about being a shitty lay.'

I blow him a kiss and he rolls his eyes. He insists we focus, and I insist I am focused, just waiting for him to start his riveting recital.

'Mind you,' I add, 'I don't think you learning an essay by heart is in the spirit of the task.'

'Well, I don't think the guy who quit school should be lecturing anyone.' There's a cheeky glint in his eye.

It's confusing. I'm cracking jokes on a bed with a guy I met off Grindr. There's very little that separates this from the beginning of a hook-up.

The air is suddenly dense. I inhale and it's heavy in my chest.

'Right.' Brad looks away. He has an essay to recite. He takes a breath and I wonder if the air feels different for him too.

'Harvey?' Dad calls. He's coming up the stairs, and his pace quickens when I call back. Soon he's at my door, bursting to tell me something...but hesitant because somebody else is here. 'Oh, hello.'

Can he tell that for a moment, the air in here was different?

No, that's stupid.

I play it cool. 'This is Bradley.'

Brad gives me a look that would make Gina proud. 'Brad.'

'I can come back,' my father says. He won't, though, because it's rare I'm home and Ba isn't. He's taken Proyiayia to her physio, mostly to perv on said physio.

'It's okay,' Brad says. 'You can just pretend I don't exist.'

Dad doesn't have an intimate knowledge of our intimate history, so it flies over his head. 'Great. With the in-conversation tonight, I wanted to run something past you,' he says.

'Shoot.'

'As you know, your father and I have been reconnecting recently.'

Brad's eyes widen.

I nod cautiously. 'I have noticed.'

It's like a slow-motion car crash. He explains that while there's a lot that needs mending, a lot of their problems stem from Ba's unrealised career. After the event, but before everyone's left, Dad's plotting to sink to one knee and present Ba with the ring he abandoned on the dresser in the Subiaco place. 'A re-engagement. A recommitment.'

Brad's eyeballs are in danger of popping out of their sockets.

'What do you think?' Dad asks.

This is what Brad warned me would happen: high hopes and hurt feelings. I need to be direct. 'No,' I say, and it cuts through him. For a second, I regret the directness. I almost soften the blow, spin it as inappropriate to repropose to Ba on Phoebe's night. But Brad's watching. I can't kick the can down the road. I tell Dad the truth. Basically, 'I didn't like how Ba was treating you, so I organised this in-conversation and made his participation conditional on him not being an arsehole,' in many, many more words.

I've never seen Dad cry before. I've never even seen him close. He blinks hard and looks away, like he can't bear my gaze. When he says he has to go for a walk, he speaks to the floor.

He retreats downstairs and Brad and I are frozen. An eternity passes before he squeezes my knee and asks if I wanna talk about it. I shake my head. I can feel myself welling up, but Brad has an essay to recite.

'I can—'

'Your essay.' I'm adamant I'm fine.

I raise the paper to block Brad's concern. After enough time for me to reconsider, he begins.

5

Ninety-seven people rock up for the launch, more than I've ever seen in the cafe, but someone's missing. When I'm on my way past with a platter of sandwiches, Gina asks where Dad is. I play ignorant and she asks if I'm bullshitting her. I shake my head. I don't think she believes me, but there's no interrogation. She tells me to go feed my great-grandmother.

We stacked most of the chairs, but lined a few against one wall. Proyiayia's seated beside a guy with a glittering Phoebe quote on his T-shirt. The sandwiches are a hit, or at least, I think they are before the guy with the arancini steals my thunder. Proyiayia returns the finger sandwich she's already bitten and helps herself to a deep-fried ball.

'Remind me, how did I get roped into this?' waiter Brad asks as we forge a path through the attendees.

'Don't act put out. You're loving this.'

'My wrist hurts.'

'You're living fifteen-year-old Bradley's dream.'

I feel the heat of Gina's gaze. She performs a series of hand gestures that can only mean *get the fuck away from each other and work the room*. No idea why she's so tense. Phoebe has paid, and she looks like she's having a nice enough time. She's nodding sincerely while a woman in her mid-fifties talks her ear off. I wonder if that's the publisher Ba's out to impress. I scan the room. My father's recounting a story to a small group by the desserts fridge. He's animated, and whatever he's saying must be hilarious, because whenever he pauses, they erupt. I catch him glancing at the woman with Phoebe.

She's definitely the publisher he's out to impress.

I don't think he notices when she looks his way.

His career was done and dusted before I was born, so I never got to meet Sam Baker. He was a just name on a spine. Before tonight. It's difficult to explain the difference between Ba and Sam. He's himself, only more. If that makes sense. Louder. Bolder.

He's got this *presence* and I'm a little sad Dad isn't here to witness it.

On the other hand, it's probably better he isn't. This is what Ba blew up their life for.

Someone lightly slaps my arse. I spin and Isabella's standing there. It boggles the mind how I could've possibly misinterpreted her interest as *interest*. I wait for her to help herself to a finger sandwich, but she's not hungry.

'Do you think I can go over and interrupt them?' she asks, pointing her nose towards Phoebe and the woman.

'You haven't said hello?'

She giggles, horrified. 'No.'

I groan and grab her elbow with my free hand. I guide her through the fans, then across the demilitarised zone between them and their idol. They're too afraid to breach the invisible barrier and get close.

She's big on TikTok, but I don't give a shit.

'Phoebe? Hi.'

'Harvey!' She makes a huge fuss about me being Ba's son.

The publisher sees the resemblance and I don't bother getting into the specifics of who donated the sperm. Instead, I push the spotlight onto Isabella.

'She's your biggest fan,' I say.

Phoebe's flattered and it takes about a minute for Isabella to manage a complete sentence. When she's okay on her own, I excuse myself to walk the remaining sandwiches around the room before Gina eviscerates me with an aggressive hand gesture.

My platter is close to empty when we make moves to start the in-conversation. There's chaos when more people wanna sit than there are chairs put out. Gina dismantles the stacks with a frightening urgency and whoever needs a seat gets one.

Brad and I stand at the back, the remaining food consolidated onto one platter. I make a dick and balls out of sandwich and arancini. It gets a laugh, then his focus returns to the night's stars.

For an in-conversation, it doesn't feel like much of a conversation. It's more of an interview. Sam Baker asks Phoebe questions, and she doesn't lob any back. He makes do. He asks her questions he wants to answer, so he has a chance to add his two cents when she's done. He's entertaining, but I get the sense the audience isn't all that interested in hearing him speak. Not when Phoebe's there. She has them in the palm of her hand, verging on tears at a moment's notice. All she has to do is drop a character's name – Devon, Michael, Orson – and the room swoons.

Brad has her number. 'Ten bucks they're all the same guy. Broody, protective, angry in bursts but the main character can change him.'

'Definitely.'

We haven't spoken about this morning and what might have happened if Dad hadn't ambushed us. I'm holding the platter with both hands, but could easily hold it with one. If I let my hand fall beside his, it could alleviate the need to speak. We'd just know.

One deep breath and I perform the manoeuvre, a subtle drop. My hand slaps his and he retracts it. Shit. I wait, wait, and while Phoebe yammers on about some anvil-chinned heartthrob she dreamt up, I feel the back of Brad's hand graze mine. It's fleeting. The next time, it's less of a graze, more of a press. He keeps it there. Eventually, I close my hand around his.

After twenty minutes, Phoebe invites questions from the audience. They ask her about the Devons and the Michaels and the Orsons, and Sam Baker sits there. He's wearing a smile, but his eyes are screaming. With each question directed at Phoebe, he looks more and more like Ba, and less like the consummate performer.

He hasn't had a chance to share his pitch, which means the publisher hasn't heard it.

I shout, 'Me!' when Phoebe announces she's only taking one last question. It's not proper etiquette, but it gets the job done. 'Are either of you working on anything new at the moment?'

Phoebe answers first. I couldn't give two shits about her work in progress. My eyes are on her conversation partner.

When it's his turn, Ba hesitates. 'Um.' Then Sam Baker clears his throat. 'This is the first time I've shared this with anybody, so you're going to have to promise to be kind.' He flashes a smile. It's a performance. He's endearing himself to them, and it's working. He pitches a love story. Boy meets boy. They'll break each other's hearts someday, but that's not the focus. Their love is. 'I think we need love now,' he says. The Phoebe stans are eating it up and I expect him to leave it there, but he gets specific. He gets very specific. He talks about his influences. He mentions Proyiayia. How when she would visit Greece, it was like his life was missing an essential ingredient. How he's now staring down losing her for good. He brings up Stavros. Her grief. The diagnosis. And the way through it.

The transition between his words and mine is so seamless, I don't notice till the end. My words have weight when Sam Baker says them. They make people cry.

I search for Proyiayia. The guy wearing the glittery Phoebe quote squeezes her shoulder. And it dawns on me that Sam Baker's just revealed her diagnosis to the room. To her.

It's definitely Sotiris Bakiritzis who sits in his childhood bedroom, waiting for his mother to scold him. He has his shoulders way forward. I'm in the hallway, about as far from him as I am from Proyiayia. She's bathed in lamplight, folding clothes and laying them on her bed. I feel compelled to ask her how she is, but I know that I won't understand any truthful answer. I don't have the vocab for it.

I hear the front door, and Gina coming up the first flight of stairs. Ba tenses. She insisted we leave her to close by herself. I assume, to blow off some steam. I don't reckon she blew off any. Or maybe there was just that much. She storms up the second flight and stomps right into Ba's room. She slams the door behind herself. As if timber can contain her.

'Are you happy? Did you get what you wanted?' she bellows, slightly muffled.

I don't expect Ba to shout his response, but I expect it to be loud enough to hear...

'How dare you!' she continues. 'You had to say something! There was a fucking procession! People we don't even know lining up to cry at her! Grown women still reading books for kids telling her she's going to fucking die?'

Ba speaks. 'They didn't say she was going to die.'

'They might as well have! She doesn't speak English!'

Proyiayia reaches into the basket, plucks out something black. She carefully folds it in the air, then presses it onto the growing pile. Without so much as a glance my way, she says, 'Áfise tin.'

I dunno what it means.

Ba's raised his voice. He says we ought to be honest with Proyiayia and Gina cuts him off.

'Don't you ever fucking speak to me again!'

The door opens. She inhales sharply when she sees me, then strides right past. She's in Proyiayia's room. She snatches something from the basket and channels all her frustration into folding it. She's gentler with the next article. Gentler with the next.

I sense Ba in his doorway, watching them.

Proyiayia asks if there's something wrong. Gina deflects, she's feeling fine, but Proyiayia clarifies. She means with *her*. It's an invitation to be frank, and Gina doesn't take it. Proyiayia sighs. She says something in Greek and Gina urges her to stop.

'Ma...' Her voice cracks.

Proyiayia has more to say. I don't understand a syllable. But Gina's crying. I wait for Ba's translation. He doesn't say a word. He's crying too.

6

Dad's on the couch in the morning. He smells like bourbon and his voice is hoarse. I brew him some tea, but he only stares at it.

'How'd your father go last night?' he asks.

Before Gina cracked the shits, Ba did have a one-on-one with the publisher. It looked cordial, but I dunno.

'I'm sorry about making you think he—'

Dad assures me it's fine. 'We were probably unpleasant to be around.'

No, what was unpleasant was seeing him get hurt over and over, refusing to even consider leaving. I wanna ask him to go. 'Quick round of Questions Without Consequences?'

He shakes his head. 'No.'

I can tell he wants me gone. Funny that.

'Remember in the park, when you told me being with Ba is your dream?' I ask.

'Harvey...'

'A dream isn't just something you have, it's something you are,' I tell him. 'It shapes you.'

'Righto.' He's not interested, but it'll take more to shut me up. This can't go on.

'If your dream is bad, it's bad for you.' I swallow hard. 'Your dream is bad.'

It's as close as I can get to asking him to leave without asking. He says he needs to get more sleep.

The plan for a Greek odyssey comes together quickly. Four weeks – some time in Athens, but most of it on the islands with Gina playing chaperone, resisting the urge to push her mother into the sea (her words).

One day, we're at the kitchen table trying to book flights, and the next, Proyiayia has her suitcases open on that same table for a last-minute check. I reckon she's packed enough to last a lifetime, but apparently not.

'Toilet paper,' she says, nudging me towards the bathroom.

I hesitate. This feels like a dementia thing. I assure her they have toilet paper on international flights.

She scowls. 'Their paper is bullshit,' she says, putting her whole heart into the swear.

I cave and when I return, she's got her arms around Dad. He's still here, avoiding Ba like the plague, but spending the odd arvo with Proyiayia when he can. They come apart. She grabs his hands and shakes them. She tells him to behave.

'I will.'

'Next time you come to Sydney, you come together,' she says.

He nods.

Ba appears with Gina's suitcase. My great-grandmother gives Dad's hands one final squeeze and calls him a good man. For Ba to hear.

Gina spends the entire trip to the airport hyperventilating about Ba's driving, and reminding me what to do in case of various cafe-related emergencies, so we have to rush our goodbyes outside Departures. We're not allowed to leave the car unattended, and we're definitely not allowed to stay as long as we do. When the airport worker in the fluoro vest encourages us to move on, I realise I'm holding Proyiayia's hand. I don't wanna let go.

What if four weeks away is long enough for her to forget me?

I hug her like it's the last time. She's wearing enough perfume to knock out an elephant. I squeeze tighter regardless. 'Na prosécheis.' It's what she'd always say before we left for Perth.

'Who cook for you now?' she whispers. 'Your father?' She pulls away to cackle, and it ends me. A tear breaks loose. I wipe my face, but not before she notices.

'Paidáki mou.' She cups my cheek, and I catch myself hoping she'll say my name. I shouldn't care. Her eyes are full of love, and that's enough.

She goes to speak, but the airport dude's getting aggro at Gina, and Gina's getting aggro right back. They need to go. My grandmother starts wheeling their bags towards the terminal, but she makes it clear she isn't happy about being rushed. Proyiayia follows. Ba and I don't budge till the doors close behind them.

We don't speak on the way back to Darlinghurst.

When he kills the engine, Ba's in no rush to hop out. I sit with him. His eyes are fixed on the back door.

Eventually, words. 'Eliza said no to the book,' he says. 'She liked the chapters, but it's too similar to another one they have coming out.' He laughs. 'I write my life and somebody beats me to it.'

It is funny, in a twisted way.

'I'm sorry, Ba.'

He doesn't react, eyes still glued ahead.

'Your father's a good man, isn't he?' he asks.

He's not after my opinion on Dad. He's asking if they should be together. I can't answer, because I don't think they should.

'He's a good man,' Ba adds.

He's made up his mind. He tells me he'll be in soon, and I leave him alone in the Mitsubishi. The back door's unlocked. I call out to Dad. He doesn't respond. I look to the couch. The suitcase is gone, and the sheets and doona are neatly folded.

TEN
The end

SOTIRIS

1

Mum said that I'd know when it was time to come back. On a picnic chair in the backyard, watching Finn pull focus with another exaggerated account of one of his exploits, I know. Jem and his mates are distracted. I rise from my chair and collect empty beer cans on my way inside.

I set to work grabbing whatever I've scattered around the house.

Jem steals moments with his mum every day, but every day, he steals shorter moments than the day before. Even though the inevitable is coming, I don't feel bad for leaving. He's settled now. He has his friends and Faye. He has people. Good people. He'll be okay without me.

When the backyard's cleared out and the barbie's been cleaned, the day ends as days do, on the floor of the living room. We've been working through the trove of board games in his mother's otherwise-empty wardrobe. Tonight, it's the one he's been avoiding.

Monopoly. Rarely fun with two people, never fun for Jem. The white box looks like it was left out in a storm.

He's divvying up the starting cash when I mention I'm thinking of booking my return flight.

He pauses. There's surprise. And understanding. He resumes the separation of coloured notes into piles. 'Cool. Cool.'

We start the game and accumulate streets. It's not the Australian edition, so I'm not familiar with any of them. Jem's quieter than usual. He doesn't even tell me it's my roll, one of my favourite pointless things he does when we're playing alone. I want to think it's because he hates *Monopoly*, but I'm certain it's because I'm leaving.

For half a month, we've existed in the limbo between on and off. There have been moments when we've felt very *on*, and not just at night, when we're lying so close I can feel the heat radiating off him. At his aunt's, when I find his hand under the table to give it a reassuring squeeze. At the park, when he rests his head on my shoulder and he is all I can smell. But we've recoiled from each other too, taken turns waiting in the bathroom for longer than we need to after sex, so that the other falls asleep before we get back. We're under no illusion. We know what this is and we know it will end.

At least, I thought we did.

I ask if he's okay. He is.

'When do you reckon you'll go?'

How much of a rush am I in? 'Um. The cheapest flight soon-ish?'

'Okay.' He stares at the board so long, I have to remind him it's his roll. Seven. He moves a plastic token that clearly didn't come in the box. My guess is it was a Rice Bubbles toy.

'What if you don't go?' He swallows. 'What if we play for it? I win, you stay another week. You win, leave whenever.'

'If you need me to...'

'It's not about need, I...' He sighs. 'We're just making the game more interesting.'

I give in, knowing full well he has the worst *Monopoly* luck. 'All right.'

I sabotage myself. I miscount when I move my token so I hit streets he owns and have to pay him *some* rent. But even then, it isn't close. He catches me buying fewer houses than I can afford. He stresses that he wants to win this fairly, but he doesn't have a chance. He powers through. Even when he's mortgaging property every turn. He refuses to be put out of his misery. There's still a chance I might land on the only set he hasn't mortgaged. I don't. He rolls two fours. Community Chest. He's safe there, but the double means he rolls again. He scoops the dice. They rattle together in his loose fist. He casts them. One and five. I count six places ahead. I own Mayfair with a hotel. I don't need to check the card to know he's lost. He sells his houses individually. If he's certain he's lost too, he doesn't want it to be over.

'Sydney only started to feel like home when I met you,' he says, voice low. 'When I'm with you, I'm at home. What if when you leave, Perth stops feeling like home?'

I start, 'Jem...'

'This doesn't have to end. I love you, Sotiris, and if you love me...Stay.' His eyes are pleading. 'We could be something.'

Acknowledgements

We Could Be Something began as a memoir project generously supported by grants from Create NSW, City of Melbourne and City of Sydney. The plan was to free myself from autofiction, and well...you don't need me to tell you how that went.

While many of the personal and professional experiences that inspired this book faded from the page with every draft, this story wouldn't exist without the people behind those experiences.

Claire Craig took a chance on a seventeen-year-old writer, and I owe so much to her and the publishers and editors who have supported me in the fifteen years since – Laura Harris, Clair Hume, Susannah McFarlane, Jess Owen, T.S. Ferguson, Chren Byng, Jeanmarie Morosin and Sophie Mayfield. I am particularly grateful to Jodie Webster and Kate Whitfield at Allen & Unwin for all they have done for me and this story this past year, and Astred Hicks for the stunning cover design.

After catching me trying to buy my own novel, a bookseller named Jace did sass me a little. We only dated a few months, and while we didn't marry and have a kid, he changed the course of my life. I knew I couldn't feel what I did for him and remain closeted forever. I cherish his enduring friendship.

I wouldn't write so much about families, and couldn't have written this particular book about families, if it weren't for my own.

My partner, Toby, has taken me writing about the implosion of a relationship as well as someone can. The kindness he has shown, and insights he has shared as the family's resident medical practitioner, have been an immeasurable comfort.

Yiayia brightens every day, whether it be with a video call when I'm on tour, or fresh spanakópita when I'm on deadline. I am so lucky to be so loved.

Finally, I hope this book makes Mum as proud as she makes me. She really is something.

About the Author

Will Kostakis is an award-winning author for young adults. His first novel, *Loathing Lola*, was published when he was just nineteen. It sold a whopping ten copies including the seven he bought himself. After a brief break to dabble in celebrity journalism and reconstruct his shattered dream, he returned with *The First Third*, which sold more than ten copies (possibly fifteen). It won the 2014 Gold Inky Award and was shortlisted for the CBCA and the Prime Minister's Literary Awards, among others. *The Sidekicks* was his third novel for young adults, and his US debut. It won the IBBY Australia Ena Noel Award. Will has also contributed to numerous anthologies, including the ABIA Award-winning *Begin, End, Begin: A #LoveOzYA Anthology*. He was awarded the 2020 Maurice Saxby Award by the School Library Association of New South Wales for service to children's and young adult literature and is an ambassador for the NSW Premier's Reading Challenge.